THE WOLF KING

TALES OF TYRRATH 1

Lauren H Salisbury

SEAMOUNT PUBLISHING

Developmental edit by J. J. Fischer | www.jjfischer.com
Cover by Moonpress Design | www.moonpress.co
Map and internal artwork by Andrés Aguirre | www.aaguirreart.com

ISBN (e-book): 978-1-915438-03-4
ISBN (paperback): 978-1-915438-04-1

To all those who think they aren’t enough:
You are!

THE KINGDOMS OF
EGREA
CRAEICK
IOCHANACK
FARWEATHER
BALEWICK MOUNTAINS
NORTHOLD KEEP
GOLDENOAK FOREST
STONETOOTH MOUNTAINS
ABBEY
TYRRATH
HAWKESDEN
LAKE ARROL
FAERSTOLMERE
MOCHYNDEN FOREST
SUMMER PALACE
NORFELD
THE WHITE CITY
OSLENGIL
BRUNLAND

Aralan
Garellion
Jadhe
Gorge City
Monastery
Iskaria
Firstport
Free Isles

Chapter 1
Maddie

Princess Madeline Dalbot dashed along the upper corridor of Northold Keep, her maid's voice still echoing in her ears above the slap of her feet on the cold, stone floor.

"You're needed in the map room, Your Highness. A messenger's arrived from the border."

The frantic beat of Maddie's heart shredded any remaining cobwebs of sleep as she tightened the robe over her nightdress and hurried down the stairs. News that could not wait till morning could mean only one thing—another village had been attacked.

Had her men been able to stop the raiders this time? Had she done enough to protect her people?

Torches flickered in their sconces at her passing, casting shadows that tugged her thoughts in ominous directions. What if she had spread the troops too thin? What if she had only exacerbated the situation, sent them to their deaths? What if…?

She halted four stairs from the bottom, her grip on the handrail so tight she could feel the grain in the wood. Her breath hitched at the images that played out behind her closed eyelids. If only—

Something clanged faintly off to her left, bringing her head sharply around. Likely one of the kitchen maids preparing for the new day, but it was enough to bring Maddie back to herself. Sucking in a deep breath, she straightened, then counted to five and slowly released it.

"Assess the facts with a clear head, seek wise council, keep the good of the people always in mind, and then make the best decision you can in the moment." She whispered the lessons of her father as she forced her legs to move once more, the mantra sustaining her as it had during the ten months since he had fallen ill.

By the time she reached the ground floor of the northern stronghold and turned to the east wing, she was ready to face whatever news the messenger had brought. The pulse in her wrist had calmed to its usual cadence beneath the fingers of her other hand, and her mind whirled with potential solutions for any number of possibilities.

Light shone from the open doorway ahead, guiding her to the sound of low murmurs beyond. She stepped inside and nodded for the guard stationed within to close the door behind her. Then she paused while she focused on the chamber's other occupants.

Tristan Kaar, Captain of the Royal Guard, leaned over one end of the long table with Maddie's most trusted advisor, Lord Elland, and a man she did not recognise from behind. The stranger wore a labourer's tunic and trousers rather than a soldier's leather armour, and her eyes snapped to Tristan, who looked up at the same time, lines of worry etching his deep black skin.

"Your Highness." He straightened to attention, despite her having repeatedly told him such formalities were not required of a childhood friend.

Lord Elland dipped his head in a short bow, revealing the balding patch on his pale, age-spotted crown, while the man opposite him spun around and froze, wide-eyed, for a moment before dropping to one knee.

Maddie's hand automatically smoothed her skirts, only to meet the soft velvet of her robe. Belated chagrin washed over her. Why had she not taken the time to make herself more presentable? A loose curl of her dark brown hair snagged in her periphery against the amber fabric, and she quickly tucked it behind her ear.

She sighed. Too late to worry about it now, and from the looks of things, she had more important issues to deal with.

"What news from the border?" she asked, walking around to the head of the table, where Tristan stepped aside to make room for her.

"We were waiting for you, Ma'am," he said. "But I took the liberty of laying out a map of the area."

Ma'am. Another moniker she hated for making her feel older than her twenty-one years. She cast him a brief smile anyway. "Thank you. The report then."

The messenger rose beside him, and the strong scent of wood smoke assaulted Maddie's nostrils. Ash hid most of his face, confirming at least one element of what he was about to say, and her hands tightened into fists.

"G-grave news, my La—Your Highness." Head still bowed, he peeked up at her, then pulled a sealed square of paper from his sleeve and held it out.

Her grip loosened, and she tugged the creased missive from his trembling fingers, passing it to Tristan as she bent into the messenger's line of sight. "What's your name?" she asked in the soft tone that calmed her shying horse and youngest sister.

"Finley, Ma'am."

"Well, then, Finley. Will you tell me what happened? From the beginning, and in as much detail as you can remember."

He gave her a shaky nod and pointed at the map spread across the table. It depicted the northern section of Tyrrath—vast swathes of forest in the northeast with the Balewick mountain range forming the edge of the kingdom until it reached the sea, and the Stonetooth range to the west, leaving a relatively short yet less clearly defined border with the kingdom of Craeick in the northwest.

"I come from Farweather, here." His finger jabbed at the largest village in the Balewick foothills on the western edge of Goldenoak Forest, leaving a slight smudge on the parchment. "We brought the animals in early, like we been doing since the raidin' started, me and the missus and our lass, and all were well till just after sundown, when we heard a cry for help.

"We live at the edge o' the village, so I eased the shutter to get a look outside. I figured one o' the Elder's boys must've been playin' a joke—he's got five, and they're full o' dragonfire, every one o' them."

He glanced up and rubbed the back of his neck, and Maddie suppressed a smile at his assessment.

"Anyway, it weren't them. Old John Baker were layed out past the old pigsties, shadows movin' all around him. I couldn't see much else on account o' it bein' so dark under the trees and… Well, I got the family to think on."

When he stopped again, she reached out and touched his fingers clenched around his cap. "You do well to put your family first. Our soldiers are trained to face the enemy. They did that, didn't they? The ones stationed in Farweather?"

"Yes, Ma'am. They turned out at the first warnin'. I heard the lieutenant giving the instructions to not let a single one o' them through. The fighting were fierce, clashing metal and yellin' all around us. The raiders pushed the soldiers right back into the village. Fought like demons, they did.

"Well, some o' the village men went out to help when it sounded like we might be overrun, and that's when they set fire to the thatch, blight on their thievin' hides. Next thing we know, they're gone. Vanished back into the night like shades, which is all any of us saw o' them. Dark clothes and face coverings, no insignias, even their blades were blackened accordin' to the lieutenant.

"Whole thing was done in less time'n it takes to skin a sow. They took half our winter hay and three o' the five sides o' pork in the general store. That's bad enough with spring still a month off, but near a quarter o' the village's roofs are gone, burned up before we could put

’em out.” He sucked in a breath and looked up. “Two o’ the soldiers didn’t make it. Five more with bad wounds, and a handful o’ scratches after that too. Sorry for havin’ to say so, Ma’am.

“The lieutenant asked me to report in seein’ as his best runner was one o’ the ones what got cut and I know the back ways better’n anyone else from goin’ out trufflin’.”

Maddie’s brain desperately tried to string together the right words to say even as her lips refused to form them. So much loss, and that was after she had stationed soldiers in each of the larger villages. She stared down at the map, willing the tiny dots along the northern border to offer up a solution, or at least bring the dead soldiers back to their families.

“What about the raiders?” Lord Elland asked.

“How many casualties on their side? Did the lieutenant take any prisoners?” Tristan’s voice sounded far away, as did the messenger’s reply.

“None, sir. If any was hurt or slain, the rest must’ve carried ’em off.”

The room fell silent, a few distant bangs and calls filtering through the door as the rest of the keep stirred.

Maddie prayed that this information did not confirm Tristan’s suspicions, but when she met his eye and he lifted one thick, black brow, that prayer crumbled to dust, less tangible than the soot that now stained her fingertips. If it was true, if the Wolf King had attacked their border rather than raiders, what hope did they have of defeating him?

She forced a smile. "Thank you, Finley. If you'd like to—"

Muffled female voices rose in volume outside, and a moment later, the door flew open.

"I'm sorry, Captain," the guard posted in the corridor said as Maddie's middle sister, Jocelyn, strode into the room, towing the youngest, Olivia, behind her.

"We heard the messenger arrive and came to see what's happening," Joss said. "How bad is it?"

Tristan gestured for the guard to stand down. "It's all right, Parker. They can come in."

Joss tutted. "Of course we can. This is my keep."

Maddie swallowed her retort. It had been her idea for Joss to take on responsibility for their northern estate last autumn. She had needed a positive focus for her excess energy, and she was only a year younger than Maddie's twenty-one. The Wolf King himself had technically ruled Craeick since he was twelve—she frowned—though his kingdom had changed much in the thirteen years since.

Breaking away from Joss, who had stopped beside Lord Elland to examine the map, Olivia rounded the table and whispered, "Sorry, Maddie. I tried to stop her, but she wouldn't wait."

"It's all right, Mouse." Maddie reached out to pull her sister in for a hug, but movement in her periphery made her pause. She turned back to the messenger. "Apologies, Finley. You must be tired after such a long night, and hungry too. Parker will show you to the kitchens to get cleaned up and eat, and I'll have a room in the guest wing prepared for when you're finished."

"Oh, please don't go to no trouble, Ma'am. I'm happy to bed down in the stables for a few hours and then be on my way."

"Nonsense," Joss said. "You—"

"You've done us a service," Maddie said, before her sister's enthusiasm scared the poor man back into his shell. "The least we can do is provide food and lodging in return."

His features relaxed beneath the streaks of soot, and he bobbed a quick bow. "Thank you, Ma'am." He started to leave but stopped and swung back, his eyes finally meeting hers fully. "We know you're doin' everything you can to help us, Your Highness, and we, well… thank you is all. And if you don't mind me sayin' so, everyone in Farweather's sorry about the king bein' ill, but we trust you to rule in 'is place."

Maddie blinked against the sudden sting in her eyes, swallowed the lump trying to block her throat. "I appreciate that, thank you."

"Make sure you get a plate of cook's griddle cakes while they're still warm," Joss added.

He ducked his head and left, the silence following his departure broken by Joss pulling out a chair and scraping the legs across the floor. She plopped into it and looked around the group. "So. Now he's gone, who's going to tell us how bad it is?"

Maddie glanced from Lord Elland to Tristan, tilting her chin for the latter to read the report and fill them all in.

He broke the seal, and while his eyes scanned the page, Maddie felt Olivia's fingers slip into hers. She gave them a squeeze, debating whether to suggest the sixteen-year-old wait for them upstairs. Was she up to hearing the details of the latest attack?

Tristan spoke before she could act on the impulse. "Craeick's forces are behind the raids." He threw the missive onto the table with a growl worthy of the Wolf King himself. "I knew I should've trusted my instincts."

An icy claw of dread scraped down Maddie's back, raising gooseflesh across her skin. Olivia huddled closer, and Maddie absently put an arm around her young sister.

"Are you sure it's them?" Lord Elland asked.

"Lieutenant Wash has seen them fight before. He's sure." Tristan pushed back from the edge of the table with a disgusted sound and scrubbed a hand over his shaved scalp. "They've been learning our defences, weakening them. And now they've stepped up their attack." His eyes found Maddie's, regret lurking in their near black depths. "They hit Anford tonight as well as Farweather. Stole most of their supplies and left the village in smoking ruins. Five dead."

Voices buffeted Maddie from all sides, questions flying back and forth across the table, but all she could hear was *five dead* repeating over and over in her mind. She sank into the nearest chair and watched the first rays of morning sunlight paint her pale fingers orange.

That was it, then. The confirmation they needed. Raiders did not plague their land; a neighbouring kingdom invaded it. One known for its undefeated army and ruthless leader. What was she to do now?

Joss's voice snagged her spiralling thoughts and brought her attention back to the conversation. "But why attack us? And why now?"

There was a beat of silence, then everyone spoke at once. Causes such as the harsh winter, the resurgence of wild dragons—which the Craeickish army would surely fight off rather than ignore in favour of attacking a peaceful neighbour—even rumours of an evil presence stirring in the north bounced back and forth.

Another possibility slithered into her mind—that they considered Tyrrath easy prey while she ruled in her father's stead—and she sprang to her feet in an attempt to banish it. The others quieted, and Tristan caught her eye, the wrinkle in his brow asking if she was well.

"What if someone's paying them to invade?" Maddie's gaze whipped to Joss, who shrugged. "What? Everyone knows they've been mercenaries for years. Any one of the other kingdoms could be behind this."

Lord Elland shook his head. "Not this time, young one." He glanced at Maddie. "I checked with my contacts, quietly, after Captain Kaar raised the possibility of their involvement. No one's paying Craeick to do this." Focusing his attention on Joss, he added more forcefully, "And our relations with the other kingdoms are strong. None of them have reason to wish us harm."

"Will they help, then?" she asked.

He rubbed his temple, the skin there lined from decades of advising his king. When he looked at Maddie, his eyes were filled with a mixture of sympathy and resignation. "No. I'm afraid they won't."

"They're scared."

Maddie grimaced at Joss's blunt assessment, though she could not refute it. She settled for sending her a warning look, to which Joss responded by raising her hands, then leaning back in her chair and picking up the lieutenant's report.

"More likely just complacent," Tristan said. "None of them share a border with Craeick, so why poke the Wolf? Easier to let us fend him off by ourselves if at all possible. Shortsighted, but—"

"Regardless, we can't let him get away with it." Lord Elland leaned on the table, staring down at the map. "We need to protect our people and show the Craeickish that they can't attack our borders without consequence."

"Agreed," Tristan said.

"Can we though? Defeat him?" Olivia asked, her voice barely above a whisper.

Maddie turned to her sister, who sat in the chair she had just vacated. Feet pulled up onto the cushion, arms wrapped around her knees, her amber eyes begged for reassurances Maddie was unable to give.

"Probably not," Joss muttered. "No one's managed it so far."

"Jocelyn!"

She looked up from the report, followed the jerk of Maddie's head towards Olivia, and winced. "Sorry, Mouse. I didn't mean that."

Doubts hidden behind a tight-lipped smile, Maddie focused on her youngest sister. "He's formidable, yes, but not invincible."

Tristan crouched down and squeezed Olivia's shoulder. "You're perfectly safe here. I promise. Our soldiers were trained by the best, and there's no sign of an army massing anywhere along the border. It's probably only a small advance party."

He stood to attention, his boot heels clacking together, and addressed Maddie. "If you want us to hunt them down, Your Highness, I can have a squadron out tracking them by first light."

Maddie shook her head. "No. They live in the mountains. They'll know how to use them to their advantage, to set ambushes or disappear at will. Your men would end up chasing the wind. No. There must be another way."

"Like what?" Olivia asked.

Joss glared at the map. "Shame the ancients destroyed nearly all the magic. We could've blasted them back to Craeick."

"Been reading Mouse's history books?" Tristan asked, relaxing his stance.

"I was bored," she muttered.

Maddie tuned them out and paced between the window and the empty fireplace, running her fingertips across the velvet of her robe as her mind worked the problem. She looked to the portrait of her father above the mantelpiece, to his wise eyes and steady smile. How she wished he were here to advise her.

But he was not. He was in Redcairn Palace in the capital, struck down last spring by a sleeping sickness no one could cure. And her mother had passed nearly a decade ago. Maddie was on her own.

The weight of rule pressed down on her shoulders, so heavy. But it was her burden to bear, and she must not let her father or her people down. With a last glance at his reassuring painted face, she straightened and turned back to the group around the table.

"The villagers must be our first priority. Take pork, grain, and feed from the royal stores to replace what's been stolen. Then arrange shelter for those whose homes have been destroyed here and at Lonthair Abbey. In fact, move as many people as possible down to the larger towns. I don't want them caught in the middle of a battlefield if it comes to that."

An idea sprouted as she spoke, and she pulled the map closer, searching for a potential location while the plan took shape. If they wanted to stop the Wolf King, they would have to outsmart him, beat him at his own game. And if he was going to play the raider, there was one sure way to draw him out. "We're going to set a trap."

Chapter 2

Luc

Lucas Sinclair, King of Craeick, thrust his sword into the gut of his opponent. The man paused, arm mid-swing, then slumped to the ground, his own sword clattering from his grip as Luc slid his free. A quick check of the callouses on the dying man's hand confirmed Luc's suspicions—this was no common field labourer. His men fought trained soldiers disguised as peasants.

Clever. But no matter. They were no match for his elite troops.

Nevertheless, he scanned the immediate area for his second-in-command. A fire in the thatch of a nearby house provided enough light to see the knots of men fighting throughout the wide lane. Shadows loomed around them, adding to the enemy's numbers, but even so, far more living bodies came against them than they had encountered elsewhere.

On either side of the packed-dirt battleground, buildings that had disgorged the enemy mere moments earlier now appeared abandoned, shutters and doors closed against the clash of metal and stench of death without. It permeated the air, a combination of coppery blood and sweat that mingled with the smoke and clung to his nostrils, familiar and centring.

His skin prickled where a gust of cold air met the heat of exertion, and he braced for an attack. After so many years of tuning his battle-senses, he knew with certainty when an itch indicated more than a mere change in temperature.

A moment later, a youth ran at him from an alleyway, short sword raised in both hands over his head, battle cry ringing with desperation. No soldier, this. He must have sneaked away from wherever the true villagers were hiding.

Luc cut him down with a slice to the neck as soon as he was within reach. The boy stumbled, momentum carrying him another pace before he fell, face first, to the dirt at Luc's feet. Blood spread in a small pool beside his head, staining the muddy slush of melting snow with swirls of red.

He should have stayed with his mother.

Stepping over him, Luc made his way along the street to his second, Aiden Munroe. Aiden fought two men at once, blades flashing in the firelight, hair flying free as he spun from one to the other. His battle mate, Rheann Braydeson, covered his back, where another foe moved in to attack, and Luc's blood sang for him to join the fray.

He was about to engage a burly fellow who cast off his farmer's tunic and appeared as if he might put up a decent challenge when a cry stopped him in his tracks. It came again, and his jaw clenched.

Flynn. What in the blazes was he doing here?

Luc followed the sounds of his young half-brother's struggles, through a gap between two houses and onto a narrower lane. By the light of a torch held by a man with his back to Luc, two others tried to manoeuvre Flynn into the rear of an enclosed cart. Flynn bucked and wriggled, kicking out and screaming at the top of his lungs. He caught the man in front of him between the legs, eliciting a sharp oomph followed by an even sharper curse.

Only Flynn could cause three grown men such trouble. Luc would have been proud of the fight he was putting up were he not so livid that the nine-year-old had ignored his express instructions to stay in their camp.

When the man raised his arm to retaliate, Luc surged forwards, sword poised to strike.

He ploughed into them, knocking the leader aside and slicing a deep line across the arm of the second, loosening his grip on Flynn and rendering him useless in the coming fight. The third must have let go to reach for his weapon, for by the time Luc had spun to face him, his brother had darted out of the way.

"Get to Aiden," Luc growled at him. "Now!"

Eyes trained on his uninjured opponents, who quickly recovered and bared their blades, he waited until Flynn disappeared between the houses in his periphery, then pulled his dagger from its sheath and circled to put his back to the nearest wall. "Let's see how you fare against someone your own size."

Neither of them made a move against him, and unease stirred in his gut. What were they waiting for? Most men would consider two against one to be good odds.

Only it was not two against one. Five or six more materialised from the surrounding darkness—too many for Luc to fight off alone. They joined their friends in encircling him, their sword points hemming him in. Cursing himself for not checking his surroundings or calling for help before charging in, he kept his weapons up and muscles loose, ready for their next move.

"Should I go after the boy?" the injured man asked.

"No," the leader replied. "We only need one. You going to surrender, or are we going to have to hurt you first?"

The taunt smarted like vinegar on an open wound, but fighting at this point would be foolish. Luc scratched his bearded jaw with the hand holding his dagger, his mind racing. Then he let out a sharp laugh and lowered his sword. This could be interesting.

They clearly had no idea who they had in their grasp. With no insignias to distinguish him from the rest of his men, and his distinctive wolf-headed sword back in their camp, why would they? Most outsiders who saw his face this close did not live to tell of it.

As the soldiers who had held Flynn gestured for him to step towards them, Luc twisted his signet ring around to hide the crest in his palm. He relinquished his weapons with only a promise of retribution should anything happen to them before he took them back, and allowed the men to bind his wrists.

Flexing his muscles while they tied the rope created some give when they were done. He tested it a couple of times, then tilted his head to the left and right, producing a satisfying popping in his neck.

Though he did not relish what would come next, the opportunity to see inside Tyrrath's defences would be worth it. Aiden knew what to do and should secure his release in a day or two, three at the most.

The man Luc had cut moved in behind him, and Luc forced his shoulders to relax. A moment later, something hard and cold slammed into his temple, and the world went black.

Chapter 3

Maddie

Maddie handed a stack of blankets and provisions to an elderly couple and gave them an encouraging smile. Waving one of the guards forward, she leaned close and whispered, “Make sure they get a place somewhere warm.”

The guard frowned, her lips twisting. “Not many left, Ma’am, but I’ll see what I can do.”

“They can stay in my room,” Maddie’s maid, Tabitha, said. When Maddie lifted her eyebrows, Tabitha grunted and slopped a ladleful of soup into the bowl a man held out to her, but pink suffused her round face. “Everyone else is already squashed three to a bed, and I could use the extra body heat.”

“Thank you.”

With a nod from Maddie, the guard shepherded the couple through the crowd in the direction of the keep, and Maddie turned to the next in line. The number of refugees seemed to grow by the moment, people pouring into the stronghold as word of the Wolf's invasion spread.

"Welcome to Northold. You're safe here."

The woman stared at the blankets Maddie held out but made no move to take them.

Setting them back down on the table, Maddie reached out and touched her hand. Icy cold. A closer look at her face revealed the blue-tinged lips and drooping eyelids of a woman about to drop. She must have walked through the night to reach them.

"I need some help over here."

By the time Maddie had unfurled the nearest blanket and wrapped it around the woman's shoulders, Tabitha was at her side with a bowl of hot soup. She held it up to the woman's lips and, when the woman gulped a mouthful down, rubbed her back and murmured soothingly as she led her around the table.

As they cleared the end, the blanket shifted at the woman's hip, exposing a little girl of no more than four. She hid behind her mother's skirts, sucking her thumb and peering up at them from wide, green eyes. Maddie crouched down to her level.

"Hello there, little one. What's your name?"

"Thara," she said around the digit.

"That's a pretty name. Where have you come from, Sara?"

"Brudick."

A three-day journey at least. No wonder her mother was half frozen, though she seemed to have ensured her daughter stayed warm. Sara removed her thumb from her mouth long enough to add, “We ran from the bad man.”

Maddie’s throat tightened. “And you did an excellent job. You’re safe now, and I’m going to make sure you and your mama get a nice rest. Does that sound good?”

The little girl nodded so vigorously that strands of matted blonde hair fell into her face.

Maddie brushed them aside and smiled as warmly as her ragged emotions would allow. “See the woman with your mama?” Another nod. “That’s my good friend Tabitha. She looked after my sisters and me when we were your age, and she always has the sweetest darley bread. If you go with her, she’ll take you somewhere warm for a nap, and then, if you ask nicely, she might find you a slice or two while your mama sleeps a bit longer. All right?”

Sara’s eyes moved slowly from Maddie to Tabitha and back. Then she nodded and scampered after Tabitha and her mother to the inn, where a couple of the largest rooms had been set aside for the most desperate cases.

Using the table for support, Maddie pushed to her feet and took a moment to stretch her back. She closed her eyes on the sea of faces, shutting out their terror and grief, but she could not stop their voices from carrying to her ears.

…destroyed everything…can’t stop them…the Wolf King…the Wolf…unbeaten…

The words and phrases rode atop overlapping waves of conversation, evidence of questions and concerns for which she had few answers. If her father were here, he would climb atop the table and address the crowd, find a way to soothe and embolden them, but doubt pinned Maddie to the cobbled ground.

If only she knew how things stood at the border… But there had been nothing new for a week, not since they had discovered who was behind the attacks.

With one last stretch, she picked up a new basket full of blankets, busying her hands, though her mind continued to churn. It kept returning to King Lucas's motives and the timing of his incursion.

Though the others in that meeting a week ago had kindly avoided it, there was only one conclusion that made any sense. It screamed inside her skull and would not be ignored—he had only invaded since she had taken up the mantle of rule. He thought her a weak target.

Which meant that she was the cause of her people's suffering. She was the reason behind all the pain and terror and death they had endured. How could they even look at her, never mind trust her to lead them?

Before long, she would likely have to order many of them farther south, or risk failing them again by running out of food and places to house them all. Would they listen to her then? Should they?

She looked around for a distraction and frowned. "Where's Joss?" she asked the nearest guard.

"With Captain Kaar, ma'am, organising the temporary shelters in the fields behind the stables."

"She shouldn't be out there." Tabitha's voice startled Maddie, and she turned to find her beloved maid looking her up and down, lips pursed. "And neither should you.

It's not right for a princess to be standing out in the cold, ankle deep in mud."

"We've been over this. I can't sit and do nothing while we wait for news." Tabitha harrumphed, but Maddie only firmed her tone. "And people need to see me, to see that I'm not scared."

The maid's brows shot up into her greying hairline. "You aren't? I'm terrified. And frozen."

So was Maddie. Scared, that was—that the Wolf would abandon his raiding tactics and attack in force, that more people would be hurt, that her plan would fail—but she could not admit any of that aloud. Not even to Tabitha or her sisters. "Why don't you go back to the keep? I can—"

"No. If you can stay out here and help, so can I." Tabitha picked up her ladle and served bowls full of steaming soup to the young family who shuffled forwards. "There you go. Get that down while it's nice and hot."

Heart warmed despite the bone-deep chill, Maddie hugged her, nearly toppling the older woman sideways. Tabitha batted her away with an exaggerated grunt, and Maddie turned back to her own task of handing out basic supplies.

A short while later—or hours, Maddie had lost track of time—sounds of a commotion drifted to them from the direction of the outer gates. Her heart flipped inside her chest, and she gripped the blanket she was holding tight to stop herself from running to find out what was happening. Was it news from the border? Had the Wolf King sprung her trap?

It had been a simple plan, but she prayed it would be enough to show him she could defend her kingdom. Wolves usually backed off at a show of strength. Hopefully, she would soon discover whether the same was true of their human counterparts. And if their quest to capture a prisoner had gone well, they could get some much-needed answers too.

A contingent of soldiers rode into view at the far side of the square, and on seeing them, her feet carried her a few steps forward. Tabitha clutched her elbow, darting a glance at the crowd that reminded Maddie of her audience.

Obliged to wait for the riders to approach, she stood on her tiptoes and tried to gauge what news they carried from their appearance, but distance and the number of people between them made it impossible. The party crawled around the edge of the crowded square, paused while the leader bent towards someone standing beyond Maddie's line of sight. Her right foot bounced against the cobbles, and she chewed the inside of her lip. Could they not move with more haste?

Eventually, the leader straightened, called something over her shoulder, and pointed in Maddie's direction. One of the others dismounted and shouldered his way through the throng while the rest rode up the hill to the keep.

The runner reached the front of the queue and stood to attention on seeing her, offering a sharp salute.

"What news?" she asked.

"I've been sent to escort you back to the keep, Your Highness."

That was it? A week of waiting, and all he could tell her was that she was needed at the keep? She dropped the blanket and set out without a word to anyone. It was only reasonable that he could not divulge any details in such a public location, but her nerves frayed as they crossed the square, people moving aside to give her a clear path.

Halfway up the steep incline, when she was certain they were beyond hearing, she stopped and turned to her escort. “What can you tell me, now we’re alone?”

He ducked his head. “Sorry, Ma’am. It’s not my place to say.”

“Soldier!” She almost growled at him. Almost.

A wince contorted his travel-stained face, and then he pushed out a breath. “We brought in a prisoner, Ma’am. Need you somewhere safe while he’s secured. Lieutenant Wash would’ve sent advance warning, but we had to move fast to keep his compatriots from stealing him back. They’ve been shadowing us since we left Berricksford.”

“Does the town guard know you were followed?”

“Yes, Ma’am. My squad leader left some men at the gate.”

“Good.” And they had a prisoner. Maddie hiked her skirts and started walking again, picking up her pace.

By the time she reached the entrance to the keep, she was puffing and hot, her corset tight, but one look at Tristan waiting for her inside the gatehouse chased any discomfort from her thoughts. His stony expression radiated anger, though with whom, she could not tell.

He dismissed the soldier with a jerk of his chin and spoke as soon as Maddie reached his side. “They caught the Wolf King.”

“What?”

“King Lucas. That’s who we’ve taken prisoner.”

Maddie’s mind spun, along with the courtyard around her. Tristan steadied her arm while she sucked in air and processed what he had told her. It could not be true. Could it? And if so, what would it mean?

“Are you certain?”

“We’ve met before. It’s definitely him.”

“But… how?”

With a touch to her elbow, he guided her inside. “I don’t have all the details yet, but from what I can tell, he was captured freeing a young lad one of the squads caught. As for the rest, I plan to find out as soon as we’ve secured the area.”

A boy? What kind of a monster would take a child into battle? “Where is he?”

“In the dungeon for now. I know he’s a king, but that’s the only place we can—”

“Good.” As far as she was concerned, king or not, the dungeon was where he deserved to stay. “I want to see him.”

The words came out of nowhere, but as soon as she said them, they solidified into a need as strong as that of breathing. She needed to face the man who had targeted her kingdom, decided she was weak enough to attack, to see for herself that he was no nightmare to haunt her dreams, just a man, and one locked in a cage.

She returned her attention to Tristan and realised he had been talking, already on the third finger of a list.

"...and on top of that, I can't guarantee he won't use your visit to his advantage somehow. He's not to be underestimated, even as a prisoner."

"What's all the fuss about? Parker practically carried me back here over her shoulder."

Joss strode through the double doors, tugging off her riding gloves. Her hair was a dishevelled mess, loose strands falling over her shoulders, and the split skirt Tabitha and Maddie insisted she wore over her leather trousers was plastered with mud.

"Oh, Joss—"

"Never mind that. What's going on?"

Tristan stepped forwards before Maddie could answer her. "Maybe we should take this discussion somewhere more private?"

Maddie snorted, then sobered. True, they had been talking in full view of anyone who happened to pass, but her sister had a way of drawing the type of attention that Maddie had spent her youth learning to avoid.

She walked into the map room and closed the door behind them. "Our trap worked better than we expected. Lieutenant Wash and his men managed to capture the Wolf King himself." She held her hand up against whatever Joss was bursting to say. "We don't have much information yet, but he's here in the dungeon, so we need to secure the town gates and make sure his men can't break him free. Tristan and I were just discussing what to do next, the first thing being me paying him a visit."

"And confirm your presence here? Did you hear nothing I just said?"

"I'm not arguing with you. I need to see him for myself."

Tristan set his jaw. "If you go in there, you have no deniability. He's the ruling monarch of another kingdom, and despite being the aggressor here, he could demand the right of treaty."

"He doesn't need to know it's you, if that's what you're worried about," Joss said.

Maddie swivelled from Tristan's angry countenance to her sister, who raised her eyebrows and shrugged as if the answer should be obvious.

"Go in disguise. I do it all the time when—"

She bit off the rest of her sentence, shooting a glance at Tristan, who threw his arms in the air and muttered something about them both being impossible. Maddie did not care. A smile tugged at her lips as she walked the few steps to her sister's side. A disguise was just what she needed.

"Help me?"

"As long as you tell me whether he really does look like a wolf."

Half an hour later, Maddie descended the steps to the dungeon, the coarse woollen fabric of her borrowed dress making her skin itch in several places. She carried a flagon of ale in one hand and a plate of bread and ham in the other. Simple fare for a king, but Tristan insisted that until the Wolf chose to confirm his identity, he would be treated as any other prisoner.

Two guards flanked the door at the bottom of the stairs, and Tristan waited beside them, his scowl no less disapproving than it had been earlier.

"Have you spoken to him yet?" she asked.

He moved to the other side of the landing, away from the guards. "Yes. Not that I got anything useful out of him."

"He didn't say anything? Not even to identify himself?"

Tristan's forehead pulled tighter, the vee between his brows deepening. "Nothing of consequence. He appears to be rather amused at his capture."

"I'll see him myself, then."

He blocked her way. "I still don't think that's a good idea."

Maddie raised her chin, giving him the imperious look her father used whenever he needed to stand firm. "I've made up my mind, now let me past."

"Please, Maddie." He reached out but stopped before their skin met and stepped back. "As you will, Ma'am, but please be careful. He's dangerous, even in chains."

With a nod to acknowledge his warning, she walked back to the dungeon door. One of the guards unlocked it, and the other offered her a lantern. "Might want a bit more light, Your Highness."

She had never visited the dungeon before. Unlike her younger sister, who had explored every inch of every residence they owned as a child, she had never felt the need. But now, she wished she had. Placing the plate of food on top of the ale, she took the lantern and ducked through the gaping maw into the gloom beyond, hearing Tristan whisper behind her, "I'll be right outside if you need me."

The room was longer than it was wide, an open space with a table and two chairs immediately in front of her and a row of iron-barred cells beyond them to the right. A single torch set high in the left-hand wall cast a pool of weak light near the doorway, but the rest of the dungeon hid in darkness.

It was cold but not as damp as she had expected, and the section of stone floor she could see was relatively clean. Only her imagination conjured the scratch of a mouse somewhere in the far corner. She hoped.

With one eye on the precarious balance of the plate and the other assessing the sturdiness of the bars on the second cell, she lofted her lantern higher and walked farther inside.

"Come to get a look at your prisoner, Princess?" The Wolf King spread his arms wide, chains clinking. "I don't blame you. I am a rare specimen."

It took everything in Maddie not to falter at his question. "I'm no princess," she said. "I've been sent to bring you some food." She lifted the bread and ale as she approached his cell.

The yellowy light of her lantern exposed his body but left his head in shadows. He sat on the floor against the far wall, one leg stretched out in front of him, the other cocked with his elbow resting on his knee. The only movement he made was his left hand, where he twisted a ring around his little finger.

"Ruling a kingdom is a lot of pressure. I don't blame you for slipping out in disguise now and then." He chuckled, a dark, dangerous sound. "Of course, I prefer visiting the local ale house and a warm wench, myself, but each to their own."

Maddie's lips pinched. Refusing to rise to his bait, she set the provisions down beside the bars of his cage and stepped back.

"So you admit you're the king of Craeick, Lucas Sinclair?"

"You first, Princess."

He sat forwards, bringing his face into the light. Piercing silver eyes grabbed hers, and Maddie swallowed a gasp. They appeared to glow, almost as brightly as the lantern, though the notion was ridiculous. Drat Joss and her imagination.

Tearing her gaze from the molten orbs, she tracked a scar from his left eyebrow down the length of his tanned face to the black scruff that hid his jaw. What could have caused such a long, thick line? It twitched, and her focus shifted to his lips, which curled in a mocking grin.

"Seen enough, or should I spin around for you?"

Her hands fisted, and she glared into his stupid eyes. He thought she was ogling him?

"This isn't a joke. You've killed innocent people."

He shrugged. "Life is hard, Princess. We all die sometime."

Silver muted to stormy grey, and he looked down at the rush-strewn floor, a deep vee furrowing his brow. What tragedy did he see there? His voice startled her when he spoke next, and on recalling who and what he was, she banished any empathy he had elicited.

"It must be eating you—excuse me, *your princess*—alive trying to decide what to do with me."

"What do you mean?"

He picked at something on his trouser leg, drawing out the silence until she thought he would not answer her.

She turned to leave, and he said, "Only that you have no good options."

Slowly, she swivelled back to face him.

The corner of his mouth lifted, and when he raised his eyes to hers, they gleamed with satisfaction. "You can't release me—because I won't stop until I have what I want—but you can't keep me prisoner either. My men will use any means necessary to get me back, including destroying half your kingdom."

Maddie swallowed. Was that true? Would they kill more innocents to get to him?

"I suppose you could kill me…" His eyes narrowed, assessing her as though he could see through to her very soul. "But I don't think you have the stomach for that, and my men would avenge my death tenfold. So, if you think about it, you're stuck."

"The guard could take you to the White City. They're neutral. They'd—"

He laughed, the sound slapping into her like a bucket of cold water. "Do you not know who I am? What I'm capable of? Move me now and you may as well release me and slaughter the men you would've sent as escort. Face it, Princess, you're caught in your own trap."

"I think you'll find that was you."

She had not meant to taunt him, but the surprise that flitted across his face satisfied, nonetheless. Unfortunately, it was immediately replaced by a snarl that made her flinch.

"Soldiers shouldn't go after lads a quarter their size."

She blinked. Right. He had been caught freeing a young boy. Yet he had the gall to blame her men for that?

"Then you shouldn't bring one onto a battlefield. A ruler should keep children safe, not turn them into killers. What kind of person does that?"

He sprang to his feet so fast she barely caught the actual movement. One moment he was sitting on the floor, the next straining to get to her with a fierceness that knocked her back a couple of steps and made her heart stutter. But the chains on his arms pulled taut just before he reached the bars. His eyes blazed through them at her.

"Rulers can't always protect their people, even when they do everything right. Have you ever seen a wild dragon atta—" He snapped his mouth shut, the muscles in his jaw working, then stepped back into the shadows. "Look at your own borders if you want proof."

She need not search so far. Evidence of his malice filled Northold, women and children fleeing through the night to escape his butchery. Her eyes stung. "Yes, well. You have your food. I should go."

He slid down the wall and returned to twisting the ring around the little finger of his left hand, as easy as if his outburst had never occurred. “See you soon, Princess.”

“I told you. I’m just a—”

“A maid. Yes. You said.”

She was almost to the door when he called out, “Next time you pretend to be a servant, you might want to scrub the scent of sandalwood from your skin.”

Cursing her mistake, she lifted her chin and strode out without a backwards glance, but the rumble of his laughter followed her up the stairs and out into the sunshine.

Chapter 4
Maddie

"You should see this. They move like they're the same person."

"For pity's sake, Joss, come away from the window."

Maddie hunched deeper into the warmth of her blanket as her sister closed the shutters and stomped over to the fireplace of their private solar. She was finding it hard enough to ignore the Craeickish soldiers camped on the hill facing the keep without Joss's commentary.

In truth, she had thought of little else since they had arrived the previous day, a dark stain along the ridgeline that had turned into a swarm of evening bugs as they lit their fires at dusk. What troops she had were deployed between them and the stronghold, a triple watch set throughout the night, but it had not eased her mind one jot. Well-trained as her men were, they were no match for elite Craeickish forces if they decided to attack.

Her only hope was that Lord Elland would be successful.

Joss picked up the poker and shoved the logs around in the grate, causing a handful of sparks to leap towards the rug. “I hate being cooped up inside.”

“I understand,” Maddie said. “I missed my ride this morning too. But with the way things stand…”

“I know. We’re safer in here.”

“Why don’t you read something?” Curled on the chair opposite Maddie’s lounger, Olivia looked up from her book of fables. “I’ve got plenty of good stories you could borrow.”

Joss grimaced. “Thanks, Mouse, but I’d rather do anything than read right now.”

She walked back to the window and peeked outside again. “They haven’t come out yet. Not that I can see anyway.”

“Joss, please.”

“Sorry.”

Maddie chewed the inside of her lip. Lord Elland had set out with a small honour guard before dawn to attempt peace talks, but there had been no news, and no movement in the enemy camp, since then. Maddie could do naught but pray the negotiations were progressing well. What if they refused Tyrrath’s terms? They would not take Lord Elland hostage, would they?

“Maybe he was right,” she muttered.

“Who? The Wolf King?” Joss crossed the room and sat down beside her, forcing Maddie to shuffle over. “Don’t let him get to you, remember? Tristan said you got more out of him than anyone else, before or since.”

“I suppose so.”

Joss bumped her shoulder into Maddie's. "No suppose about it."

"Yes. Thanks to you, we know why he's invading," Olivia said.

"Maybe. I got the impression there was more to it than just dragon attacks." Maddie glanced towards the closed window. "And it doesn't change the fact that over two hundred of his men are out there, poised to strike."

Olivia shifted in the chair. "But Lord Elland will stop them, right? Make a deal so they stand down?"

"That's the plan." Maddie searched the room for a distraction, and her eyes lit on her sister's favourite game. "In the meantime, how about a round of Knights?"

Joss jumped up and fetched the board, giving Olivia a quick squeeze on the way back. "Don't worry, Mouse. We'll think of something if that doesn't work. We always do."

They set up the game on a stool between them, and Olivia won the right to go first.

She had just used a dragon card to send Joss's fourth piece home when someone knocked on the door.

"Come in," Maddie called, laughing at Joss's disgruntled muttering.

Tristan walked in, and all merriment evaporated.

"Has Lord Elland returned?"

"Not yet, Your Highness. Against my better judgement, I'm here to convey a request to see you from King Lucas."

Maddie blinked. "King Lucas? What does *he* want?"

"Maybe to make peace after all," Olivia said.

The Wolf's calculating eyes flashed through Maddie's mind, and she winced. Unlikely, unless he had had a significant change of heart since the previous day.

Tristan caught her gaze. "He wouldn't say, Ma'am, but whatever it is, I'd advise against it. I don't trust him one inch."

Needing space to think, Maddie stood and paced the length of the rug, but a clatter of horse hooves in the courtyard below broke her focus. She ran to the window, Joss right behind her, and threw the shutters wide in time to see Lord Elland dismount.

"He's back," Joss said.

Maddie spun to Tristan. "Let's hope he has good news."

The wait was interminable, though it could not have been more than a short while.

Olivia returned to the game, but Joss declined her turn. She bounced from the window to the fireplace and back again, making Maddie's head spin. Maddie sank onto the lounger and folded her hands in her lap to prevent herself from fidgeting.

When Lord Elland arrived, the slump of his shoulders and tight line of his lips told Maddie everything she needed to know before he opened his mouth to speak.

"Will you join us?" She gestured for him to take a seat, but he refused with a shake of his head and a rueful glance at the mud-spattered cloak he still wore.

"Thank you, but I should change first. I'm sorry, Your Highness. I did everything I could, but the Craeickish general refused to see reason."

Joss handed him a cup of water, and he took a sip before continuing. "Their approach to negotiations is completely counter intuitive. Anyone would think they were the ones with a hostage. They demand their king's release and vow to destroy one of our settlements every day until he's returned, starting tomorrow. I'll have a full report for you within the hour…"

Anything else he said was lost on Maddie. An image of the border villages burning one by one played across her vision, and try as she might, she could not dislodge it. She had failed her people. Again.

Vaguely aware of Lord Elland taking his leave, she raised a hand in farewell, then walked to the window and pulled the shutter wide. A blast of cold air hit her face, and she breathed it in, clearing the fog from her thoughts.

"Can we beat him, if it comes to war?" Joss asked.

It took a long moment for Tristan to reply. "It'll be difficult if they come here in force. His army's notorious for a reason."

Maddie looked over her shoulder at him, and he grimaced.

"I wish it wasn't true," he said, "but they wiped out Lord Bann's forces when they worked for Valek last year. We'd have to muster all our reserves to stand even half a chance against them."

She looked down at the courtyard, where a handful of youths practiced their swordplay, sticks clacking back and forth, then out past the walls to the hill beyond and the mass of brown tents spread across the slope. Tiny figures trained for war beside them, each one wearing the dragonhide armour of Craeick's elite troops. Their swords flashed in the sunlight, their movements fluid, as precise and deadly as Joss had claimed.

"Think, Maddie," she muttered, considering her options like moves on a Knights board.

Much as she hated to admit it, the Wolf King had been right—she was as trapped as him. If she kept him prisoner, his army would destroy her kingdom until he was released. But if she let him go, he would return to them armed with additional knowledge and invade in earnest. Either way, her people suffered, and there was little she could do to stop it.

Only one thing remained. She turned to Tristan and smoothed her skirts. "I'll see the prisoner now."

"Are you going to convince him to make peace?" Olivia asked at the same time as Tristan said, "I still think that's a bad idea."

Maddie focused on her sister. "I doubt it'll make a difference, but I'll try."

She had little other choice.

Joss touched her arm, understanding shining in her eyes. "Do you need the dress again?"

Lifting her chin, Maddie shook her head. "Not this time." This time she would visit the Wolf King as herself.

She made her way downstairs and across to the dungeon entrance, Tristan close on her heels. He did not attempt to dissuade her from her decision, but the set of his mouth and the white-knuckled grip he kept on his sword made his feelings on the subject plain.

When they reached the landing at the bottom of the stairs, she turned and said, "I think you should wait here." She put a hand up before he could argue. "You two clearly antagonise each other, and I don't have the energy for games today. Please, Tristan."

His eyes narrowed, jaw working, but he gave a single, short nod and stepped aside.

"Thank you," she mouthed. Then, taking the lantern one of the guards held out, she swallowed her nerves and walked through the door into the dungeon.

A whistle echoed from the darkness within, and she could feel the Wolf's eyes on her, though she could not see his face. Suddenly, the rich emerald gown she had chosen to wear that morning made her feel too exposed, the gold embroidery around the cuffs and hem too expensive against the rough stone and stale rushes.

"More light, please?" she called through the open doorway, forcing her feet to stay put.

The same guard brought several torches inside and, lighting them from the one by the door, set them in brackets along the left-hand wall.

"Thank you," she said, and waited for him to leave before proceeding farther into the room.

The Wolf stood, leaning against the same section of wall beside his cot, his face hidden in shadows even with the additional light.

"No pretending to be other people today?" he asked.

"There doesn't seem much point, does there?"

He shrugged, a slight movement. “Shame, but fair enough.”

“What do you want?”

He did not answer, and the silence between them drew taut.

“I suggest you say whatever it is you wanted to tell me before I change my mind and leave.”

“Tch, tch, tch. So testy today. Is my army causing you trouble, Princess?”

She spun to leave.

“Fine. I have a proposition for you.” He walked forwards, stopping just before the chains on his wrists reached their limit. The wicked gleam that had haunted her sleep was missing from his eyes, but a prickle at the base of her neck warned her not to trust him.

“I’m listening.”

“I take it from the circles under your eyes that my men have arrived, and I assume you’ve sent someone—probably your best—to negotiate my release. But I can tell you now, it won’t work. He’ll be safe enough under a flag of truce—my men live by the rules of engagement—but they have strict orders never to accept terms on my behalf.” He met her gaze directly. “This will be the only offer you get from Craeick. Understand?”

He could not know the negotiations had failed already. She kept her expression blank and hands still, wondering what deal he could possibly wish to make.

“Go on.”

“You want to save your kingdom from all-out war. I want out of this cage, and access to resources I can’t get in Craeick. Release me, give me enough land to build a fort and a small town, and I'll call off my men and ensure no enemies ever come against you again."

She mulled over his terms, so simple, so reasonable. Where was the catch?

"Tell me why you attacked."

His eyes darkened, black brows drawing together, but after a long moment, he flicked a hand through the air and said, "Dragons are returning in greater numbers, and winters are harsher than ever before. We can't stay in the mountains much longer."

"Then why not treat with us in the first place?"

He blinked. "Why ask for what you can take?"

"Because it's not your—" Biting off her retort, she blew out a slow breath and unclenched her fists. "Never mind." There was no point arguing if he was willing to negotiate.

"Don't mistake me, Princess. I'm not bargaining. I'm offering you a way out. Take it or leave it. I didn't plan to get caught—obviously—but now I'm here, it presents a unique opportunity. A short cut, if you will."

If she could glare any harder at him, it would surely burn holes in his wrinkled black shirt. She ground her teeth and asked, "What guarantee do I have that you won't attack as soon as you're released anyway? It's what you promised yesterday."

"My word is good. But if you need more than that, Tyrrath has three princesses, does it not? None of you betrothed."

He inspected his hand as if bored with the direction of their conversation, picked at what looked like dried blood crusted around his nails. Maddie took an involuntary step back as realisation stole the volume from her reply. "You propose marriage."

"It would bind our kingdoms to the pact."

"I… I suppose it would."

"Then we're agreed?"

He looked up, the silver of his eyes pinning her in place.

Some small part of her was aware of Tristan storming into the room, shouting, "Don't you do it, Maddie," but his voice floated to her from far away, his hands grasping her arms barely registering beneath the weight of the Wolf's scrutiny.

A single step brought her nemesis within arm's reach, though a voice at the back of her head reminded her that chains prevented him from breaching his cell. She scrambled for an alternative solution, finding nothing but walls as thick as the dungeon around them.

"There would be stipulations," she blurted.

"Go on." His voice mocked her earlier impatience.

Tristan's face appeared in her line of sight, breaking the connection between her and the Wolf. He tugged her out to the landing and said, "I can't let you do this. We'll find another way."

"There is none. Any other option would put more lives in danger, and I'm not willing to do that when a treaty will stop him."

"But marriage? It's for life, Maddie. With that man."

He pointed towards the cell, and an involuntary shudder ran through her. She swallowed, lifted her chin. "Many royal marriages are arrangements between kingdoms. All three of us know this and have been prepared for the eventuality."

"But—"

"This is the way, Tristan. This is how I protect my people, by making a bargain with the Wolf. Now, please, let me go. Your objections only make this harder."

His jaw stiffened, and he looked down at the floor, then rubbed the back of his scalp. "This is my fault. I let you down by not seeing the danger sooner."

She reached out and touched his arm. "No. If it's anyone's fault, it's mine."

His head snapped up. "How is—"

"Are you really going to make me argue with you about this? You know I'll win."

He stared at her a moment longer, then the corners of his mouth twitched, and his muscles relaxed as he blew out a breath. She made to walk past him, but he stopped her with a touch to her elbow. "You know I'll always be here for you?"

"Thank you." Despite the situation, a grin took over her cheeks. "Who would've thought I'd be fighting this hard for a wedding treaty with the Wolf of Craeick."

He shook his head but gave her a lopsided smile and stepped aside.

She smoothed the fabric of her dress and marched back to the Wolf's cell, where he waited exactly where she had left him. "The marriage would be in name only for at least a year," she said, as if they had never been interrupted.

"Done."

"And the terms of our agreement must be signed and witnessed by both sides."

He sighed. "Fine."

"And your men will surrender their weapons and remain in their camp until after the wedding."

A growl escaped his throat, but he nodded.

Maddie swallowed. Creator forgive her, but, "Then, yes. We have a deal."

"Good."

She was about to leave when he added, "Not that it matters, but which princess will I be marrying?"

The thought of Joss or Olivia marrying the monster who had terrorised their kingdom was too much to even contemplate. This was her mess, her fault, and she would be the one to suffer the consequences. For the sake of her people, and her sisters, she had no other choice. Straightening her shoulders and lifting her chin, she looked the Wolf King directly in his cold, calculating eyes.

"Me."

Chapter 5
Maddie

On the morning of her wedding, Maddie woke with a crushing headache. She stumbled out of bed and over to the window, where she eased the curtain aside to reveal sagging, grey storm clouds and the miserable patter of rain on the rooftops. It figured.

She turned back to her bedchamber, achingly empty on a day that should, under normal circumstances, have been filled with joy. No mother, no sisters, only her faithful maid would be here to help her prepare.

Joss had barely spoken to her since she announced her engagement, muttering plans for rebellion and insisting they should have found another way to end the Craeickish invasion. Worse, Olivia's eyes had filled with tears whenever they crossed paths. Maddie had taken to avoiding them both, praying they would come around if she gave them enough time. It appeared three days was not enough.

But she needed them with her now, or she feared she would not be able to go through with it.

Someone knocked on the door, and Maddie crawled back under the covers, calling over her shoulder for Tabitha to enter. Maybe if she went back to sleep, the nightmare of the last few months would be over when she woke again.

"Can we come in?" Olivia's tentative voice, not Tabitha's, halted Maddie's quest for oblivion. She lowered the blanket and peeked out.

"We came to help you get ready." Joss held up an armful of winter flowers—hellebores, bloodroots, and Maddie's favourites, wild snowstars.

A lump formed in Maddie's throat. Her sister must have scoured half the nearby woods to have found so many of the delicate blooms, and with the Craeickish forces camped less than two miles away. Reckless, loveable girl.

Joss set the flowers on the chair beside the fireplace and launched herself at the bed, landing beside Maddie and wrapping her in a tight hug. "Sorry we reacted so badly. We just…"

They had hoped for more for her. She knew it even without looking at their faces, though they both attempted to smile. Sitting up, Maddie stretched her lips into the biggest grin she could manage, which only worsened her headache. She let out a low groan and leaned back against the pillows, rubbing her temples.

"Ach, my head."

"I have just the thing for that." Tabitha backed through the door bearing a tray laden with three cups of hot dakka and a heaped plate of griddle cakes. "I had a feeling I might be bringing breakfast for three today."

She deposited the tray on the end of the bed and put a blessedly cool hand to Maddie's forehead, then tutted and thrust one of the cups into her hands.

"Drink that. It'll soothe your nerves."

Maddie obeyed while Tabitha bustled about the room, adding a log to the crackling fire and brushing invisible lint from the dress Maddie had chosen to wear. Soft burgundy wool rippled at the maid's touch, and the vines embroidered along the gold ribbon edging the neck and hem appeared to come alive in the firelight.

It was a beautiful gown. Shame it would be wasted on the—

No. Maddie cut off the thought and focused instead on her sisters tucking into the steaming griddle cakes.

Joss juggled one between her hands, alternating between blowing on it and saying, "Ah, ah, ah," before tossing it back on the plate. She glared at the buttery round, then looked up, pointed at it, and said, "Still hot."

Maddie and Olivia burst into laughter, and the knot in Maddie's stomach loosened a little. It was good to have her sisters back. Whatever happened with the Wolf King, she could endure it if she had them by her side.

As soon as they finished breaking their fast, they bundled her out of bed and into a tub, then brushed and braided her hair, banishing the last of her headache with the tangles. By the time Tristan came to fetch her, she was dressed, her hair adorned with sweet-smelling flowers, and her mind focused on what she had to do.

Olivia opened the door to his firm, double rap, and Maddie stepped forwards to meet him.

He took her in and blinked. "You look… I mean…" He cleared his throat. "You look lovely, Your Highness."

"Thank you, Captain Kaar. Ready to give me away?"

She tried not to wince at her question but could not stop the memory of her father's still form, eyes closed in perpetual sleep, from flooding her thoughts. That should have been his role. If only he were here…

She took Tristan's arm and set off along the corridor. If her father were here, she would not need to be marrying at all. The Wolf would not have invaded in the first place, and all the unfortunate decisions that had led them here would never have been made.

But it was too late for regret. Maddie knew her role and would do her best to live up to her obligations, however odious. She pasted on a smile as they descended the stairs to where the witnesses who could be assembled on such short notice had gathered.

"Is everything in order?" she whispered to Tristan.

"No movement in the Craeickish camp, and the Wolf—King Lucas's wedding party is waiting at the chapel. Parker checked them for weapons before she let them through."

"Thank you."

"Your Highness." A gruff voice pulled her attention to the left, where a burly man wearing a brown, fur-trimmed cloak brushed off his companion and stomped towards her. "I can't believe you're going through with this farce."

The quality of his clothing combined with the fierce scowl carved into his rugged features suggested he was one of the border lords, but his name escaped Maddie's memory.

"Lord Walling." Tristan's low tone held a clear warning, and he placed himself partially in front of her.

Lord Walling—his lands abutted the western side of the Craeick border, his village one of the first to be targeted.

"How can you marry that dragon spawn?" the lord demanded, his hand gripping his sword hilt as though ready to avenge them at a moment's notice. "He slaughtered my people."

Guilt rolled through Maddie's gut, until she considered the many other villages under her care.

Nudging Tristan aside, she met the older man's eyes. "I understand how you feel, Lord Walling, truly. But what's the alternative? Resist? Counterattack? Face an all-out war?" She stepped closer and rested her hand on his arm, softening her voice. "And what of our people then? More families would be ripped apart, more lives lost."

He winced, his shoulders slumping as his hand fell from his weapon.

"The treaty includes reparation and protection from outside forces in future. No one can bring the dead back to life, but this is the best solution we have to stop further violence."

A sound somewhere between huff and grunt escaped him. But he lifted his gaze to the ceiling, loosed a breath, and moved aside, albeit with a grumbled, "I still don't think it's right."

Neither did Maddie, but she would do what she must, for her people. For her father. Lifting her chin, she returned to Tristan's side, smoothed her skirts, and nodded for them to continue.

They led the bridal party—her sisters directly behind her, Lord Elland, Lord Walling, and a handful of the other Northern lords falling in at the rear—through the main residence's double doors and out into the courtyard. The sky had stopped its tears, but dark clouds still hung low overhead and the ground was damp.

Four royal guards stood to attention outside. They saluted, then took up positions on either side of Maddie and Tristan as an honour guard. When they were ready, Maddie lifted her skirts and allowed Tristan to guide her around to the chapel.

She had done away with most of the trappings of a royal wedding, favouring speed over formality under the circumstances, but Tristan had insisted on at least this much, not trusting her groom one jot when it came to her protection.

"It's not too late, you know." His lips curved into a half smile, and he tilted his head towards the stables.

Maddie chuckled, then assumed a serious expression. "I'll let you know if I need to leave in a hurry."

"Maddie, I—" He shook his head. "I'm here if you need me. For anything."

He looked ahead, and his muscles jumped beneath her hand. She followed the direction of his gaze to find her soon-to-be husband waiting for them outside the chapel, flanked by two more of her guards and his own small wedding party. Her steps faltered, but Tristan kept her upright, his solid warmth at her side steadying in more ways than one.

She had not seen the Wolf—Lucas, she must think of him by his name now they were to wed—since she had accepted his offer. He had met with his second, a man of medium height and build with golden brown skin and twinkling eyes, that same afternoon. Then he had moved into respectable yet secure rooms at the far side of the keep, where he had remained under the watch of Tristan's most trusted guards until the treaty signing the previous evening.

Lucas wore a long black cloak, his matching hair swept back, brushing the fur collar. He seemed different in the light of day, more human, until he cocked his head and caught her in his cold stare, the scar standing out more vividly against his clean-shaven face.

Drawing fresh air deep into her lungs, she widened her smile, nodded a greeting, and approached the small portico where she would be married to the Wolf of Craeick.

The ceremony was brief, containing the bare minimum to be considered legal, and within an hour, Maddie was sitting at the high table in Northold's great hall beside Lucas Sinclair. Her husband.

The savoury scent of roasted meat wafted from her plate, but her stomach rebelled at the thought of eating anything. She closed her eyes on the pitying looks cast her way by servants and guests alike. She was doing this, had done this, for them. But it was so much harder when they treated her as if going through with the wedding had sealed her doom.

She touched the ring on her fourth finger, a plain band fashioned by the keep's smith until a family ring could be retrieved from Craeick. It felt cold, strange, heavy.

Joss squeezed her arm, and Maddie straightened and looked up—directly at a portrait of her parents. Unlike the formal poses commissioned for most great halls, it showed them sitting atop her father's favourite horse in the hills overlooking Arian Bay. Her mother straddled her father's lap with her arms around his neck and her head thrown back in laughter. And he looked down on her with such love, such confidence, it made Maddie's chest ache.

She had dreamed of a marriage like theirs, but it was not to be, and that was that. A glance around the hall, at the people chatting and eating, her people, eased the pain. She could stay strong for them, and her sisters. Better the ring was on her hand than either of theirs.

"I'm glad you're both here," she said, turning to face them at her left.

"So are we," Olivia replied.

"How do you feel, now it's all done?" Joss rested her fork on her plate and scrunched her lips to the side, eyeing Maddie closely.

Maddie lifted one shoulder. "It's not so bad, really."

She stole a look at her husband, who was talking to his second, General Munroe, and a stern woman with pale skin and bright copper hair seated to their right.

Maddie had to admit, Lucas cleaned up nicely, though there was still an air of danger about him.

The bloodstained clothes he had worn to attack Berricksford—and spent two nights in her dungeon wearing—had been replaced by a fresh shirt, doublet, and trousers. The black fabric stretched over his shoulders and bunched at his elbows where he had pushed his shirtsleeves back when they sat down to eat. Her gaze climbed higher, to the silver embroidery edging his doublet and the ends of his hair that curled in different directions at the base of his neck.

Her mouth twitched at the sight. He was not entirely controlled, then.

"They certainly know how to make everyone else uncomfortable," Joss said.

Maddie spun back to find her sister glaring a hole in his spine, and her cheeks heated, though she could not say why.

One of the musicians providing the after-dinner entertainment played a short scale on his pipe, and Joss's face lit. "Oh, let's dance. That'll cheer everyone up. Come on."

She grabbed Olivia's hand and dragged her from her seat, ignoring her protest and towing her around the table to the clear area in the centre of the room. At Joss's nod, the quintet struck up a lively tune, and she twirled Olivia across the floor.

Others joined in, and soon laughter, whistles, and the stomp of feet vied with the music filling the hall. Maddie tapped her toes to the beat and waited to see if Lucas would ask her to dance. She watched him from the corner of her eye, picking at the food on her plate, but he continued to talk to his officers as if she was not there at all.

For a few moments, she was not sure what to think about him completely ignoring her, but she eventually settled on relief. It meant he was sticking to their bargain that their marriage would be in name only.

A young boy of around nine or ten sat at the far end of the high table—Lucas's half-brother, according to Tristan. He shared the shape of his brother's nose and mouth, but his hair was a mass of deep red curls, and his eyes were green. He gave her a shy little wave. Then, at her warm smile, he slid off his seat and walked along the row towards her.

"Hello. I'm Flynn."

"Hello, Flynn. I'm Maddie."

"I know. I heard your name when you married my brother." He glanced up at Lucas, worship in his gaze. "You'll be glad you did. He's the best swordsman in the world, and the best brother. He always finds the juiciest caeldon berries."

Whatever Maddie had expected him to say, it was not that. "You get on well, then?"

"Oh, yes. He taught me how to ride and fish, and he saved me from—"

He bit his lip and looked anywhere but at her, and she pressed her lips into a thin line at the reminder of Lucas's reprehensible actions in bringing the boy to a battle.

"From my men?"

A nod of his head set his curls bouncing. He peered up at her from beneath his lashes and said, "I wasn't supposed to be there. I thought it was a dragon-hunting party, so I followed them when they set out from home. And when Luc found out, he told me to stay in the camp." His head drooped even lower. "But I followed again. If I hadn't disobeyed, he never would've been caught."

His head snapped up, eyes wide. "But then you never would have met him, so I suppose it worked out after all."

The Wolf King had not brought Flynn to the battle? Maddie studied her husband, trying to fit the disparate pieces of information about him together.

"It's a shame my parents aren't here. Roasted boar is my mam's favourite. But Lucas says they'll come later, when the pass thaws enough for the carriage. Can we go to the coast sometime?" Flynn asked, clasping his hands together and bouncing on his toes. "I've never seen the sea."

His guileless enthusiasm wormed past her defences, and in that moment, Maddie's heart melted for him. She promised herself that whatever happened between her and his brother, Flynn Ross would always have a warm welcome in Tyrrath.

"Then we'll have to visit Arian Castle. Everyone should see the ocean at least once. It's magical."

If possible, the boy's eyes stretched even wider, his jaw hanging open, and it occurred that he might have taken her description literally. She was about to explain when his brother's attention fixed on them.

"Stop pestering the princess, Flynn."

"Yes, Luc."

Flynn scampered back to his seat before she could object, and with a dismissive flick of his eyes in her direction, his obnoxious brother returned to his conversation. Maddie locked her hands together on her lap, her fingernails pressing into her skin. If Lucas Sinclair thought her unworthy of his attention, that was fine by her, but to force his brother to ignore her as well was ridiculous.

She watched Flynn, hoping to silently reassure him that he was always welcome to talk to her. He reached for his cup with both hands, then paused, eyed Lucas, and straightened, copying his mannerisms. Lucas raised his goblet to the boy, and Flynn returned the gesture, beaming like the sun itself had noticed his presence.

Maddie scoffed quietly, casting her husband a brief look that fell on his officers and lingered. They also appeared relaxed in his company, laughing and even teasing him. It showed more than mere respect for his position. She studied him anew.

Maybe there was more to him than just the fearsome warrior. Maybe he did not warm easily to strangers, and she needed to get to know him a little better. Anyone who could inspire such devotion was surely not entirely bad.

A greying head of hair snagged in her periphery, and she glanced at Lord Walling, reminded of those killed during the border raids. No, the Wolf of Craeick was not to be trusted. She picked up her wine, and the ring on her finger clinked against the side of the goblet, making her pause again.

Who was Lucas Sinclair? Was he the dangerous predator the old lord feared—she looked back at Flynn—or the hero his brother idolised?

Her head began to ache. Regardless of past conflicts, they were married. If she wanted the treaty to succeed, they would need to start building a different relationship.

But how? How did one talk to someone who was both stranger and husband? Talking to her sisters was easy, but the man beside her was a completely different animal, and one she had no idea how to approach.

Some time later, after a tale from a travelling bard and a few more rounds of dancing that Joss and Olivia and even Flynn joined in, Maddie's eyelids began to droop. Prolonged tension and lack of decent sleep the previous night combined with too much wine, no doubt, though she had only consumed a couple of goblets full. Nevertheless, she found herself struggling to focus and stifling a yawn.

"If you will excuse me," she said to the room at large, rising from her seat, "I will retire for the night."

Joss ran over from where she had been dancing with one of the border lords, cheeks flushed and eyes sparkling in the torchlight. She put a hand to her chest while she regained her breath, then said, "Goodnight, Maddie, dearest. Will you be..."

Her gaze drifted to Lucas, and Maddie squeezed her hand, speaking before Joss could finish the thought. "All is well. Have you seen Olivia?"

"She left while you were dancing with General Munroe."

"Ah." Maddie squashed a chuckle. Their youngest sister had a knack for slipping away without notice. "Then I'll leave as well. Goodnight to all."

Someone at the near end of one of the side tables raised a toast to her health, and she nodded her thanks before heading for the door to the royal apartments to the sounds of cheering.

When she arrived at her room, Tabitha was already there, turning back the covers and crying softly. "Oh, Your Highness. I don't know what to say."

Neither did Maddie. She was married, though not in any way or to any one she would have envisaged. She threw her arms around Tabitha and rested in her warm embrace, breathing in the scent of lavender, until another yawn broke loose.

Tabitha pulled away and rubbed Maddie's arms. "Come on, child. Let's get you ready for bed. I'm sure the wedding night nerves will have you wide awake in no time."

Maddie's heart kicked, then settled when she recalled that there would be no wedding night. Not a normal one, anyway. She and Lucas had kept that aspect of their arrangement from everyone, aside from her sisters, so she mumbled a vague agreement and allowed Tabitha to guide her to the chair by the fireplace and remove the flowers from her hair.

It was brushed and half plaited when a sharp triple knock at the door brought Maddie's head up. It opened before she had a chance to ask who was there, and Lucas walked into the room.

His presence expanded around him, pushing her farther into the cushions at her back. He looked around, his gaze wandering over her with little more note than he gave the bed or wardrobe, and gestured to someone outside.

A youth entered carrying a chest, and Lucas pointed to the far corner. "Put it over there for now."

Maddie jumped to her feet, wrapping her arms around her middle. "I didn't expect—"

What had she expected? That they would marry and he would continue to sleep at the other side of the keep? They had agreed to make a public show of unity to ease the friction between their kingdoms. That would hardly work if everyone knew they continued to live as strangers.

She glanced at the young man, who deposited the chest on the floor with a solid thud. "I'm surprised to see you join me so soon. Thank you, Tabitha. I can see to the rest myself."

Tabitha gave Maddie's arm a gentle squeeze. Then she bustled Lucas's aide out and closed the door behind them with a soft click, leaving Maddie alone with her new husband.

No iron bars separated them today. If he chose, he could easily break his word and take what was now his by right. She spun to the stool where her robe warmed in front of the fire and dragged it on over her dress, tying the cord tight.

Her room in Northold had no adjoining one, so until they returned to Faerstolmere, they would have to make do. She eyed the fleece under her feet, gauging its size in relation to the man towering before her.

"I'm sorry we don't have more space."

"No matter." He stripped off his doublet and pulled his shirt over his head, tossing it onto the chest as if he were alone.

Maddie spun to face the opposite wall.

A few moments later, the bed creaked behind her, and she turned, mouth gaping. He stretched out on his back, filling half the mattress. Thankfully, the covers were pulled up over his chest, but the arm folded beneath his head was bare.

"What are you doing?"

"Trying to get comfortable."

"I mean, um—" She took a deep breath and smoothed her robe over her hip. "I assumed you would sleep on the floor."

"Why would I do that?"

Inside her head, she yelled, *Because we had an agreement!* Physically, she only blinked.

He propped himself up on one elbow, the covers sliding down to reveal the broad expanse of his muscular chest. She stepped back, flinging her eyes up to his face, and his mouth curved into a lazy smirk that tugged at the scar bisecting his cheek.

"What's the matter?" he asked. "Afraid I'll have my wicked way with you?"

Her mouth dried, and all her words fled.

The bed protested as he flopped back down. "Relax, Princess. I've no interest in bedding a reluctant woman, but I'm not sleeping on the floor for anyone."

She stood awkwardly by the dying fire for another few moments, trying to think of a way to make him move, but he only closed his eyes and settled his head into the pillows, his breathing deepening.

What now?

He did not seem inclined to take advantage of her, which was a relief, but there was no way she could sleep beside him—and no way to drag a fully grown man out of bed if he did not want to move. She inched closer and peered at him, jumping when he turned onto his side.

Her eyes drifted to the floor. Could she sleep there? The thought made her want to cry.

She clenched her jaw and glared at him. No! She was dead on her feet, and if he was indifferent to sharing a bed with her, well, then, so could she be. She shrugged off her robe and draped it over the back of the chair, knocking something onto the floor with a loud thud.

The hairbrush.

The Wolf shifted, making the bed creak again, and she snatched up the brush, brandishing it like a weapon. He settled, and she breathed out once more.

Would climbing into bed disturb him too? She stilled. Frowned. This was *her* room. If he didn't want to be woken, he should have slept on the floor—or elsewhere.

She removed the rest of her clothes, donning her nightdress as quickly as her trembling fingers would allow, and slid ever so carefully under the covers, keeping one eye on him. Perched on the edge of the mattress, as far away from him as possible, she stared at the beamed ceiling, ears attuned to the slightest movement beside her as her heart banged against her ribcage.

Sleep refused to come. For a long time, she listened to the sounds of revelry drifting up from below, then, as it died down and silence blanketed the keep, to the low snores rumbling through the bed. Not daring to move in case she woke the Wolf and he changed his mind, she clutched the blanket around her chin and counted the hours till dawn.

Chapter 6
Maddie

Maddie's eyes were closed when the mattress shifted beneath her. Closed! She popped them open, her entire body stiffening. Had she fallen asleep? Had the Wolf taken advantage? Slowly, so as not to alert him to the movement, she twisted her head enough to watch him sit upright.

He stood and stretched, his outline barely visible in the thin, pre-dawn light sneaking around the curtains. Then he yanked one of them aside and crossed the room to his trunk. As he padded past the end of the bed, various lines on his body caught her eye, some thick and red, others thin and white with age. They could not all have been from the attacks on her land.

"Where did you get all those scars?"

He glanced at his arms and shrugged. "Training. Battle." He tossed a black shirt over his head, and it dropped down his torso, covering the evidence of his wounds. "Life isn't easy in the mountains, Princess. Not like here."

She bristled at his assumption, but with the brutality of his life so clearly displayed on his flesh, how could she argue that hers was not one of comparative comfort and luxury?

"Where are you heading this morning?" she asked, rubbing the grit from her eyes.

He met her gaze but did not answer straight away, pulling on a thick, leather jerkin and fastening the straps, then reaching for his boots. The all-black ensemble made it appear like he gathered the shadows about him rather than dressed for a new day.

"I'm going to see to my men." When he finally spoke, the low rumble of his voice made her start. He speared her with a mocking grin. "Now they're allowed to leave their hillside prison. So I won't disturb you if you want to sleep longer, like a fine lady of the flatlands."

She opened her mouth to refute him, but fatigue chose that moment to catch up to her, producing a yawn too big to hide. He chuckled and let himself out, leaving her caught between impotent irritation and an overwhelming need to sleep.

"I haven't slept for two days," she called after him, but his heavy footsteps had already faded along the landing. "Thanks to you," she mumbled, snuggling back under the still-warm blankets.

The last thought she had before dropping off was that they smelled of leather and musk instead of sandalwood.

The next time she woke, it was to bright sunshine flooding the room. Tabitha hummed as she tied the curtains back, picked up Maddie's discarded gown, and moved her slippers closer to the flickering fire.

"How are you feeling today, Your Highness?"

Maddie sat up and stretched. "Better. What time is it?"

"Almost midday—"

"What?" She threw the covers aside and scrambled out of the bed. "Why didn't you wake me sooner?"

Tabitha held out the robe, which Maddie ignored in favour of running to the wardrobe to find a fresh dress.

"I looked in at dawn as usual," the old maid said, "and again a few hours later. But when you still didn't stir… Well, I know it's not like you to sleep so late, but I thought you might need your rest this morning."

A groan escaped Maddie, and her search became more frantic. "Lord Elland and the others must have given up on me by now. We were supposed to discuss the rebuilding plans this morning."

The Northern lords were far more straightforward in their dealings than the royal council, but they would still frown on tardiness.

"I'm sure they'll understand in the circumstances." A moment later, Tabitha tutted. "What are you doing, child? You're getting them all creased."

She nudged Maddie aside and set about straightening the dresses she had riffled through. Then she pulled out a midnight blue one with silver edging and pointed Maddie towards the ewer and basin. "Wash first."

When Maddie made to protest, she held the gown out of reach. "They've waited this long; they can wait a little longer. You need to be presentable on your first day as a married woman."

That made Maddie pause. She looked down at the ring on her fourth finger but gave herself a little shake and focused on getting ready instead. "Have you seen Joss and Olivia this morning?" she asked as she poured water into the bowl and picked up the soap.

"Olivia's with her tutor. He brought a stack of history books from Faerstolmere that should keep her occupied till you're ready to head home."

Good. "And Joss?"

Tabitha handed her a towel. "Joss is out in the woods. But she'll be fine. Captain Kaar sent Parker with her, and if anyone can keep up with Joss, it's her."

Maddie clutched the cloth, twisting it between her fists, then pushed out a breath and forced her fingers to loosen. There was no logical reason to keep Joss inside the keep any longer, and she would have only sneaked out had they tried to stop her. Still, it was hard not to worry, no matter how well-equipped she was to handle herself.

"I wish sometimes Papa had never encouraged her to pick up a bow and arrow."

"She'd have found one eventually. That girl's got archery in her blood." Tabitha raised a brow, her eyes flicking to Maddie's hand. "And you can be just as headstrong when you choose."

"That's completely different, and you know it." Maddie snatched up her dress and stepped into it, turning her back for Tabitha to fasten the laces. "Now help me get ready so I don't waste any more of the day."

Less than a quarter hour later, Maddie rushed down the stairs and around to the map room, but when she arrived, only Lord Elland and one other lord were there.

"Your Highness," they said in unison, standing to offer polite bows that she returned with a nod.

"Apologies for my lateness, gentlemen. The other lords left?"

"I hope you don't mind," Lord Elland said, "but I suggested we reconvene at a more convenient time, Ma'am. We shouldn't have requested your presence so soon after your wedding."

Maddie felt her cheeks heat. "Yes. I suppose I should have considered that myself." She turned to the other man. "You still wish to speak with me, Lord Grayston?"

"Ah, yes, Your Highness. The land chosen for the Craeickish settlement abuts my estate. I wanted to ask… That is…"

"Your land will be safe, Lord Grayston. Safer than anywhere on the continent, I imagine. The terms with King Lucas are very specific, and the fort he's building here in Tyrrath is for our protection as well as those of his people who choose to settle in the adjoining town."

She glanced at Lord Elland, whose sharp eyes twinkled, then stepped closer to the other lord and lowered her voice. "In fact, they'll probably be in need of much help in the coming months. A good opportunity for his closest neighbour to build trust and establish trade, yes?"

"Yes." Lord Grayston stroked his short beard, staring into the middle distance for a moment. He looked back at Maddie and bowed again. "Thank you, Ma'am. You've given me much to think about. If you'll excuse me, I'll pass on your reassurances to my family."

"Of course."

Lord Elland joined her as she watched him leave. "He'll go straight to his steward with instructions to begin negotiations with King Lucas's man."

"Then we'll have one less terrified lord to deal with and be one step closer to peace again." Maddie caught his smile and frowned. "What? Did I do something wrong?"

He twisted to fully face her. "On the contrary, Ma'am. Your father would be so proud of you."

Warmth spread through Maddie's chest even as tears pricked her eyes. She swallowed, having no words to thank him. "So, what now?" she asked when she was able.

Lips pursing, he looked to the window, and Maddie finally noticed the lack of noise filtering through from outside. Not entirely silent, the usual clang of hammers from the smithy and raucous chatter of the stable hands and guardsmen training in the courtyard was nevertheless subdued, as if a thick blanket smothered their activities.

"Have the Craeickish soldiers broken camp?"

"Most of them left around mid-morning, heading south-west to the land we gave them…"

"But some stayed." Maddie could well imagine her people's reaction and closed her eyes on the painful image.

"It would help for the townsfolk to see you. Set them the example."

She straightened, gave him a tight smile. "I'd planned to visit the inn this afternoon anyway. That should be the perfect opportunity to ease some concerns." Though forgiving wounds—and worse wrongs—would understandably take far longer.

Her stomach rumbled, and she pressed a hand against it, stilling. "Sorry. I haven't eaten yet."

Lord Elland let out a laugh and patted her free hand. "Maybe break your fast first then. Diplomacy is always best attempted on a full stomach."

He walked her to the great hall, then left her for the study, where he intended to spend the afternoon working on the plans for the new town. Located in Hawkesden, a fertile valley in the foothills of the Stonetooth mountains, it would provide Lucas's people with everything they needed to establish a settlement in Tyrrath. She only hoped the rest of the local lords would be as amenable to the arrangement as Lord Grayston had been.

Meanwhile, she would stop by the kitchen for some bread and ham, then visit the refugees and let her people see there was nothing to fear from her husband and his men.

Half an hour later, her stomach full of fish stew, smoked pork with saffron cabbage, and a large slice of spiced apple pie that Tabitha had made her eat, Maddie fastened her cloak around her shoulders and walked through the double doors into the courtyard. The air was crisp and the sky clear, though the cobblestones were still a little slick after the previous day's downpour.

The stablemaster paused his conversation with a young stable hand and bowed in her direction. "Afternoon, Your Highness. Want me to saddle Midnight for you?"

"Not today, thank you." She tilted her head towards the town. "I'm on a mission."

"Right oh, Ma'am."

She continued past them and approached the gate, where one of the guards on duty peeled off to accompany her. Maddie waved her off. An armed escort would hardly send the right message.

"Captain's orders," the guard said.

Maddie's teeth clenched, but she exhaled and smiled brightly. "Then I'm overruling them. I won't leave the town, but I *will* go alone."

The guard stood to attention, her heels clicking together. "Yes, Ma'am."

She re-joined the others, and Maddie left the confines of the keep for the first time in over a week. She walked down the hill, filling her lungs with fresh air and revelling in the simple freedom of being alone. Off to her left, the stream that fed the keep from the mountains at her back burbled over its rocky bed, finally throwing off winter's chill. Soon it would find others and become a river, winding across her kingdom to the sea.

The urge rose to mount Midnight and chase its course, but Maddie squashed it. Duty called louder. She was responsible for the plight of her people—arrangements for their welfare must come first. And the possibility of healing some of the deeper wounds the conflict had wrought.

As she descended into the town and buildings blocked her view of the rolling landscape beyond, she straightened her back and lifted her chin, determined to greet everyone she encountered with a friendly smile and an encouraging word.

Unfortunately, her efforts were wasted. Only a handful of people braved the main street, far fewer than usual for that time of day, and unease bled through their stilted movements and whispered conversations. The palpable undercurrent threatened her resolve, dimming her smile and slowing her steps.

She was passing the apothecary when a boy of no more than three or four ran out from the alley beyond it and straight into her legs. He let out a small cry, clutched her skirts to steady himself, and looked up.

His eyes rounded, and he blurted, "You the princess." Then his little forehead bunched. "You married a bad man."

Maddie could only blink at the accusation in his tone. Was this how the townspeople perceived her marriage? The strength of their feelings such that even a child picked up on it?

Before she could devise a response, a woman with several strands of hair escaping her cap and what appeared to be a blob of batter stuck to her cheek ran up and caught him by the arm. She dipped a curtsey, mumbled a quick apology, and dragged him back the way he had come, leaving Maddie staring after them.

She glanced around, relieved that no one had witnessed the incident, and set off again, more determined than ever to calm the tension simmering within the town.

More people filled the square, but still nowhere near the bustling crowds she was used to seeing. She almost faltered when a couple of Craeickish soldiers rounded a corner in front of her, black, dragonhide armour polished to a dull, scaly shine, shoulder-length hair tied back from their faces with metal-tipped cords. Even without their weapons, they were a formidable sight.

They strolled towards the inn, their relaxed demeanour at such odds with those around them that it sent a shiver across her skin. She pulled her cloak closer and forged ahead, noting some of the nearby mumblings shift from fear to hatred and disbelief.

Someone shouted, "Go home, you murderers!" but when she spun to find them, there was no sign of anyone having spoken, only a scattering of groups with equally hunched shoulders, and a space widening around the northerners.

Maddie peered at them.

They walked at the same pace and chatted in the same tone as before, either indifferent to the label or disciplined enough to ignore it. Either way, the likelihood of a clash diminished with each passing heartbeat, and Maddie relaxed her taut muscles.

She bit the inside of her lip. Maybe allowing Lucas's troops access to Northold had not been such a good idea after all. She had hoped it would show her people they were no longer a threat, but that had clearly been the wrong decision. A glance at the tormented faces around her proved as much. Would they stop at heckling or push things further?

More importantly, what could she do to prevent the tension from worsening? To soothe nerves and foster peace?

A flash of black drew her attention to the far side of the square. Another group of soldiers headed towards the main gate, her husband easily identifiable among them, though she could not pinpoint why. They disappeared between two buildings before she could call out, so she veered in their direction and picked up her pace, an idea forming as she went.

"Um, good day, Your Highness."

A broad-faced man bowed in front of her, clutching his cap in both hands. Several fragments of hay clung to the sleeve of his plain brown tunic, and sandy hair stuck out from his head at odd angles.

"Good day."

"Begging your pardon, Ma'am, but I wanted to thank you again for your kindness last week. It were much appreciated. Much appreciated indeed."

Maddie wracked her brain for the connection, drawing a blank. Then he ducked his head and rubbed the back of his neck, and it hit her—the messenger from

Farweather. She barely recognised him without soot covering his face.

"How are you faring now… Finley?"

"Not so bad, considrin', Ma'am." He looked off to the right, and his face lit. "Can I introduce my wife and our lass, Ma'am?" he asked, waving someone over.

Tamping down the need to be on her way, Maddie followed his gaze in time to see a little girl running towards them trip on a cobblestone and fall. She held herself still and silent for a double heartbeat, then her face crumpled, and she let out a wail that would have made a dragon whelp proud.

"Oh dear."

Before Maddie could rush over to offer aid, her mother scooped her up and, after a brief exchange, lifted the girl's smock to reveal a small gash on her knee. The woman cupped the area and closed her eyes for a few moments. When she opened them and lifted her hand away, the skin on her daughter's leg was completely healed.

Maddie stared in awe. A mage.

The continent of Egrea had once been ripe with magic, accessed freely by the dragons that roamed the land. Then humans had arrived.

At first, they befriended the dragons, living in harmony with them and learning to harness their vast power by somehow bonding with them. The history books were hazy on what happened next, but the most common theory said that between the mage wars and attempts to tame the dragons, magic had all but died out nearly a thousand years ago.

Nowadays, dragons fell into two categories—those subdued and used as domesticated animals by the neighbouring kingdom of Brunland, and those in the far north, wild creatures that only ventured south to hunt. And mages—they were rare now, capable of far less than their ancestors, the magic having been bred out of their lines as surely as with the dragons of old. To see one in action was fascinating.

Questions bubbled through Maddie's mind, but she clamped her lips closed and concealed her curiosity behind the polite mask her tutors had drilled into her. Princesses did not gape like fish, especially not in public.

The woman hoisted the tot onto her hip and continued walking towards them as if the incident had never happened. Safe in her mother's arms, the little girl scrubbed her damp eyes, looked up, and beamed at Maddie.

An answering smile crept past Maddie's defences. "I remember you."

Beside her, Finley's head swivelled between them. "You've met?"

"Pretty lady and her friend give me darley bread," the little girl, Sara, said. "Can I have some more?"

"Sara!" The woman put a hand to her face. "I hope she didn't cause you too much trouble the other day."

"Not at all. It was the least I could do." Maddie looked at Finley, whose eyes had grown round and jaw hung slack. "This is your family?"

The woman also turned to him, absently brushing the hay from his sleeve. "You know each other?"

Finley swallowed, his features frozen in abject horror. "This is Princess Madeline, Bron. Ma'am, my wife, Bronwen."

"*Princess*?" Bronwen squeaked, the truth dawning in her eyes as she took in the quality of Maddie's plain cloak. "Oh, Your Highness. I'm so sorry. I didn't know." She dropped Sara to the ground and dipped into a deep curtsey, her hands shaking so much her skirts trembled.

"Please don't fret," Maddie said. "I've had far worse introductions at court." When the other woman did not rise, she leaned closer and whispered, "An Iskarian ambassador once found me with my sisters in the garden and thought I was their tutor. He tried to buy me for his daughter. Took my father an entire week to convince him I was the crown princess."

Bronwen snorted, then looked up. "Really, Ma'am?"

"Creator's truth." Maddie guided her to her feet and asked, "How did you do that? Heal Sara's knee?"

"Mage on my mother's side," Bronwen replied, animation returning to her voice once more. "Twelve generations back, but I have enough of the magic to heal scrapes and cuts, don't I, love?"

She stroked Sara's head, and the little girl raised her arms to be lifted again. Finley swept her up and spun her around, eliciting a giggle, before tucking her into his side. She rested her cheek on his shoulder and stuck her thumb in her mouth, eyelids drooping.

Maddie glanced down at her leg. Not even a bruise marred the skin where she had cut herself.

"Incredible. I've never met anyone with the gift before. Can you do anything else? Light fires, or move objects?" A list of abilities danced through her mind, exotic tales from Brunland and Garellion, passed on by academics who studied the arts of the mages but had no magic in their lines.

Bronwen shook her head. "As far as I know, most of us can only do one thing. For me, that's healing flesh wounds. My great-great-grandfather could mend bones as well, but all I can do is knit broken skin together."

"Still, it's a useful skill to have. Will you go home to Farweather now?"

"Not much to go back for," she said.

Finley shuffled, not quite meeting Maddie's gaze. "Ours was one of the houses taken by the fires, Ma'am. The pigs too." He stilled and his voice took on a faraway quality. "Lucinda was the best truffler this side of the Goldenoaks. Don't know what I'll do without her. A plague on that Wolf King!"

Bronwen gasped and dug her elbow into his side. He blinked, then froze, his expression stricken. "I'm so sorry, Your Highness. I didn't mean..."

A pang of guilt-laced sympathy speared Maddie's chest, and she had to force her hand not to rise to the spot. "Please. I'm the one who's sorry. You've lost so much."

She watched Sara, sleeping on her father's shoulder, and her mind raced for a way to redress the loss. Fortunately, inspiration struck. "You're a truffle hunter, you say?"

"Yes, Ma'am." His chest puffed out. "One of the best."

"Then you should come and work in Mochynden Forest."

"The royal woods," Finley whispered, eyes widening.

Maddie nodded. "Our cook is always in need of experienced suppliers." And the vast estate could easily accommodate one more truffler. If not, she would ask Lord Elland to find something else.

"It won't be your own living, but it comes with a cottage, and I'm sure Bronwen could find a position with one of Faerstolmere's healers."

Bronwen clasped her hands to her chest. "Oh, that would be wonderful. Thank you, Ma'am. We won't let you down. We're hard workers, both of us."

"Well, then. Here." She unfastened the small brooch she was wearing and pressed it into Bronwen's resistant fingers. "Come up to the keep tomorrow and show them this. I'll have the arrangements made."

Maddie's heart felt lighter as she repaid their hasty bow and curtsey with a dipped head and turned back towards the inn. No doubt there would be many more such cases among the refugees, and she would not be able to create positions for all of them, but she had made a good start, a very good start indeed. And if she could convince her husband to join her efforts, they might not only repair the damage his invasion had caused but build a stronger kingdom in its wake.

Chapter 7

Luc

Two days after the wedding, Luc swept his sword through a series of movements, his body falling into the familiar rhythm as naturally as breathing. The grip below the wolf-headed pommel, worn by years of use, perfectly fitted his hand, and it felt good to hold his own weapon again. He came to a stop, muscles singing, sword tip held steady at shoulder height, then gestured for Flynn to join him in the centre of the small training yard.

"See? You need to move with the blade, from here." He twisted his hips. "Not swing from your elbow. Now, try again."

His brother hefted his weapon, a wooden practice sword Aiden had carved to fit his small frame, and stared straight ahead. His lips moved silently for a few moments, breath puffing in the cold air, then he copied the sequence Luc had just demonstrated. Each move was slow but far less jerky than the last time.

"Good. Again."

After Flynn's next attempt, Luc stepped in and adjusted his brother's stance, nudging his feet farther apart on the packed dirt. He was about to review the downwards strike when a rustle of fabric behind them made him spin around.

The princess stood by the wall of the keep. Her soft smile prickled like burrs under his skin, and he gritted his teeth. Training was no place for female sentiment.

With a jerk of his chin, he set Flynn to practising again, and stalked over to the woman. If his brother caught sight of her, his focus would be completely destroyed. "What do you want, Princess?"

She straightened, her expression smoothing into a blank mask. Impressive, he absently noted. "We need to talk."

"I'm busy."

"This cannot wait."

A grunt escaped his throat. He sheathed his sword and, putting finger and thumb to his mouth, whistled a short, two-tone note.

Rheann Braydeson, his most trusted lieutenant, jogged around the corner, hand on hilt. She stopped beside them, glanced at the princess, and raised a brow. "Sire?"

"Take over with Flynn." Luc tilted his head towards his brother. "And watch his hold on the downward swing. It needs work."

With a single nod, she walked into the training yard, and Luc turned to the princess.

Her eyes darted around them, and she fidgeted with her skirts. Dragons' breath! If she wanted to talk, why could she not get on with it? He steered her towards the nearest doorway—a store attached to the smithy—and ducked inside.

"Out. Now," he said to the lad polishing weapons by an open window at the far end.

The boy jumped, then scrambled through a door opposite the one Luc had used, letting it close behind him with a dull bang.

Luc gestured to the princess and walked farther in to give her space to enter. Folding his arms across his chest, he leaned against the wooden bench and waited for her to speak. Again.

She scanned the room before settling her gaze on him. "I've been looking for you since yesterday."

His brow rose a fraction. He had assumed she wanted as little to do with him as possible and had gladly obliged, resuming his habit of taking a solitary, late-night walk along the battlements, and rising an hour before dawn to train with his men.

"Well, now you've found me. What do you want?"

She wet her lips, drawing his attention to her mouth. "We need to spend more time together."

A smirk tugged at his cheeks, and he looked her up and down. Soft hair, full lips, curvy figure. He pushed off the bench and stepped towards her. "I'd be happy to get closer if that's what you want. Just say the word."

Eyes the colour of wet peat rounded, and she shuffled backwards half a pace before stopping and lifting her chin. "Not like that."

"Then I've got training to get back to."

He made to leave but she blocked his way out.

"Our people need to see us together. To see that we've put aside any hostilities and are at peace."

"Didn't the marriage solve that?"

"Yes, to an extent, but… Less than a week ago, you were attacking our villages, and now your men are—"

"Are any of them causing trouble?" He had given express instructions for how they were to conduct themselves in the town and made clear what would happen should they defy his orders.

"No. They're actually surprisingly restrained, but—"

"Then I don't see the problem."

"You would if you let me finish," she growled, her forehead wrinkling like a wolf pup kept from a plate of meat. She pushed out a breath, and the lines disappeared. "People are anxious. They look to us as their leaders to set the example, so we need to show them there's nothing to fear, that the alliance is real and the fighting a thing of the past."

"I'm not changing my plans to coddle your subjects."

Her eyes narrowed, and he could not help imagining the wolf pup preparing to pounce. "I'm not asking you to change your whole day, just to spend some time together in public. This afternoon, maybe. How does it look if we ignore each other?"

Ah, they came to it at last. "You care too much about what people think of you."

"And you care too little," she snapped.

Control slipping, he crowded her space. "On the contrary, Princess. I care a great deal. I just limit my concern to the people that matter."

She flinched, and he spun to leave through the second door, done with wasting his time.

"Like it or not, we're family now," she called out behind him. "Husband and wife."

Something shifted in his chest at her words, and he paused mid step. He had not fully considered it before, but technically, their marriage *had* made them family. She shared his name, which was more than even his mother did since her marriage to Flynn's father. But that meant… what?

He frowned, twisting the signet ring around his finger as he tried to shake the feeling creeping through him.

Her hand touched his arm, startling him from his thoughts. "It was your idea for us to marry in the first place. Can't we at least *try* to get along?"

Could they? He put family—his brother, mother, and stepfather—above all else, and if she was part of that now too, her welfare—maybe even her happiness—was his responsibility. Was it not? No. This was just an arrangement, a means to an end. And yet. Family. That connection tugged at him.

Dammit! He slammed his fist into the wall, bringing a rain of dust motes down from the ceiling. Slowly, he turned around, but she was already gone. The door swung closed behind her, leaving an empty room and a conflicted man in her wake. He scrubbed a hand over his face and followed her out, watching from the doorway as she crossed the courtyard in the direction of the keep.

They *were* family, whether he liked it or not, which meant he would have to make amends, starting with appeasing her fear-riddled, lowland-softened people.

"I see you're charming your new wife already."

Luc whipped his gaze over his shoulder as Aiden stepped up beside him, attention fixed on the princess and the hint of a smirk edging his features. He folded his arms across his chest and tossed Luc a knowing look. "What did you do?"

Lips pressed into a tight line, Luc stared ahead, avoiding both his friend and the princess's retreating figure.

"You're the one who decided to get married instead of taking the land we need in battle." Aiden cocked his head. "But I can see why. She *is* pretty."

"Shouldn't you be overseeing the morning training?"

Aiden's grin spread wide. He stretched his back and said, "I sent them on a run. Came to ask if Flynn wants to join us for archery practice."

Luc was about to answer when movement in his periphery caught his eye. Captain Karr jogged over to the princess, stopping her at the bottom of the steps to the keep. He gripped her shoulders and bent until their faces were barely a hand span apart. Then the princess waved her arms in expansive gestures while he nodded and stepped even closer. Luc snorted, though it sounded more like a growl.

A moment later, the captain stiffened and looked up. The glare he fixed on Luc burned across the courtyard, and Luc clenched his teeth.

"Looks like you made another friend," Aiden said.

“I’m talented that way.” Luc turned his back on the pair. “He’s nothing I can’t handle if it comes to it.”

Aiden scratched his jaw. “I wouldn’t be so sure about that. I’ve heard he’s a skilled swordsman.”

“What? Him?” Luc jerked his thumb over his shoulder in the general direction of the captain.

“Yes. His father trained him until his mid-teens.”

Luc stared blankly at his friend, and Aiden tsked. “You really should’ve paid better attention to your tutors. Altan Kaar… Golden Blade of Iskaria. Hero of Bakri…”

“One of the five legends of the ages,” Luc finished. He twisted around and studied the captain with narrowed eyes as the man laughed at something the princess said. “Impressive lineage. But it doesn’t mean he inherited his father’s talent. And no matter how well-trained, a guard dog is no match for a wolf.”

Aiden’s hand landed on his shoulder. “Is that confidence or jealousy talking?”

“Jealousy?” Luc shrugged free. “Why would I be jealous?”

Backing up, Aiden spread his arms and glanced at the captain and princess entering the keep arm in arm. “Because your wife runs from you but smiles at him.”

Luc jabbed a fist at his so-called friend, missing by a fraction. He would have followed through with another strike, but Aiden sprang out of reach, his grin far too self-satisfied. Rather than fuel his addle-brained notions, Luc gestured in the direction of the training grounds where his men spent their mornings.

"Go set up the targets before I make you join the men on their run."

Aiden straightened, all traces of humour gone save a glint in his eyes. "Should I set one up for Flynn?"

"No. His form still needs work. Rhee will stay with him."

A grimace flashed across Aiden's features, and he muttered, "Poor kid," as he turned towards the gate separating the barracks from the main keep.

Luc followed but could not help glancing over his shoulder before ducking through the archway. Though the princess was long gone, her words lodged in his flesh like a splinter, and he rubbed at the ache in his chest.

She was his wife, his responsibility. If any man was going to see to her needs, it should be him, not Tristan Karr.

Chapter 8
Maddie

"Are you sure you don't want to come with us?" Maddie asked her sister.

Olivia peeked through the window at the blustery sky and wrinkled her nose. "No thanks. I'd rather stay in the library." Her eyes lit. "I found a book on the mage wars that's got a whole chapter on Galisia."

The corner of Maddie's lips twitched. "Haven't you read everything there is to know about her by now?"

"But she was our ancestor, and so incredible. All those things she could do…"

"That she was. Just make sure Tabitha knows where you are, all right?"

With a little nod and an absent wave, Olivia walked away.

Maddie watched her for a few moments, smile tender and heart full. Her little sister could lose herself in books for days if no one reminded her to eat or sleep. But she was growing up fast, the same dark hair and delicate features as their mother, and almost as tall as Joss since her latest growth spurt, though all elbows and knees.

Making a mental note to speak to Tabitha about adjusting Olivia's hems again, Maddie focused on her own plans for the afternoon and swung her cloak around her shoulders. She had several refugees to visit after her trip to the market, and Lord Elland would need her to sign the documents he was working on while she was gone.

She stepped outside to a gust of frigid air and pulled the cloak close. Oof! Maybe Olivia had the right idea after all.

"Hurry up, will you?" Joss stood in the centre of the courtyard, bouncing on her toes, tendrils of loose brown hair swirling around her face.

Maddie threw her a quick frown before pulling on her gloves and joining her.

"I'm coming."

"About as fast as a snail," Joss grumbled. "I've been waiting for ages."

Ages? Joss barely knew the meaning of the word, flitting from one thing to the next as soon as she grew bored. "You try running the kingdom. See how much free time you have."

Joss only grunted.

"You could be more help you know, especially as you're supposed to be responsible for this region."

"That was before—"

A black mass loomed at the edge of Maddie's vision, and she spun to find Lucas standing beside them. She blinked. How had he appeared so suddenly?

More importantly, what was he doing there at all? He was the last person she had expected to see so soon after their altercation that morning. Her mind raced for an explanation, but he was as fathomable as the wind tugging at their garments.

"Do you two need a moment?" Joss asked.

He flicked a glance at Maddie, his stony features giving nothing away. "I'm here, as requested."

"To go into town with us." The confusion in Joss's tone made the statement sound more like a question.

"If that's what we're doing."

"You don't know?" Her eyebrows bunched together as she eyed them both in turn.

He pushed out a breath. "The princess asked me to join you, so here I am. But I need to be back with my men in an hour, so let's get on with it."

"I see." Joss gave him an assessing look that Maddie prayed would not turn into more questions, then turned to Maddie. "Come on then."

She set off, and after an awkward moment, they followed.

When they neared the gatehouse, Parker slid a helmet over her plaited blonde hair, detached from the group of guards, and walked forwards, but Joss waved her off. "It's all right, Parker. King Lucas is coming with us. I doubt anyone will try anything with him around."

Maddie could not prevent her gaze from straying to the wolf-headed sword at his hip. Indeed. They would be foolish to try.

Parker stood to attention as they passed under the archway, her grey eyes following their progress, and

Maddie gave the guard a grateful smile. At least she would not have to keep track of Joss for the afternoon.

Outside the gates, a thick layer of icy slush covered the lane. They trudged through it, the cold soon penetrating Maddie's leather boots.

Joss dropped behind for a few steps but caught up on Lucas's far side with a wink. Maddie would have glared at her but feared her husband would assume it was directed at him and turn back. The silence between them pressed in on her and she searched the freezing landscape for a way to break it.

Clearing her throat, she asked her husband, "Is there anything you need while we're in town?"

"No."

"Oh. The market here has most supplies, though we usually have to wait until the spring thaws for anything specialised."

No response. Maddie looked over at Joss, who shrugged.

"I want to see if the smith has any throwing knives," Joss said.

"You train in combat?"

Lucas's question startled Maddie so that it took a moment for the disbelief in his tone to register.

Joss straightened. "Yes. Why?"

He stopped walking. "A princess of Tyrrath, trained for battle?"

Her cheeks flushed, and Maddie silently cursed his derision.

"Just archery."

"Mm-hm."

"But Parker let slip my aim's as good as our top marksman, so I thought I'd try something else."

He looked at Maddie, one black brow lifted. "And you, Princess?"

She merely shook her head. She had no interest in handling weapons. That was Tristan's domain.

Lucas's eyes slid to her hip before he turned away, as if in confirmation that no weapon bulged beneath her cloak, and she could have sworn she saw a trace of disappointment in his gaze.

They continued on, their feet sloshing through wet snow and the wind tearing through the bare forest the only sounds until Lucas spoke up again.

"Why not get a set from your armourer?"

"Because Tristan would find out and forbid it." A mischievous grin spread across Joss's cheeks. "But he has no jurisdiction over the town smith."

Lucas barked a laugh, and they fell silent once more.

Maddie attempted to engage him in conversation a couple more times, but his terse responses soon sapped her will to try. Yet despite his clear reluctance to talk, he matched his long stride to hers, and when she slipped on some hidden ice, his arm was instantly there to steady her.

"Be careful, Princess. Unless you're asking to be carried the rest of the way?"

"Oh, n-no. Thank you." She forced a smile to her lips, despite the heat burning her cheeks, but he had already turned away. Balance regained, she focused on the ground beneath her feet and pondered his behaviour—just one more odd piece of the puzzle that was her husband.

By the time they arrived at the market, word of their outing had clearly spread through the town. People milled around the stalls in the centre of the square, some casting them sideways looks, others staring openly, their murmurs rumbling beneath the whistle of the wind.

Maddie straightened her cloak over her skirts and edged closer to Lucas, ensuring her posture remained relaxed and her smile warm. This was the point, after all. To set an example for her people and let them see they had nothing more to fear from Lucas or his men.

Joss made a beeline straight for the smith's workshop at the far-left corner of the square, and Maddie followed behind, acknowledging a few greetings along the way. When she and Lucas arrived, he opened the door for her, and she beamed at him before ducking inside.

The heat from the forge hit her like a wall after the icy cold outside, making her cheeks tingle and the ties on her cloak feel too tight. She loosened them and looked around, finding Joss already engrossed in a selection of slender knives the smith was laying out on a wooden counter bisecting the room.

Stepping aside to let Lucas enter behind her, Maddie scanned the rest of the space. She had never visited the shop before, and the light shining through the windows revealed a veritable trove of metal objects. Hanging from the walls, standing on the floor, and piled in various barrels were nails, hinges, spoons, knives, hoes and scythes, a single helm, and several deadly-looking weapons.

Lucas wandered around, running his fingers over a few of the items on display, but Maddie remained by the doorway, unsure of the correct etiquette. Did the smith mind his wares being handled, or did he prefer his customers make known their specific needs so he could serve them?

A hum drew her gaze to her husband, who had picked up a dagger. He turned it this way and that, inspecting it from different angles and checking its weight and balance the way she had seen Tristan do with new recruits' swords.

"Where's this from?" he asked without bothering to face the smith.

The man looked up, darted a glance at Maddie, and said, "I made that myself, sire. Right here."

"Impressive piece." Lucas pressed his thumb to the edge. When he lifted it, blood welled along a thin line across the pad, but he did not even flinch. "Keen as a Craeickish blade."

"The iron came from the Stonetooth mines, sire. Finest ore I've ever worked with."

Lucas placed it on the counter and tossed a simple leather sheath on top. "I'll take it."

Again, the smith looked to Maddie, and she gave him the slightest nod.

"Of course, sire. That'll be five silvers, and a copper for the sheath."

Fabric rustled, coins clinked, and Lucas swept his purchase into the folds of his cloak. Maddie sucked in a slow breath as the smith dropped the sum into a strongbox beside the forge. Her husband had paid the full asking price without so much as a quibble—whatever problems Craeick had, they were clearly not financial.

A short while later, Joss made her selection, and they emerged into the bitter cold once more. Maddie had planned to visit each of the stalls in the market, but between the shifts in temperature and Lucas's puzzling actions, her head had started to ache. By the time they reached the cloth merchant and Joss had decided to buy a ribbon for Olivia, she felt as miserable as he looked trailing after them.

Still, she could not fault him. For whatever reason, he had decided to comply with her request, and the mere fact that he was there was enough. Maybe, in time, they could learn to work together after all.

She was about to release him from his escort duty when his head jerked up and he looked at something behind her. She twisted to face the same direction and spotted his second-in-command and the sullen redheaded soldier at the edge of the square.

General Munroe made a strange gesture with his hand, and Lucas reciprocated, then focused on her.

"I need to go. I trust that was enough hand-holding to appease the peasants."

Maddie ignored the jibe. "I appreciate you accompanying us this afternoon."

"I'm sure you do." He made to leave but stopped and turned back to her. "Before I go, here."

He held out the dagger he had bought, and when she did not reach for it, picked up her hand and placed it in her palm. "I noticed you don't wear a weapon."

Slowly, her eyes rose from the blade to his equally sharp gaze. "I thank you, but I'm well-guarded. I have no need of one."

"Everyone should be able to defend themselves. You never know when it might be necessary."

Maddie studied his face. His features held no emotion, no particular care for her, but he wanted to ensure she was safe? If they had a hundred years together, she might never understand him.

The longer they stood there, the more attention they drew, onlookers gathering, their stares boring into Maddie's skin. She curled her fingers around the dagger, and Lucas let go, cold rushing to fill the space left by his hand.

He spun on his heel and walked away without a backwards glance, leaving her holding a weapon she had no idea how to use from a man she had no idea how to read. She stared after him, watching the crowds jump apart at his approach and trickle back into the gap left in his wake.

Joss bumped her shoulder and looked in the same direction, though Lucas was already lost to sight. "What're we looking at?"

"Nothing. Lucas had to leave."

"Wait. Is that the dagger that..." Joss let out a low whistle, her eyes leaping to Maddie's. After a moment of intense scrutiny, she dropped her gaze back to the dagger and chuckled. "Interesting."

Prickled by her insinuations, Maddie clenched her jaw and shoved the dagger into her skirt pocket. It hung against her leg, its weight both dangerous and warming.

She pinched the bridge of her nose, but when she dropped her hand, Joss was still grinning like a court jester.

Maddie groaned. "Leave it alone, Joss. There's nothing going on here."

"If you say so."

Joss sobered, linking her arm with Maddie's and tugging her to the side of the square. When they were out of earshot of the market goers, she dropped her hand and bit her lower lip. Maddie adjusted her cloak and let her sister sort through whatever it was she wanted to say.

"I've been thinking," Joss said. "I know we agreed that I'd move up here and be responsible for the northern region while Papa's ill, but after everything that's happened… I want to go back to Faerstolmere with you when you leave. If that's all right?"

Maddie opened her mouth to argue, but the way Joss shuffled and glanced in the direction Lucas had gone made her pause. So many things would change now she was married to Craeick's king, and it would be good to have both her sisters with her for a while.

She nodded, and Joss wrapped her in a tight hug.

"All right. Put me down before I run out of air."

"You won't regret this. I promise."

Someone cleared their throat beside them, and Joss let go. Maddie smoothed her clothing and turned to the person, a young man in royal livery who thrust a square of paper at her.

"Your Highness."

She took the note, unfolded it, and scanned the contents, then read them again more carefully.

"What is it?" Joss asked, thankfully not attempting to peek over Maddie's shoulder for once. "Is it Papa?"

Maddie met her gaze. "No. Nothing like that. But it looks like we'll be leaving sooner than we'd planned. Come on. I need to get back to the keep."

Chapter 9
Maddie

Maddie rubbed the tightness from her forehead and offered Lord Elland a weak smile as he gathered the papers they had just finished reviewing. "That's the last of it, then. We're ready to leave as soon as the wagon's loaded."

"Try not to worry, Madeline. All will be well."

She released a breath. "I know. I just…" She spread her hands. "All this."

"Issues often breed more issues. That's the way of these things. Your father once ruled on a border dispute between brothers and ended up having to relocate an entire town to avoid flooding because of it."

Her brows rose, but she was too preoccupied to follow up on the diversion.

When she had read the message from the capital the previous day, she had wanted to scream. How could the news of recent events have become so distorted, the truth been mixed with such outlandish falsehoods? That rumours had spread so far and so fast did not surprise her, but the content, and the unrest in the capital they had prompted, made her head pound all the harder. As did her councillors' inability to ease people's fear-fuelled anger.

The only recourse left was to return and let them see that neither she nor her sisters had been kidnapped by bandits or attacked by wild dragons. They would believe the truth from her own lips—and her husband's—and cease their calls to exact revenge on non-existent threats. Though the reality was sure to cause consternation as well.

"I wish you could come with us," she said.

Lord Elland leaned forwards and patted her hand, his soft skin wrinkled and stained with ink. "I'll follow behind as soon as things are settled here. It shouldn't take more than a week or two, three at most, and I'll have Lieutenant Wash to keep me safe.

"Besides, you won't need me. You're a capable leader, Madeline—your father would be proud of you."

Maddie steeled her spine, smoothed her skirts, and stood. "Well, then. I'll see you in Faerstolmere."

He rose as well, dipping into a bow as she rounded the desk and walked out of the study, head held high.

She made her way along the corridor to the great hall, her skirts whispering against the stone floor. The low rumble of conversation ahead told her people had begun gathering and they might be able to depart on time after all.

She reached for the door, which had been left ajar, and was about to swing it open when a shadow darkened the gap and something heavy thudded to the ground on the other side. Her hand jerked back, and in that moment, someone spoke.

"Found out last night," a young, male voice said. "I'm gonna be joining the king's guard detail in the capital."

Maddie debated opening the door, but indecision held her captive.

"How'd you pull that off?" a gruff, older voice asked.

"He worked hard." The third man's tone suggested the answer should have been obvious.

"Imagine. I'm gonna be serving under the Wolf himself!"

Pride and excitement coated the youth's statement. Her husband was revered by his men. She eased closer to the crack in the doorway to hear more.

"Well done, lad," the third man said. "You can go anywhere from there."

"Exactly. I'll learn so much from him."

"If you survive." The older man laughed, and the others joined in.

The youth sobered first. "Worth it, though, to train with him."

"Aye. As long as you don't have to serve his bride." The older man's words struck the air from Maddie's lungs. The scratch of fingers against bristles sounded overloud in her ears. "I can see it now. 'Fetch this. Hold that. Stand here while I tie my ribbons just so.' Don't know what the Wolf was thinking."

"I do," the third man said. "You seen her up close? I wouldn't kick her outta bed, that's for sure."

Maddie's cheeks burned, and she clenched her fists, indignation and mortification vying for dominance over her racing heart.

"Really? Looks too stuck up to me." Grunts and guffaws followed that she did not want to interpret. "Oh, Madeline. Wake up, Madeline. Hah. Be like bedding a dead fish."

She closed her eyes against the jibes and turned to leave.

"If you say one more word about my wife, it'll be the last you ever utter." Lucas's voice cut through the laughter, and despite her opinion of the men, Maddie flinched at the threat it carried.

"Sorry, Sire. I didn't mean—"

"One. More. Word."

She heard scuffling sounds but dared not look through the gap.

"General," Lucas snapped.

"Aye, sire."

"See that these… soldiers"—he spat the word like an epitaph—"are put on night watch for a month and chosen by every man in the unit for sparring practice. And this one is no longer required in the capital."

"Aye, sire."

Footsteps receded, and silence hung heavy for a few moments before the young man muttered, "Thanks a lot. You could've said he was behind me."

"He only just showed up," the older one said. "Besides, you didn't exactly tell us to stop, did you?"

"Leave him alone. He just lost his one chance at promotion. Sorry, lad."

However the youth responded, it was not verbal.

Clatters and grunts suggested the soldiers readied to depart, but Maddie waited until she heard them walk away to sag against the wall. Her mind spun in a million directions. Much as Lucas's men respected him, they clearly cared little for her. But he had. Grabbing that thread to quiet the maelstrom, she mulled over his reaction to their comments.

Her heart warmed at his defence of her honour, though a shudder ran through her at the severity of his response. She had no doubt those men would suffer greatly for their crassness. Which brought her back again to the question of why. Why had he chosen her over them, reacted so strongly, when he barely tolerated their marriage or her presence?

Why did he have to be such a puzzle?

And then it struck her. Hidden in the dim corridor, leaning against the cold, stone wall, she realised that she had been so busy trying to solve the riddle of the Wolf King—and using him as a prop to ease the minds of her people—shame bit deep at that—that she had forgotten to simply get to know him.

A smile tugged at the corners of her mouth. Maybe she could begin on the journey home. Straightening, she peered through the narrow gap and, finding the way cleared, opened the door and strode through. She tried not to seek out the men who had been discussing her, but her ears tuned into every gruff, male voice, thankfully finding none familiar that she did not already know.

The hall was bustling with people preparing for their departure. Soldiers waited beside bulging packs, and maids and grooms carrying various supplies rushed in and out of the open double doors to the wagons outside. A hound with half a chicken in its mouth darted through the throng and was chased out by a couple of youngsters.

Maddie snagged one of them on his way past. "Thomas, go and ask Master Longwick to saddle my horse, please."

"Yes, Your Highness."

He ducked his head and scampered off after the others, and Maddie headed for her room. Hopefully, she would have enough time to change her clothes without holding everyone up.

She had barely ridden since they arrived at Northold, and the more she thought about it, the lighter her steps felt. Fresh air and exercise would clear her head and get her heart moving—just what she needed.

But more importantly, it might give her an opportunity to spend some much-needed time with her husband.

Chapter 10
Maddie

Less than an hour later, Maddie mounted her horse, Midnight. The air was crisp but clear, only a few wisps of cloud trailing the horizon. A good day for travelling.

Olivia climbed into the royal carriage a few paces away with Joss right behind her. Maddie did not envy them the jolting, stuffy ride, and Joss's sour expression confirmed that she felt the same way. Guilt ate at the edges of Maddie's good mood.

"You could have ridden as well, Joss."

Her sister paused with one foot inside the carriage, the other still on the steps leading up to it. "And leave Mouse on her own?"

"Where's Tabitha?" Maddie searched the crowds for their maid.

"Said she'd ride with the old couple from Anford."

It took Maddie a moment to place them. "Ah." A dozen or so of the refugees from the border villages had chosen to travel to the capital with them, hoping to start again in safer environs.

Joss cast her a half smile. "It's all right. You deserve a bit of freedom after being cooped up here for so long. And I went hunting last night, so I could do with the rest."

She covered a yawn with her hand, then winked. "See?"

From inside the carriage, Olivia said, "Hurry up, Joss. You're letting the cold in."

"I'm coming."

Joss climbed in and closed the door with enough force to startle Midnight. He sidestepped, and Maddie smoothed her palm down the solid warmth of his neck.

"We'll be on our way soon enough. Then we'll have a good run, yes?"

A grey stallion appeared alongside her, Lucas astride its back. He focused on her waist and nodded—noting she wore the dagger he gave her?—before meeting her eyes. "You're not joining your sisters?"

"Not today. I thought I'd ride."

The flap at the window pulled back, and Joss stuck her head out. She looked from Maddie to Lucas and back and let out a long, knowing "ah."

Maddie threw her sister a quelling stare and tried to ignore the grin plastered across her face.

"Are you going to ride together?" Joss asked Lucas.

His face scrunched like he had eaten an underripe gooseberry and then smoothed so quickly Maddie might have imagined it. "If she can keep up," he said.

"I'll do my best."

"Maddie's an excellent horsewoman," Joss added. "She's been riding since she was little, and she's better than most of the guards we race—"

"Yes, thank you, Joss." Maddie spun to Lucas, cheeks flaming at the secret she had failed to prevent Joss from spilling. Still, she had decided to open up to her husband, and riding was part of who she was, so she shrugged in response to his widened eyes.

His answering smirk promised a challenge she would readily accept. Blood singing with anticipation, she heeled Midnight and set off.

She kept their pace steady as they left the confines of the keep and rode down the hill to the town for the last time. Tristan caught up first, muttering about her waiting for her guard detail, followed closely by Lucas and his cadre, Flynn's mount tied to Rheann's. The carriage rumbled along behind them with the supply wagons in its wake and the rest of their company trailing at the rear.

The main thoroughfare was lined three deep, the people of Northold and those villagers staying on waving at her and her sisters and wishing them farewell, though their cheers quieted into sullen silence before the Craeickish. Many of the displaced souls who had taken refuge here had already returned to their homes, and others had joined the convoy to travel south, but a few would remain under the care of Lord Elland until places could be found for them or their lives rebuilt.

As soon as the convoy left the cobbled street behind and the last of the crowd's cheers was carried away on the breeze, Maddie pushed Midnight into an easy trot and glanced over her shoulder.

Lucas met her gaze, his eyes gleaming, and he spurred his horse to overtake Tristan. She did not wait any longer but rode ahead, eyes fixed on the lane winding down the hillside. If she could hold him at bay until they reached the valley, they could cut cross country and put their skills to the test.

When the ground finally flattened out, they were side by side a good three lengths ahead of the others. Tristan would no doubt berate her for leaving them behind when they stopped for the night, but finding a common interest with her husband was worth a lecture. She reined in and pointed at a ridge in the distance.

"Race you to the giant sycamore on that hill there. There's a stream just beyond where we can stop to water the horses." They had rested at the spot on their journey north, and it would not be so icebound now.

"All right, Princess. Let's see what you can do."

Without another word, they broke into a run as one, their horses keeping pace with each other as if they had been doing so their entire lives. Maddie gave Midnight his head, and he sped across the ground, his muscles bunching and stretching beneath her, muddy divots flying up behind them.

It took but a moment to match his rhythm, and they were soon galloping at top speed, all sounds other than the puff of their breaths and the wind whistling past her ears ripped away. She let out a whoop and bent low over his neck, urging him on as Lucas's grey stallion pulled ahead to their left.

She eased Midnight back into a canter for a small hill, knowing there would be a hedge to jump on the other side, but Lucas continued at breakneck speed up the slope, only slowing at the apex. It gave him the edge he needed to beat her to the sycamore that stood on the next rise, but she did not care. Cheeks stinging, bodice sticking to her skin, she drew up beneath its naked branches a handful of heartbeats behind him, spreading her arms and dipping her head to acknowledge his win.

They walked down to the stream at the other side of the low hill, breathless and spent.

"You're good," Lucas said, allowing his horse to quench its thirst.

Maddie directed Midnight a few paces farther along, then stopped as well. "Thank you. You're not so bad yourself."

He barked a laugh. "My father had me in a saddle before I could walk. You?"

"My mother taught me." Her smile turned wistful, and she rubbed Midnight's neck. "She knew how gruelling life in the palace could be, so she insisted each of us have an outlet, a way to escape the pressures of the court. For me, that was horses. For Joss, archery. She's the most like our mother—wild, carefree, so mischievous…"

"And Olivia? She's the youngest, correct?"

"Yes. She loves to tend the garden, though she spends most winters huddled in the library." Midnight tossed his head, and Maddie refocused her thoughts. "What about you, your family?"

His lips slanted to the side, bunching the scar bisecting his cheek, and he turned his horse away from the water, walking him slowly along the bank. She slumped as she followed his lead, assuming he would not answer, but he glanced back at her over his shoulder and said, "Flynn takes after our mother. He has an easy way with people that I… do not."

"He's your half-brother."

"Yes. His father's my most trusted advisor. He helped my mother rule on my behalf until I reached my majority, and they married when I was fourteen."

Maddie did a few quick calculations in her head. A couple of years after Lucas became king. "You had an older brother as well, didn't you?"

His posture stiffened. "I did, but that was a long time ago. Let's ride."

He spurred his horse on, and she cursed herself for the insensitive question. They had been doing so well until she ruined it. "Lesson one, Maddie. Don't mention his deceased family unless he does."

Lucas crossed the stream and cantered up the opposite slope, cutting an impressive figure even with the tension still radiating from him. Loosing the regret from her mind, she dug her heels into Midnight and chased after him, determined to reclaim the joy of their ride.

The next day, Maddie stayed with the carriage, riding alongside and chatting with her sisters through the open window. Spring had arrived in earnest in the lowlands, and the farther they travelled from the northern mountains, the milder the weather became. The air lost its bite, the ground softened beneath the horses' hooves, grass replacing snow, and Maddie removed her fur collar and opened the folds of her cloak.

Lucas joined them in the afternoon, whistling as he pointed at the pig farms that dominated the rolling landscape. "I should call you Pig Princess."

Maddie only blinked, causing Joss to erupt with laughter—until he added, "Does the whole kingdom smell this bad? It's worse than dragon dung."

"Maybe you shouldn't have invaded then." Joss smirked at him from the safety of the carriage, and Maddie nudged Midnight forward to block their view of each other.

She drew in a breath, the familiar scent of manure tingeing the air. "Pork and leather are Tyrrath's main products. This is where they come from."

"So I see." He grimaced. "But knowing that and smelling it are different things."

"You can go home any time you want," Joss muttered.

He grinned, an unreadable curve of his lips that could equally have been amusement or predatory.

"I've battled dragons," he said. "I'm sure I can handle a few pigs." He spurred his horse to a canter and joined his men at the head of the line, leaving Maddie with a disgruntled sister and an odd sense that he had purposefully blunted his barbs.

On the third morning, when they were within sight of home, she rode ahead with Lucas again, racing across the plain with her hair whipping out behind her.

The city of Faerstolmere rose in the distance, Lake Arrol shimmering on its right, Mochynden Forest stretching out to the left from the rear of the hill, and fields of wheat rippling between those of livestock in the foreground. Red stone buildings climbed up the slope to the palace at the top, seemingly no larger than a child's play set, but Maddie could almost feel the bustle of the streets and see the carved facades and palace gates soaring into the sky overhead.

A track split off the main road just over a mile from the city, and she led Lucas along it towards Mochynden Forest. The path wound through the trees, taking them deep into the heart of the private woods and around to a little-known rear entrance to the palace complex.

"Interesting route we're taking," he called from behind her.

She twisted in her saddle to meet his gaze, trusting Midnight to follow the familiar path without direction. "We'll be surrounded by people soon enough, and we won't be able to escape them. I thought you'd appreciate putting it off for as long as possible."

He grunted in a way that she was beginning to recognise as approval, and she faced forward again to hide the smile playing at the edges of her mouth and soak in the peace of the forest. New leaves burst forth on the gnarled, ancient fingers overhead, dappling the canopy with bright shades of green. The sun filtered through them, warming her face as she tipped it up to catch its rays.

She breathed deep, and the scent of rich, damp earth filled her lungs and soothed her soul. She had loved these woods since she was a little girl, exploring with her sisters and playing hide and seek with Tristan and a few of the other palace children. Pointing out various landmarks to Lucas, she travelled back to a time where the cares of the crown seemed naught but a distant cloud on the horizon.

The horses clopped past the stream where she had learned to swim, a small glade they had defended from imaginary trolls, and the giant oak that Joss had fallen from and broken her arm. But at last, they came to the palace wall and the unassuming gate half hidden behind a thicket of brambles.

Maddie dismounted and approached the wooden portal on foot, pulling a key from the pouch at her waist. It slid into the keyhole with ease but scraped inside the lock and stuck for a moment. She jiggled it twice, and the bar thunked home. The door creaked as it opened, and she gave up on secrecy and led Midnight through, Lucas and his stallion directly behind.

They walked along a narrow passage and emerged into the courtyard, which hummed with activity. A groom was the first to spot them, dropping the end of his shovel and spilling manure across the stone slabs.

"Your Highness-es!" he stammered, his eyes darting from her to Lucas as he ducked a hasty bow.

"Be at ease," she said. "Here."

She held out Midnight's reins, and the groom rushed to take them from her. Others stopped to bow or curtsey, a ripple of bobbing heads racing the murmur of their greetings around the yard.

Maddie straightened under their gazes and brushed a stray twig from her skirt. She led Lucas over to the palace's main entrance, and they had just mounted the first few steps when the sounds of cheering announced the rest of their party approaching the gates from the road through the city. With a quick glance over her shoulder to confirm her sisters' carriage was well, she climbed the last of the stairs and marched through the oversized doors.

The interior was cool so early in the season but filled with light from the huge windows fronting the building. A young lad balanced on a ladder to polish the glass while the new steward stood behind him, pointing out where to rub. The steward, a thin, hawkish man appointed after his predecessor broke his hip, and whose name Maddie had not yet learned, glanced over at their intrusion and started.

"Your Highness! We weren't expecting you so soon—get down—can I fetch you some refreshments?"

He shooed the boy away, managing a low bow from the waist at the same time.

"I'll take some mint tea," Maddie said. "Upstairs. I want to visit my father. Lucas?"

"Ale. In..."

"I've had the east wing made ready for you, Sire. Ma'am. I took the liberty of preparing the rooms and moving your things when I heard of your nuptials."

Her jaw clenched, despite her best efforts. She would have preferred to make the decision herself, though she had to admit the move made sense. Lucas could hardly stay in her old chamber with her sisters next door, and the only other alternative was the dowager suite, a dreary set of rooms in the north tower with a perpetual draft.

"Thank you…"

"Hodges, Ma'am."

"Hodges. We'll be upstairs when the drinks are ready."

She made to leave, but Hodges cleared his throat, drawing her eyes back to him.

"Begging your pardon, Ma'am, but would you like me to show King Lucas to the east wing? You mentioned visiting your father…"

They *were* on opposite sides of the palace.

Before Maddie could respond, Lucas strode around her. "I'll go with him. You see your father." He leaned closer and added, "I'll see you later, Princess."

He started up the stairs, forcing Hodges to run to catch up and leaving Maddie staring after them like a landed fish. Something in her chest tugged at the sight of Lucas's retreating back, but the moment she tried to identify it, it dissipated. The men reached the landing and turned left, and she started up after them, rubbing the spot.

She pondered the odd sensation as she walked along the quiet hallway to the right, but when the guards flanking the gilded double doors at the end snapped to attention at her approach, she took a deep breath and cleared her thoughts.

Gesturing for them to be at ease, she turned the handle as gently as possible, opened the door, and slipped inside. The room was softly lit by a fire glowing in the hearth and a single candelabrum on the nightstand. She stepped forwards, listening for the regular exhales that indicated her father still lived, seeking the slight rise and fall of his chest when her eyes adjusted to the low light.

A maid rose from the chair beside the bed and dipped into a curtsey before silently retreating into the side chamber. On Maddie's orders, they had long since stopped reporting the king's condition whenever she visited. It had remained unchanged since the morning he failed to wake, and she could not bear the torment of having her hopes dashed each time they started to speak. They would inform her the instant anything happened, and that was enough.

"Hello, Papa," she said, sitting on the edge of the bed and taking his hand in hers. "I have so much to tell you."

Chapter 11

Maddie

The next evening, Maddie stood outside the royal entrance to the great hall and peeked between the curtain and the archway into the room beyond. Representatives from all the other kingdoms in Egrea gathered inside, waiting to scrutinise her every move. She smoothed her hands down her embroidered, maroon skirt once, twice, as desperate to remove the knot from her stomach as the sweat from her palms.

Neither her sisters nor Tristan were anywhere in sight, though she had secured a promise of attendance from each that morning. All three were known for avoiding formal receptions, though for vastly different reasons. While Olivia was shy and Joss craved freedom, Tristan loathed what he called the 'pomp and deception' inherent in such events.

Still, they should have been there by now. Maybe she should send a maid to find them, but that might leave the servants in the hall shorthanded. She smoothed her skirts again as she mentally checked each detail of the arrangements.

"What are you doing?"

Startled by Lucas's voice behind her, she spun around and nearly bumped into him. He quirked his brow and looked down at her hands, which she balled at her sides to break their movements.

"Sorry." She dropped her gaze as well. "Nervous habit. This is the first reception I've hosted without my father or Lord Elland to guide me."

She clamped her mouth shut. Why had she told him all that? She had not intended to admit more than the first three words, but the rest had spilled out unbidden.

A glance up at his face revealed a deep furrow etched between his eyes. She flinched and could have sworn a low growl emanated from his chest, though it could as easily have been a groan. Biting her lip, she searched for something benign to say, but her mind blanked when he took her hand and wrapped her fingers around his arm.

"They're just people," he said, then tugged the curtain aside and walked her out into the hall.

The lord chamberlain leaped to attention as they swept past him, his words tripping over each other in his haste to announce their arrival. "Lords and Ladies, His Majesty, King Lucas Sinclair of Craeick, and Her Highness, Princess Madeline Sinclair of Tyrrath."

That he had replaced Dalbot with Sinclair threw her for a moment, but she recovered and looked around.

A sea of eyes turned their way, and she tightened her grip on Lucas before she realised what she was doing. She eased her hold and exhaled slowly as they mounted the short dais and made their way to the thrones at the centre of the high table.

"I see you didn't wear your dagger tonight," he said, distracting her from the murmurs circling the room.

Her gaze jumped to his. He expected her to wear it everywhere? "This is a formal reception."

"You can never be too careful."

She shook her head and took in his outfit. Unrelenting black met her gaze, his doublet, trousers, and boots bearing not a single adornment. A lone sheath hung from his belt, also made from simple black leather, holding a blade far too long to be a customary eating knife.

Maddie could not help but laugh. "I see you dressed for the occasion."

"Would you rather I look like a peacock"—he tipped his chin at a man wearing a riot of pink, purple, orange and green— "and strut about the palace as if I own it?"

"I'd rather you'd stayed within your own borders," she drawled.

She peeked at him from the corner of her eye. Had she taken it too far?

He leaned close, eyes gleaming, and whispered, "But then I wouldn't be the Wolf King."

"Your Majesty. Your Highness." The lord chamberlain bowed before them, drawing both of their attention, and lifted his arm towards a familiar young man standing to his right. "May I present Prince Raiman Sakanin, nephew of Iskaria's ki—"

"Raiman." Lucas said. "How're your plans coming along? Need my help again?"

The prince smiled. "We've been making good progress lately, though there is something I want to show you…"

Maddie's muscles locked. Had Lucas agreed to fight for Iskaria? She glanced at the couple from Garellion, who stared at him with stony expressions. Tensions between the two kingdoms had always been fraught, Iskaria's technology-based society an antithesis to Garellion's reliance on nature and magic, but open warfare? Surely not.

And she had married him, potentially risking Tyrrath's good relations with the mage-ruled kingdom.

She had known she was binding herself to a mercenary, but the full implications of that had faded into the background of the threat she had faced at the time. She surveyed the rest of the room, passing over several courtiers who appeared awed by Lucas and a few ladies who blushed behind their hands.

But here and there among the curious stares of the majority, some cast calculating looks his way while others studied him with an air of trepidation and, in one case, bald fury. What had she stepped into? Navigating the tapestry of relationships with the other kingdoms had been delicate enough before, but now…

Now the tangle of knots grew in her mind, threatening to rip her previous work apart.

"Then I look forward to it," Prince Raiman said. "Congratulations on your nuptials, King Lucas, Princess Madeline."

He tilted his head to Lucas, then her, and as he strolled away, the lord chamberlain brought forwards Crown Prince Fredrick of Brunland.

Maddie focused her attention on her closest ally and long-time friend, her smile feeling less forced.

"You've been busy, I see." She gestured to the chain swinging from his waist, where several new tokens had been added, each denoting a dragon he owned.

"Hardly. That's what I have the dragons for." He laughed, then turned to Lucas. "I'd better keep them away from your husband, though. Don't want them skinned for their hides."

"Brunnish dragons are too small to be worth the effort. Besides, there's no honour in besting a tame beast," Lucas said.

Though his comment was genuinely dismissive, rivalry over dragons was far preferable to potential warfare. As they continued to argue the merits of taming versus killing the creatures, the tension in Maddie's heart eased.

That evening, she would concentrate on getting through the line of people waiting to formally congratulate her and Lucas, and in the morning, she would discover what damage had been done and begin to repair it.

Later, after the feasting had ended and the tables been cleared away, Maddie found herself strolling around the room, arm in arm with Joss. They moved on from a group of nobles eager to ingratiate themselves with Lucas by paying her court—a futile scheme, if they only knew it—and searched the crowded hall for Olivia.

"I'm sure I saw her not long ago." Joss stood on her tiptoes to peer over a portly friar's head, and Maddie tugged her back down.

"Stop doing that. It's unseemly."

"Well, how else are we supposed to find her?" They skirted a group of men raucously arguing the merits of Brunland's dragons over Iskaria's technology and greeted but did not stop for a couple of local nobles' wives. "She's probably hiding in a corner somewhere with a book."

"True. But I'd still rather know."

They headed for the nearest bay window, Maddie's protective instincts buzzing. Though their father had been encouraging Olivia to attend more public events since she turned fourteen, they were still difficult for her. Maddie and Joss usually made sure she was within sight of at least one of them in case she needed them, but with the size of the gathering and the curiosity regarding Maddie's marriage, they had lost her.

The bench beneath the window was empty, but Maddie caught a slice of brown skirts poking out from the next alcove along. "There."

While they were still a few yards away, Lucas stepped away from a group in front of them and walked over to their sister. He sat down beside her, legs stretched out in front of him, body blocked by the angle of the wall.

Had he deliberately sought her out? Why? They had not spent more than a few hours in the same room before, and Olivia had avoided him then.

Maddie walked faster, but with only a handful of feet to go, Aitha Malz of the Free Isles ship, Dauntless, stopped them. The wide leather belt cinching in a white shirt at her waist thankfully carried only one knife that Maddie could see, though the first mate often hid a small blade in the thick coils of hair gathered in a thong below one ear and hanging down her chest. A wide grin stretched across her deep black face.

"Princess Madeline, Princess Jocelyn, I'm glad I caught you."

"Aitha. How long have you been here?"

"A week. I hitched a ride up the river on a merchant vessel and stayed when I heard about the wedding." Aitha poked Joss in the side. "Wasn't sure which one of you got shackled till I got the invitation to this thing."

Maddie smiled at Joss's oldest friend and shifted to keep Olivia in her line of sight. Her sister's head was bowed, but should she look up, Maddie would be able to tell if she needed aid.

Joss leaned closer to Aitha and lowered her voice. They were likely planning some wild scheme or other that would cause Maddie a headache later, but she ignored them in favour of observing her youngest sister and husband.

Fortunately, Lucas did not modulate the volume of his voice. "So, you're the one they call mouse?"

Olivia nodded, a small dip of her head.

"Why is that?"

She glanced away but shrugged.

"Not a fan of people, huh? He waited only a single heartbeat before continuing. "Me either. I always used to hide in the stables during these things when I was young."

He shifted, blocking Maddie's view of Olivia. She moved half a step towards them, but froze when Olivia murmured, "I like the library." She peeked up at him. "I've read most of the books in…"

Maddie gripped Joss's hand, dragging her attention towards the pair. Olivia had not spoken more than two words together in public for years, yet here she was, sharing her favourite story with a man who, until a week ago, had terrified her.

True, she had not seemed distressed by his appearance in her hiding spot, but never would Maddie have thought he would be the one to bring her sister out of her shell. She studied what she could see of her husband—or that he would have opened up to her.

"You're not scared of me?" he asked Olivia.

"Not anymore."

He rubbed his jaw. "Hmm. Why not?"

"I researched wolves when you married Maddie and found out they're pack animals. We're part of the same pack now. Besides, they only hunt for food, and I'm not worth eating."

Lucas laughed—tipped his head back and laughed with complete abandon. The deep, rich sound burrowed into Maddie's chest, and when it stopped, it left the tiniest ache behind. Her hand rose to the spot. How could his mirth affect her so?

She searched the back of his head for the answer and found the unruly little curl at the nape of his neck. Her lips twitched up at the corner.

"I think you're starting to like your husband."

Joss's voice startled her, and when she spun to protest, Joss was studying her with far too appraising an expression.

Maddie glanced around for an alternate topic. "Where's Aitha?"

"Gone to find something to drink. Well?"

Flicking a hand through the air between them, she said in as light a tone as she could muster, "We're learning to work together, nothing more."

"If you say so."

"What are you talking about?" Olivia said behind her.

For the second time in as many jolted heartbeats, Maddie found herself the subject of a sister's curious gaze, though Olivia's was considerably less calculating.

"Maddie's feelings for Lucas," Joss said.

Maddie gaped at her. "I have no such things." She glanced around, desperate to confirm he had not overheard. Thankfully, he was nowhere within sight.

"But you could, with the right encouragement."

"Leave her alone, Joss, please," Olivia said while Maddie was still trying to formulate a response. "It can't be easy, getting married like that."

Olivia shifted her weight from one foot to the other, and Maddie pulled her into a tight hug, giving Joss a pointed look over her shoulder. "Thank you, Mouse."

Lucas joined them as they moved apart. He pointed at the lord chamberlain hovering nearby and said, "I think we're expected to lead the first dance."

Maddie instantly recalled his declaration that he did not care what others thought or expected of him. As if reading her thoughts, he added, "In this case, I have no objection—if you don't."

She stepped away from her sisters, and he took her hand in his, his calloused fingers warm, her sudden awareness of them disconcerting. Pushing Joss's insinuations to the farthest corner of her mind, she walked to the centre of the cleared area in the middle of the room.

Others joined them, and when the musicians tucked away in the upper gallery struck up a lively tune, she and Lucas swept along the row, close enough that her skirts brushed his legs with each step.

"I heard you back there," she said as they made room for the next couple. "With Olivia."

"Eavesdropping, Princess? Tch, tch, tch."

Her cheeks flamed, but she pressed on with what she needed to say. "Thank you. She finds these events hard, and… Well, thank you."

"It was nothing."

But it was. To Olivia, to Maddie, it was another step forwards. She focused on their current steps, a twisting figure of eight around each other and the adjacent pair, and then she watched Lucas for a few beats. He moved with surprising grace, light on his feet, his hands perfectly placed to meet hers or support her back.

"You dance well," she said when they faced each other again.

"My mother insisted. In case I ever wanted to sweep a princess off her feet." His sardonic grin made an appearance. "But it's a useful skill for a warrior, helps with coordination and balance, timing, stamina…"

She stopped listening, but he must have noticed, for his fingers tightened on hers.

"Am I boring you, Princess?"

They separated to circle around the neighbouring pair and return to each other once more. "Not at all. I love hearing about ideal battle traits when I'm dancing."

He smiled—not a smirk, there was no hint of derision or scorn in the silver of his eyes—a genuine, mirth-filled smile. The first he had given her.

Beaming back at him, she released all the worries from her mind and let herself get lost in the rhythm of the dance.

Chapter 12

Luc

Restlessness plagued Luc as he walked along a deserted palace corridor, his feet sinking into an overly thick runner streaked with moonlight from the windows to his left. His nightly walks usually settled his thoughts, but in the four days since the formal reception, he had not been able to banish his wife from his mind.

Maybe the palace grounds were not as calming as the battlements at home.

Or maybe he was beginning to like the princess.

He balled his fists and lengthened his stride, stalking through the darkness like the predator he should be. Her wellbeing was his responsibility, and he had accepted that burden, had even made an effort with her sisters. They were all joined by the marriage, after all. But more than that?

A growl rumbled in his throat, and he veered towards the library the steward had pointed out when Luc first arrived. Whitlow's *Treatise on the Art of Warfare* should prove diversion enough if they had a copy—there was always something new to learn from the tome.

The door opened smoothly and silently, the hinges well-oiled, and inside, a soft glow emanated from a small table beside it. He lifted the lamp, only marginally surprised to find it already lit, and looked around the room.

Shelves lined the walls, broken by a large fireplace farther along from where he stood and two windows opposite. Between them, chairs surrounded a table piled high with books, and several loungers filled the space beyond, blankets tossed haphazardly over their backs and books strewn about their feet. It looked inviting, cosy even, completely at odds with the ordered functionality of his library back home.

He could almost see the princesses here, reading and chattering loudly enough to wake the dead. Had his wife spent rainy days on one of those loungers, flipping through a book while wishing she could be riding outside instead? A smile stole over his face, but he swiped it away.

Her happiness was not his concern, only her physical wellbeing. He need not, should not, care for her. What he needed, the voice deep inside his head reminded him, was to focus on his true goals for coming here, the duty he had to his people.

Turning his back on the scene, he strolled along the wall of shelves, looking for something to read. A section on continental politics caught his eye, and he stepped closer. One of those would do.

He was pulling a volume down when a soft voice startled him. "That's one of my favourites."

He spun around, swallowing the curse that sprang to his lips and letting the sword he had half drawn slide back into its sheath.

The princess stood before him, enticing as a cool stream after a long day of battle. Her hair tumbled over her shoulders in magnificent disarray, drawing his eyes to her chest, where she clutched a shawl around her nightdress.

He flung his gaze up to her face and said, "What are you doing here?"

She flinched, and he cursed himself again for the aggression in his voice, but before he could modulate his greeting, she straightened. Her chin lifted to a regal angle, and she gestured around them. "Same as you. Getting a book to read."

"Of course." He offered her a half smile, and her shoulders relaxed.

After a moment of awkward silence, she pointed to the book in his hand. "He has an interesting perspective on cooperation between kingdoms."

It took Luc another beat to catch her reference. "Maintaining a skewed balance in favour of the other party to encourage reciprocation?"

She nodded, and her smile lightened something in his chest. Dragon's breath, she was dangerous. He dropped his gaze to the floor, only to note her bare toes poking out from beneath the lace-edged fabric of her nightdress, which sent images of enfolding her in his protective embrace swirling through his head. Swallowing the impulse, he turned back to the shelves and tugged another volume down to cover his discomfiture.

"What about this one?" He held it up without even glancing at the cover.

A hint of sandalwood teased his nostrils as she stepped closer to read the title, and he clenched his jaw against the desire it evoked.

"I don't care for it. Too reliant on the element of surprise."

What? He inspected the title—*Battlefield Strategies in the Second Era*—and grunted. He had thought the same when Lord Ross had made him read it.

"Seems we've read many of the same books."

"That makes sense." She lifted one shoulder, causing her shawl to slip. "We were both trained to rule."

He dragged his gaze back to the leather-bound book between them, mulling over her words. It had not fully penetrated before that they would have received the same education, been exposed to the same philosophies and tactics, though on reflection, it explained much.

"Did you have to study Gerick's *Anatomy of a Kingdom*?" he asked.

"And Osmund's *Founding of Egrea*, and the *Complete Histories of the Mage Wars*."

A groan escaped at her mention of the loathsome series. "Don't remind me. It took me half a year to get through those." He had been nine and had spent most of that time trying to avoid reading the dusty old texts.

She laughed, the warm sound washing over him like pure water over a blackened stone. "I can well imagine. You preferred to be outside, yes?"

“Of course. Politics was almost as boring as mathematics, though not nearly as useless.”

Her brows rose, a challenge in the tilt.

“You don’t believe me?” He faced her fully. “All right, tell me, how many times have you used Alathogus’s theorems outside the schoolroom?”

A wrinkle appeared over the bridge of her nose, and his fingers itched to smooth it away. He tightened his grip on Battlefield Strategies.

“You know, I don’t think I have,” she admitted. “But I enjoyed the mage war histories. My ancestor was mentioned in them.”

With a shake of his head to cover the crook of a smile he could not suppress, he stepped over to the table and placed the lamp atop a stack of books.

“I learned more from my first year of rule than I did from any books,” he said, then clamped his lips together. Why had he told her that? “But even as a boy, I’d rather learn from experience. I’d take a few hours of physical combat training or a dragon hunt over reading about it any day.”

He glanced at her, and after only the briefest hesitation, she joined him by the table, a grin spreading across her face. “I can see it now—six-year-old you sneaking out while your tutor’s back was turned and joining the soldiers outside who let you stab at a practice post with a small knife.”

He chuckled along with her, recalling several incidents close to her description but choosing not to mention that he had climbed through the window or that the knives had always been full-sized and sharp.

Their eyes met, the lamp's flame flickering in her warm brown orbs. They pulled him in, made him forget why he should not want more. Visions of a large family returned, stronger, more alluring than ever. Being with her felt good… right.

She covered a yawn, her eyes squeezing closed and breaking the spell. "Oh, I'm sorry. I'd better get some sleep." Her gaze flicked to his face and away, a blush staining her cheeks. "Are you coming?"

Thoughts still tangled, he gave himself a mental shake, clearing his throat before saying, "I'll be there soon."

"Very well." She offered him the tiniest smile, which he returned in kind, and tightened her shawl as she walked to the door.

He watched her leave, seeing the smile that graced her lips, the twinkle that lit her eyes as they talked as clearly as the shawl clinging to the curve of her hips. Something flickered in his chest, and he closed his eyes and gripped the back of the chair beside him to stop himself from following her.

But why? Why should he not go after his wife? They were legally bound, after all.

"It's just a treaty, not a real marriage."

But it could be.

The thought whispered through his mind, tempting him with images of a loving wife, more siblings, and maybe, one day, children of his own.

His fingers twisted the ring on his left hand while his mind wandered the problem. Maybe he could have her *and* fulfil his duty. He had come to Tyrrath with a specific goal in mind, but that did not necessarily prevent him from caring for the princess. He was already starting to.

Both. He allowed the idea to take root, the possibility, at least, and the tumult in his head cleared. Snatching up the lamp, he dropped the book in its place—he had no need of it now—and strode to the door. Then, after depositing the lamp on the table where he found it, he left the library and hurried upstairs to fall asleep beside his wife.

Chapter 13
Maddie

Maddie drifted in a state of warm bliss, more rested and content than she had felt in a long time. But as consciousness slowly tugged at her, something solid and heavy registered across her middle. Had Tabitha laid the breakfast tray on her while she still slept?

She slitted her eyes open and looked down, but blankets blocked her view. The tray was under them? Why would her maid do that? Thoughts still muddled with sleep, she slid her hand beneath the covers, felt around, and froze, her eyes popping wide.

The weight was not a breakfast tray.

Lucas's arm draped her waist.

Instantly wide awake, she snatched her hand away and catalogued where else their bodies touched. His chest pressed against her back and his legs curled around hers. Heat prickled her skin at the discovery.

How long had they been like this? Did he know? They must have found each other in their sleep, for she was certain they had been on their own sides of the bed when he had blown out the candle the previous night.

Cautiously, she shifted her position, but he did not stir. His breath ruffled the hair by her ear, the deep, even cadence that of sound sleep. It tickled at first, but the steady rhythm combined with the warmth of his body around hers soon eased the tension from her muscles. And the longer she lay in his arms, the more comfortable it felt.

Assured that her movements would not wake him, curiosity spurred her to feel under the covers once more. His arm, covered in coarse hair, rose and fell in time with her breathing, his hand curled into her stomach. Her fingers found a thin scar, and she traced it over the curve of his forearm, thoughts wandering to the childhood he had described in the library.

What had caused the puckered line? And when? Had it caused him much hurt?

He shifted beneath her touch, and she pulled her hand away. Too late. With a sleepy yawn, he rolled onto his back, his arm slipping from her waist, then stretched. "Morning, Princess."

He tossed the covers aside and sprang from the bed, the muscles in his back rippling in the pre-dawn light slicing through a gap in the curtains. Metal rasped against stone, and a moment later, a faint glow emanated from his tinderbox. He lit the candle from the small flame, then pinched out the splint and snapped the tinderbox shut. In the brighter light, the ridges and planes of his chest appeared as if sculpted of stone, shadows pooling in the grooves of his stomach.

When he walked to the wash basin, wearing only his trousers as usual, her eyes followed him, more aware than ever of his toned physique.

"I slept pretty well last night," he said, meeting her gaze in the mirror with a knowing smirk. "You?"

Cheeks burning, she gave him her back. "Um, y-yes. Fine, thank you."

His chuckle shivered through her, and she gripped the sheets with both hands. It was not honourable to tease her so. Then again, he had never claimed to be a man of honour. Water splashed behind her, then the faint rasp of cloth on skin followed by the sounds of him donning his boots.

She peeked over her shoulder at him and, on finding him fully clothed, twisted back around.

A few moments later, he stood and strapped his sword belt around his waist, then looked up once more. "You can watch me any time you want, Princess. I don't mind one bit." One side of his lips quirked. "But next time you want a cuddle, just ask."

"Me? You were—"

He strolled to the door, and Maddie threw a pillow at his back. It missed.

"You snore," she called after him as he slipped out, only to hear masculine laughter trailing his receding footsteps.

The door had barely swung closed when one of the maids walked in and narrowly avoided stumbling over the pillow. She frowned down at it on her way to the bed, tray in hand, and Maddie grimaced.

"I'll get that later," she said.

"It's all right, Your Highness. I can get it."

The maid deposited the breakfast tray on Lucas's side of the bed and retrieved the pillow before Maddie could argue. Then she walked to the other side of the room, drew back the curtains, and began stoking the fire.

"Where's Tabitha?" Maddie asked, pouring herself a cup of hot dakka from the pot.

"With her granddaughter, Ma'am. She got word the lass was sick last night and went to see to her. Sent a note for me to cover for her this morning and said she'd be back by noon. Hope that's all right."

"Of course." Maddie made a mental note to check on them as soon as possible. If Tabitha had only said something, she could have arranged for the royal physician to go with her.

Having coaxed the fire to life, the maid set the bathtub beside it and arranged Maddie's clothes and a towel over rails to warm. She glanced at Maddie every so often, her eyes twinkling and a knowing smile lifting her mouth.

"What is it?" Maddie asked at length.

"Oh, sorry, Ma'am." The maid ducked her head. "It's just that… You look happy, if you don't mind me saying so. Nice to know the rumours are true for once."

Rumours. In the palace, there were always rumours. Still, it was always wise to know what people were saying. Maddie lowered her cup. "Which ones?"

The maid bit her lip, and Maddie beckoned her closer. "Please. Tell me. You're not in any trouble."

"You're sure, Ma'am?" Maddie nodded, and the maid sucked in a deep breath. "Well, some say the trouble in the north was a cover for the two of you to meet in secret. But others saw a few refugees come back with you, so they think the Wolf—I mean King Lucas—helped you defeat the bandits attacking the border, and that you fell in love during the battle and couldn't wait to be wed." She sighed. "It's so romantic."

Maddie said nothing, stunned by the conclusions people had jumped to in her absence.

"Is that what happened, Your Highness?"

Nothing could have been further from the truth, but Maddie knew better than to try to quash the falsehood. That only ever lent them more weight. She met the maid's gaze and said, "Not exactly."

Two hours later, Maddie was in the council chamber dealing with the third crisis of the morning when she caught Hodges hovering in the doorway. Calling a halt to the discussion, she took a sip from her goblet of honeyed wine and beckoned him forwards.

He walked around to her chair and leaned close before whispering, "The representatives from Garellion have arrived. They said they would wait in the antechamber, but they seemed agitated, so I took them to the morning room."

Maddie pressed her lips together. On any other day, the meeting running late would have mattered little, but the Garellis had taken issue with her marriage to 'that warmonger' as they had called him during their conversation two days prior. She had intended to assuage any further fears that morning, not keep them waiting while she dealt with land disputes and banditry.

Glancing around the members of her council, who showed varying interest in her steward's interruption, she said, "Gentlemen, if you'll excuse me, I'm needed elsewhere. We'll reconvene tomorrow morning."

Then she rose and followed Hodges out of the room, gesturing for Tristan to join her.

"The Garellis are here," she told him when they were outside.

They walked across the grand entrance hall, where Hodges left them to oversee the delivery of refreshments, and along the east hallway in silence. Drawing to a stop not far from the morning room, Tristan turned to her and said, "I don't like it. They seemed fine when they left the other day."

"Mmm." She looked up from her study of the patterns in the rug. "They requested another meeting. I can only assume my assurances weren't enough to ease their concerns."

She walked to the door, where Tristan made her wait while he entered first, made a brief scan of the room beyond, and held his arm out for her to join him.

"Lucas is only training the Iskarians. Your alliance is not at risk," she murmured to herself. "Keep a clear head and remember your training." Then, wishing Lord Elland were there to offer guidance, she stepped inside with her head held high.

The Garelli ambassador and her fifth-level guild mage stood as Maddie entered, causing her lips to twitch. The way the ambassador towered over her counterpart never failed to amuse her, though she would never admit as much.

One was tall and willowy, her height only accentuated by the bright yellow dress she wore and the tight, black curls piled atop her head. The other was short, not stocky but by no means lean, her straight, black hair tied back in a simple plait. Her plain, fawn coloured dress would have blended into her surroundings but for the guild's dragon-etched medallion resting on the fabric below the neckline. The only parts of them that matched were their warm-brown skin and their nervous smiles.

"Lady Imogen, Mistress Nessa. It's good to see you again. Apologies for keeping you waiting."

"Not at all, Princess Madeline," Imogen said. "We should be the ones to apologise for taking up more of your time, but what we must share is of the utmost importance."

"Oh?" So, this was not about Lucas. That was a relief. Maddie took a seat at the small table by the fire and gestured for the women to join her. Tristan brought a third chair for Nessa, then stood back, leaving them to talk in relative privacy.

"We believe magic is waking across the continent," Nessa said as soon as they were comfortable.

Maddie paused in straightening her skirts and met each woman's gaze in turn. "Magic? But how can that be? It was virtually extinguished aeons ago."

"We know." Imogen spread her hands. "We thought the same, but there have been incidents recently, surges of mage powers that suggest..."

Nessa took up the narrative. "We've been receiving accounts at the guildhall for the last six months. One or two isolated cases at first—mages noticing stronger abilities or greater control when they used their gifts. Then came stories of non-gifted displaying powers, one or two with significant consequences."

A series of potential disasters flitted through Maddie's mind, and she grimaced. "You say this is happening across the continent?"

"In small pockets, yes. We've had reports from Brunland, here, Craeick." Nessa dropped her gaze for the briefest of moments. "There's no discernible pattern that we can see, and even the Free Isles have been affected, but the first cases were in the north, and several outposts in the Balewick Mountains have had a number of incidents."

Maddie stared unseeing into the fire, trying to reconcile what they were telling her with truths taught for hundreds of years. "I thought you were here to talk about Lucas again," she absently noted. "After hearing this, I almost wish you were."

Imogen sat forwards, drawing Maddie's attention back to them. "We've got our best minds working on what's causing the resurgence, and the guild is offering training to any who discover powers, but we need the support of the monarchs to encourage people to come forward—"

"And to stop the influence of Iskaria's mage hunters. Bad enough their own people believe us to be dragon spawned without them convincing anyone in the other kingdoms to hand new mages over."

Nessa ground her jaw, her grip on her armrest so tight Maddie would not have been surprised were it to splinter between her fingers.

"The sooner we have the full picture," Imogen said, "the better we'll be able to help the outliers who…" Maddie's brain supplied the word 'explode' in the heartbeat it took for Imogen to choose the phrase 'cannot control their powers'. "But to do that, we need information."

Controlled once more, Nessa continued. "By the time accounts reach us, they're often days old, and there's nothing we can do. When we heard about the flooding along your border with Brunland, we knew we had to speak with you."

Maddie started. She had been discussing that very issue with her council only half an hour earlier. It was a terrible situation, but one most of her advisors had attributed to natural causes. Could a mage have the power to burst dams? If so… Her mind balked at following the thought like a horse at an unfamiliar, dangerous jump.

"What can I do?" she asked.

Imogen replied, "Send out word that people shouldn't panic but should contact the guild if anything unusual happens. And with your permission, we'd like to set up guildhalls in each of Tyrrath's provinces so we can gather information faster and help where needed."

Guildhalls in Tyrrath. While her kingdom had never rejected mages, and certainly did not condone them being hunted, they had not had a formal presence within its borders since before the mage wars. Many of the remote villages did not even believe such powers still existed. Maddie glanced at Tristan, but his gaze was fixed on the wall above their heads, and a passive expression hid his thoughts on the subject.

She returned her attention to the Garelli women. “Let me think on it.”

Nessa opened her mouth, but Imogen spoke first, placing a hand on the mage’s arm. “It’s a big decision. We understand. But, please, don't take too long.”

Maddie nodded and rose. She needed to consider her next steps carefully.

Tristan had the door open before she reached it, and she strode through with him close on her heels. As if she did not have enough to deal with. Now magic? “It could be worse,” she said aloud. Craeick battled dragons.

“We’ll have to inform the council, and sooner rather than later.”

“I know.”

Her feet carried her towards the staircase leading to her father’s chamber. If only she could ask his advice. Or Lord Elland’s. Every time she thought she knew what she was doing, something happened to throw her off kilter. She exhaled, repeated her father’s mantra—clear head, wise council, people first, best in each moment—and hardened her resolve.

“Can you ask someone to arrange for them to reconvene in half an hour? I need some time to think first.”

“Of course, Ma’am.” Tristan stood to attention, the clack of his boots meeting loud in the quiet hallway, then jogged away before she could scold him for either formality.

Mock glare melting into a grin, she looked aside to where a bust of her ancestor, Galisia, sat in a small alcove. "Did you have this many problems to deal with?" she asked.

The stone face stared blankly back at her.

"No. I suppose having mage powers of your own helped."

"Are you talking to yourself?" Joss called from farther along the hallway. She strolled towards Maddie, leather trousers peeking out through her split skirt, throwing knives attached to her belt.

"Please don't let anyone see you dressed like that, Joss." Though fine in Northold, it would raise more than a few eyebrows in the capital.

"You'll drive yourself mad if you keep working so hard without a break," Joss said, blithely ignoring her. "Do you want to be locked in the north tower like the weeping lady?"

Maddie lifted her eyes to the ceiling. "You do talk such nonsense. Where do you even get these stories?"

Joss gave her a sideways hug. "I read. Sometimes. But I'm serious about you taking a break once in a while. You've barely stopped to breathe since we got back." She stepped back and sucked in an 'oh', eyes gleaming. "You should come out to the forest with me. We've not gone swimming together for an age."

"I'd love to, but I can't. I have to meet with the council again this morning."

Joss harumphed. “Well, at least go for a ride later. I’m worried about you. Think I see a few grey hairs in here.” She poked at the plaits coiled around Maddie’s crown, forcing Maddie to bat her away.

“Wretched girl,” she said through a smile, patting her hair to make sure none had come loose.

Joss backed away a few steps, hands raised, then winked and sauntered around the corner that led to a private entrance not far from the forest gate.

With one last check of her hair, Maddie straightened her skirts and headed for the council chamber. Joss was probably correct, much as she hated to admit it. A ride would do her much good. She considered inviting Lucas to go with her that afternoon, and her steps lightened at the prospect. But first, she had business to see to and a few mages she wanted to visit.

Chapter 14
Maddie

Maddie had not immediately thought of Bronwen, the refugee with the healing gift, when she heard of the resurgence of mage powers, but she sent a message to the family as soon as her meeting with the council broke for the second time. Having invited them to the palace the next day, she set out to find her husband and was pleasantly surprised when he agreed to an afternoon ride together.

When they arrived back at the palace, word was waiting that his family would soon set off from Craeick to visit, and he and Flynn spent the evening answering her and her sisters' many—in Joss's case—questions about them. Maddie met Lucas's eyes more than once during their conversation, and a smile passed between them each time.

They settled into a routine after that, waking together before dawn, fulfilling their respective duties in the mornings, spending a few hours together after lunch, then returning to their scheduled meetings until dinner, and relaxing in the evenings with their siblings.

Not that playing Knights with Lucas and Flynn was particularly restful. The little boy was an astute strategist, and Lucas played to win every game. Nevertheless, a new sense of normalcy suffused the palace, and Maddie began to hope that her marriage could someday be more than the desperate treaty she had entered into. Her only regret was that she was unable to introduce her husband to her father.

The weather improved along with their relationship, the land throwing off the last traces of winter, new leaves turning the tree outside her study from brown to green. She finished the last of her daily correspondence one morning and looked up to find pink buds dotting its branches, the sky clear, and sunlight pouring through the glass panes.

It seemed a shame to waste such a glorious day sitting inside. The impulse to invite Lucas to lunch in the woods fluttered through her, and she grinned at the idea. Roguish ways aside, he had allowed her to see a side of him she doubted many others ever saw, and this would be the perfect way to reciprocate. They might even be able to go for a swim.

She tidied her papers, set the stack of letters aside to be delivered, and barely contained her gait to a walk as she left her study.

Halfway along the corridor, Tristan looked up from a guard he was talking to and lifted one brow. “Your Highness?”

"Captain Karr," she returned in kind, slowing her pace in front of the other guard.

Tristan fell into step beside her and asked, "Going somewhere special?"

"I'm going to see if Lucas wants to eat by the stream."

His lips flattened. "You'll need an escort."

"To the woods? Surely not if Lucas is there?"

"It's my job to protect you, Ma'am. Your father would have my hide if I let anything happen to you. So would mine if he were here."

Maddie winced. "You're right, of course. Help me find him, then?"

He chuckled, shaking his head at her. "You're becoming as difficult as Joss."

"Never! Now do you know where Lucas is or not?"

"Yes, Ma'am."

They made their way to the rear of the palace complex, where Lucas had taken over part of the guards' barracks and training yard for the dozen men he had brought with him. A crowd gathered at one side of the open space outside the porticoed building, and the clash of swords rose over their intermittent cheers.

Maddie and Tristan pushed through to the front, where they found Lucas sparring with a young soldier. Leather jerkins protected their torsos, but their arms were bare, their sleeves rolled back to the elbows.

"Why aren't they wearing more protection?" she asked Tristan.

He answered without looking at her. "It's just a training match."

Oh.

The man fighting Lucas could not have been much older than Joss, yet he appeared to be holding his own. Eyes locked on each other, their limbs moved equally smoothly in the deadly dance, and neither wore the bloody symbols of defeat.

The men around them shouted encouragement, a few placing bets as the battle ranged back and forth. Off to the right, she caught Flynn watching from beside one of the pillars lining the front of the barracks. Should he have been there? He looked around and waved at them, giving Maddie a huge grin as he pointed at his brother and shouted something she could not hear.

She lifted a hand and nodded anyway, then turned her attention back to the match just in time to see the soldier land a glancing blow along Lucas's forearm. She sucked in a sharp hiss as her husband swiped a thin line of blood from the cut, smearing it across his sweat-soaked skin.

The young man fighting him stepped away and lifted his sword to the crowd in triumph, then walked a small circle, soaking in their whistles and calls. Scratching the Wolf, it seemed, was worthy of much note.

"Lucky hit," the man beside her said to his companion.

"Aye, and he'd do well not to enjoy it so much. The Wolf won't stand for that."

Maddie studied her husband more closely. His features darkened, and he attacked his opponent without warning, his sword moving so fast she could barely keep track of the strikes. Metal clanged and rasped against metal as he drove the young man back.

She glanced at the men around her, some wincing, others appearing rapt by the brutal display. Fear for the young man crept up her spine. Her husband fought without mercy, a snarl twisting his features into those of a wolf indeed.

A thrust found a gap in the soldier's defence, which weakened by the moment, and scored a line across his thigh, but Lucas did not stop. Would he gravely injure the man over a small cut and wounded pride? Surely, he could not be so… so vengeful.

The soldier stumbled and fell, scrabbling backwards to escape his commander's relentless onslaught. Though the crowd quieted, none intervened.

But she could.

She would not let Lucas kill another man while she stood and watched.

"Stop." Hitching her skirts with one hand, she lunged into the makeshift arena.

Tristan grabbed for her, but someone jostled him, and she managed to evade his grip, ignoring his command to stay back. She felt him chasing behind her and pushed forwards with all the strength she had.

"Lucas, no."

Lucas's sword glinted in the sunlight, high above his left shoulder, then swung down towards the young man on the ground at the same time as she reached for her husband's right arm. Her cry drew his lethal gaze, and the arc of his sword changed, slicing around to the right, towards her.

She instinctively raised her arm to protect her face, but the blade only tugged at her sleeve and was gone. Bewildered, she looked up into eyes that tore through several emotions before settling on fury.

That was all she saw, for Tristan spun her around by the shoulders, a slight tremble in his firm grip. "What were you thinking? You could have been seriously hurt." He looked her over. "Are you well?"

"I—"

"You're bleeding." He glared at Lucas and growled, "You cut her."

She was? He had? She peered down at the ruined fabric of her sleeve, at the dark stain blooming on the fine, sapphire wool, and at the trickle of blood wending around her fingers to drip onto her skirt. Pain registered—a sting that burgeoned into a burning flame along the outside of her forearm and made her clamp her lips between her teeth.

"We need to get this tended to," Tristan said more gently, lowering his head to meet her eyes.

"I'll see to it," Lucas gritted from right behind her.

Tristan straightened. "The princess is my responsibility."

"But she's *my* wife."

They hemmed her in between them, stealing the air from her lungs, neither even looking at her any longer. Then a hand clamped around her uninjured arm and tugged her towards the barracks, and for the space of a heartbeat, she was unsure which of them it was. But Lucas's grip was nothing like Tristan's—firm and unyielding, though nowhere near as terrifying as the expression on his face when she glanced at him. Thunder resided there, furrowing his brow and compressing his lips into a flat, tight line.

The crowd scattered at their passing. Men melted into shadows, doorways, the far reaches of the training yard as if nothing out of the ordinary had just happened. Only Tristan and Flynn trailed them, Flynn asking, "Doesn't she know not to interrupt a fight like that?"

She did now.

He trotted up beside her as they reached the barracks and said, "You'll be all right. Lucas stitches really good."

Grimacing despite her best efforts, she started to answer him, but Lucas tugged her across the threshold and shut the door behind them, leaving Flynn and Tristan outside. A few soldiers hustled out through a second door farther along the same wall, and they were alone.

Still, Lucas did not speak. He left her by the entrance and gathered some supplies from a chest, depositing them on a table beneath the window between the doors. Then he poured some water into a bowl, added a few drops of something from a small bottle, and pulled a stool out from the table, scraping the legs across the floor.

He did not meet her eyes, only angled his body towards her and waited, which she took as indication she should sit. Not willing to break the silence lest he unleash his thoughts and tell her just how badly she had erred, she took the seat, facing the window so she could lay her injured right arm on the table beside her.

When he peeled back her sleeve and lifted her wrist to inspect the wound, his touch was much gentler than she had expected, and some of the tension in her shoulders eased.

"This will hurt," he said, and a moment later, a wet cloth pressed against her forearm, setting the fire burning again.

She clenched her teeth together, determined not to cry out.

The cloth disappeared, and the sounds of him rinsing it filled the space between them. Then the scent of cloves and rosemary reached her as he returned the cloth to her arm once more. Tears stung her eyes, and she squeezed them shut, counting the heartbeats until the pain receded and blessed numbness took its place.

Freed from the focus of the pain, she peeked up at Lucas while he worked. Anger still radiated from him, though whether for her getting in the way or being injured, she could not tell. But something else bloomed too—awareness of him.

Her skin tingled at his proximity. His breath warmed her shoulder as he worked to clean the cut, his face mere inches from hers, and his fingers felt both warm and rough against the sensitive skin of her forearm. She swallowed the dryness that parched her throat.

Searching for a way to break the tension, she blurted, "You know, with most married couples, this is done the other way around."

"I can tend my own wounds." His expression softened, and he pulled the cloth away, inspecting the cut carefully. "It's my responsibility to look after you."

She glanced at her arm, and a laugh burst out of her mouth. The grunt he emitted only worsened her fit of giggles, and he dropped the cloth into the bowl of water.

"I don't see what's so funny."

Maddie swallowed her mirth and shifted to meet his eyes. Assured the danger had passed from them, she said, "In that case, you might want to be more careful where you swing your blade."

A scowl darkened his expression. "And you might want to avoid running into the middle of a swordfight."

"I was trying to protect him—and you. You nearly killed him."

"I did no such thing."

She gaped at him. Could he have forgotten so quickly? "He cut you, and you went wild. Vengeance should never enter a training ground." She had heard Tristan's father state that fact more times than she could remember as a girl.

"Is that what you think I was doing?"

The stunned indignation written across his widened eyes and raised brows made her pause, and when her throat unlocked, her response sounded more like a question than assertion in her ears. "Yes."

He closed the space between them. "I was teaching him a valuable lesson. Or trying to until you got in the way. One cut doesn't bring down a foe, which is why a soldier should never take their focus from the enemy until they're truly beaten. A mistake like that on the battlefield could have cost him his life. He needed to learn that."

Maddie frowned. “And the best way to teach him is to attack without mercy?”

“When he’s crowing like a fool while I barely bleed? Yes!”

His breath came in heavy pants that lifted the fine hairs around her face.

“It’s how I was taught.” He snatched up a bandage and gauze. “This doesn’t need stitches,” he said, smearing honey from a small pot over the cut and wrapping her forearm.

She glanced at the visible scars on his arms, the one down his face, and flinched. Such a hard life he had lived. So different from her own experiences.

“This bothers you?” He pointed to his cheek, and a pang of regret sliced through her chest.

She looked into his eyes and told him the truth. “I hardly notice it anymore.” But she was curious. Mustering her courage, she asked, “How did you get it?”

His brow furrowed, pain etched into the deep groove, and the muscle in his jaw ticced.

Regret bit deep. Why had she pried? She wracked her brain for a distraction, but before she could think of another topic, he let out a long, low sigh, and said, “Dragon attack. When I was young.”

“I’m sorry.” Whether for the boy who was hurt or for dredging up the memory, she was not certain.

“Not your fault.”

They sat in silence for an endless heartbeat, until he turned aside and broke their connection. He tied the bandage off like he was swaddling a babe, tucking the ends under one of the folds just so. Then he cleared his throat and spoke in an undertone.

"You could have been seriously hurt today. I'm sorry I cut you." He looked up at her. "Promise me you won't do anything that stupid again. Promise me, Maddie."

"I promise." Her brain took a moment to unscramble what had just passed between them, but when it did, a grin tugged at her lips.

"What?" he asked.

"That's the first time you've called me Maddie."

A growl rumbled through his chest, but laughter danced in his eyes, assuring her that his anger—and alarm—had truly dissipated. He picked up the supplies, then bent close to her ear as he stood, and whispered, "Don't get used to it, Princess."

Chapter 15
Maddie

Despite Maddie's insistence that her arm was well enough to ride, Lucas refused her woodland picnic invitation. Instead, he led her back to the palace, where they ate their lunch in the library over a game of Knights. Only after they finished two large bowls of fish stew and a platter of cheese and fruit did it occur to her to have Bronwen heal her wound. She called for a servant to fetch the mage, and a short while later, a knock on the door preceded the regular palace healer entering the room.

He bowed low, dropping his bag to the floor, and said, "Apologies, Your Highness, but Bronwen left to visit family yesterday and isn't expected back for several days. May I be of service?"

"Oh." If the wound could not be magically healed, was it worth disturbing the bandaging?

"Yes. Look at my wife's arm," Lucas said, drawing Maddie's focus. He did not meet her gaze, but his brow had furrowed, and his lips formed a tight, flat line.

"Of course, Your Majesty."

The healer bustled in Maddie's periphery, unwrapping, examining, and rewrapping her arm, but she could not look away from her husband. He followed the healer's movements with the intensity of a predator ready to strike, only relaxing when the man straightened and addressed them.

"Whoever tended the wound did a fine job, Ma'am. I couldn't have done better myself. Rest your arm for a few days if you can, and call on me to change the dressing if it gets wet or leaks."

Lucas cleared his throat. "I'll see to that myself."

"Very well, Sire. Will that be all?"

"Yes. Thank you," Maddie said.

The healer offered a quick bow and slipped out of the room, leaving them alone once more.

Maddie ducked her head and studied Lucas from beneath her lashes, while he studied the board between them as if real lives depended on his next move.

She sighed, and his gaze jumped to her. "Do you need anything? More wine, a pillow for your arm?"

"No." She hid a bubble of mirth behind what she hoped was a reassuring smile. "I'm well, thank you."

He studied her for a long moment, then said, "I'm sorry about what happened."

Waving him off, she searched for a way to ease his concern. "I was the one who charged into a sword fight without a weapon. Not even Joss would do something so reckless."

Finally, he chuckled. "You might be foolhardy, but you're certainly brave. I can admit that."

They returned to their game, and she was about to defeat his dragon when the door burst open and her sisters spilled inside.

"What happened?" Joss asked. "We heard you were injured."

They rushed over to her side, and Joss lifted her arm to inspect it, though there was little to be seen through the bandage. She spun on Lucas and said, "What did you do to our sister?"

He winced but lowered his goblet of wine to the table and looked Joss directly in the eye. "I accidentally cut her when she tried to stop a training match. I—"

"The Wolf of Craeick, greatest swordsman of our time, and you can't tell your opponent from your wife?"

"I'm the one to blame, Joss," Maddie said before the exchange became heated. "I shouldn't have got in the way."

Joss's brows shot up, twin bows at full stretch. "How is it your fault? He was the one holding the sword."

Maddie tugged on her arm, and after glaring at Lucas for a moment longer, the tension drained from her body and she sat down, scooting her chair closer to Maddie's.

"Are you in pain? Can we get you anything?" Olivia stood motionless, her hands clenched together so tightly the knuckles had whitened.

The sheen in her eyes made Maddie's heart twist, so she held out her free hand until Olivia stepped closer, then gave her fingers a squeeze. "I'm perfectly well. Lucas treated the wound himself."

"Least he could do," Joss muttered.

"It's a clean cut," he said. "Your sister should heal in no time."

Olivia glanced at him and edged closer to Maddie, kneeling on the floor and burrowing into her side. Then she frowned up at him with an expression as close to approbation as she had ever mustered.

Maddie stroked her sister's hair and whispered, "I'm well, Mouse. Truly."

While Olivia nodded, Joss sat forwards, studied the Knights board, and said, "Whose move is it? I'll play the winner."

They spent the next few hours keeping Maddie entertained and fussing over her whenever she so much as inhaled sharply. When she reached for one of the books stacked on a nearby table and winced, Lucas and Joss both jumped up from their seats.

"I'll help you, Maddie." Joss shouldered Lucas aside, saying, "*You* can't even control a blade."

He glared at her, the muscles in his jaw bunching. "That's the third time you've attacked my competence."

"And?"

"It's twice more than any man would have survived."

Joss snapped her mouth closed, and Maddie did her best to suppress the urge to laugh at her sister's stunned expression.

"Madeline," he said, turning to her and softening his voice. "I think it's time we retired for the evening." He glanced at her sisters. "If you'll excuse us…"

He did not wait for a reply, simply set the table aside and drew Maddie to her feet. She looked over her shoulder as he led her to the door, flashing Olivia a reassuring smile and shaking her head at Joss to prevent her from following them. It seemed wise to let tempers cool for a while.

When she and Lucas reached their room, he settled her in a chair by the fire and sat opposite her, his long legs filling the space between them.

He said nothing, only stared into the empty hearth, and the silence grew thick and heavy. Maddie picked at the edge of the blanket he had tucked around her.

"I apologise," he finally said, startling her. "I'm an experienced warrior, not some raw recruit. There's no excuse for not controlling my blade in time."

"It's not your—"

The glower clouding his face darkened. "I shouldn't have hurt you. Family are the only people I'm supposed to care about."

Supposed to? She frowned. "What do you mean?"

"My family and my kingdom. Isn't that the way it's meant to be?"

Maddie studied him. Such a heavy burden he carried. Craeick was neither as prosperous nor safe as Tyrrath, and he must have faced so many difficult decisions throughout his rule. "They're important, yes, but there's room for other things too." She drew a breath and firmed her resolve. "I accept your apology—on one condition."

He straightened, his eyes darting to hers.

"That you let it go." She lifted her bandaged arm. "Dwelling on this serves no purpose for either of us. It was an accident, and I'm none the worse for wear. Let's put it behind us and move on. No more apologies."

He blinked. Once. Twice. Then the corner of his mouth twitched up, and when he nodded, the tension in her body finally eased.

She pointed at her wardrobe, where the old Knights set her father had given her as a child poked out from the bottom shelf.

"Now, if you want the chance to salvage your dignity in our tournament, you could fetch the board." She lofted a brow in challenge, cleared a stack of books from the table, and tried to pull it closer without wincing.

Barking a laugh, he stood, hefted the table into position with far more ease than she could have managed even without her injury, and strode across the room.

"You're going to regret challenging me, Princess."

But even though she lost, she did not regret it at all.

They talked until the sky outside the windows darkened, their conversation ebbing and flowing through a range of topics. She told him about falling from her horse when she was six; he told her about the first time his sword master allowed him to fight with a real blade; they avoided mention of the scar on his face or his father's death.

When Maddie's stomach grumbled, Lucas left briefly and returned with a tray of bread, ham, dried fruit, and a dakka pot. He handed her a mug of steaming brown liquid and watched as she took the first sip.

It tasted so vile she almost choked, coughing and spluttering behind her hand.

“What is that?” Her mouth contorted in a vain attempt to remove the disgusting flavour. “It tastes like tree bark and tar and pig guts.”

He laughed.

The sound, deep and rich, almost distracted her from the foul concoction assaulting her taste buds. Almost. But the amusement soon fell from his face, and he said, “We use it in the army. Tastes like a rotting dragon’s carcass, but it’s good for healing, so you need to finish it.”

Grimacing again, she pinched her nose and tipped the rest down her throat. When the mug was drained, she set it on the table and took a gulp of her wine, eliciting another chuckle from her husband.

But when her eyelids began to droop and she could no longer contain her yawns, he tucked her into their bed, where, for the first time, he wrapped her in his arms before sleep, her injured arm cushioned atop his broad chest.

The last words she heard as she drifted off were “I’ll protect you from now on, Madeline. I swear it.”

The next time she opened her eyes, a hint of light limned the curtains and Lucas was already awake, his back propped against the headboard, the candle beside their bed lit. He studied her face, his expression soft, and asked, “How are you feeling this morning?”

“I’m well.” Why should she not be?

She pushed herself upright, and pain shot up her right arm, reminding her of the previous day's events and the cause for his concern. She bit back a hiss, but he must have noticed, for he handed her more of the foul-smelling tisane. Tabitha would have added honey, she absently noted.

He inspected the bandage while she drank. "Looks good, but it'll need changing soon. I can—"

"Tabitha can see to it." Her heart sped at the thought of him touching her wrist again, blowing gently on her skin. She gave him a weak smile and sought a reasonable explanation for her refusal. "She's been mending my scrapes since I was born. She's more than capable of changing a bandage."

He twisted his lips as if he were about to argue.

"Please. You must have plenty to do today without playing nursemaid. And this"—she lifted her injured arm—"was my own fault, remember, not yours."

Their eyes met and held, his shining with… was that admiration? She could not fathom what she had done to deserve such esteem, but before she could enquire, he reached out and ran his fingers down the side of her face.

The air shifted between them, growing thick and charged with static that raised the fine hairs on her unbound arm. He leaned forwards, slowly, and her heart bucked in her chest, pounding loudly enough for half the palace to hear it. She held still while he hesitated, his face a finger's breadth from hers, and then his mouth touched hers.

His lips were firm, warm, and slightly prickly where he had not yet shaved, but none of those sensations explained her reaction to the kiss. Heat, breathlessness, a skein unravelling deep in her belly, longing for more—it was too much to process all at once.

She leaned into him, wanting, needing more.

And then, without any warning, it was over.

He pulled back, and she stared at him, stunned, while a grin slowly edged across his face. "What? Nothing to say, Princess?"

The way he said 'princess' was different than before, like a caress that she felt down to her toes. He chuckled and climbed from their bed, and the sight of him did more strange things to her stomach.

She looked away and focused on regaining control, trying to ignore the sounds of him readying for the day. When the bed dipped under his weight and she brought her gaze back to him, his expression was serious.

"Rest that arm today. It didn't need stitches, but it will if you overextend it."

Unable to find her voice, she nodded her assent.

"I have a busy day ahead, so I probably won't see you until this evening." He reached out and swept a stray lock of her hair behind her ear, the tips of his fingers grazing her skin and leaving a trail of tingles behind. "Maybe then we can discuss a renegotiation of our treaty agreement, hmm?"

He winked and was gone, leaving images of more kissing in his wake.

She was scrambling out of bed when the door latch rattled again. "Can you help me change this dressing?"

she asked without looking. "I've got so much to do today."

"Not until you've eaten," Joss said, dumping a tray laden with food on the table before the fire.

Olivia followed behind her, carrying a pot of dakka and three cups. "We thought you deserved breakfast in bed after…" Her eyes trailed to Maddie's arm, and she bit her lip.

Shoving her good arm into her robe and easing it over the other, Maddie rounded the end of the bed and hugged them both in turn. "I'm fine. Truly. But I'll never say no to breaking my fast with you."

She dropped into one of the chairs and picked up a slice of sweet darley bread—a treat indeed—breaking small pieces off it to pop into her mouth. Her gaze drifted to the fire, where Joss toasted a slice over the flames on the end of a long fork. The pain in her arm was a distant throb, her sisters were by her side, and her husband…

"What are you daydreaming about?" Joss asked, startling her back to the present.

"Hmm? Oh, nothing." Heat in her face belied her words, and she silently cursed her inability to hide a blush.

Joss slathered butter over the crispy toast, handed it to Olivia, and jammed another slice on her toasting fork before spearing Maddie with a narrow-eyed look. After a moment of intense scrutiny, her eyes widened, and she pointed a finger at Maddie. "Something happened with Lucas, didn't it? Tell us everything."

Maddie avoided her probing gaze, but Olivia peered at her from where she had curled up on the floor as well. Cheeks burning hotter than a forge fire, Maddie stood and walked over to the wardrobe.

"Did he kiss you?" Joss asked. "He did, didn't he? What was it like? Did you—"

Maddie threw the last of her darley bread at her, satisfied when Joss barely lifted her arm in time to deflect it from hitting her face.

"Come help me, Mouse." Maddie turned her back and pretended to be engrossed in choosing a dress for the day.

Unfortunately, there was no way to block out Joss's mumbled, "It must have been some kiss."

When Maddie finally made it downstairs, Tristan was waiting for her. His eyes flicked to her arm, where a fresh bandage bulged beneath the pine-green sleeve, and the muscle in his jaw ticced.

He said nothing about it, instead holding up a creased piece of paper and asking, "Did you know about this?"

"What?"

"The queen mother of Craeick and her husband, Lord Ross, crossed into Tyrrath yesterday. They'll be here within the week. And according to my scout's report, they have a small army with them."

Within the week? Maddie stilled. She had not pressed Lucas for the exact timing of their visit, in small part, she had to admit, because she feared their reaction to recent events. The manner of her marriage to their son hardly fostered good relations—if he had informed them of the particulars. But surely, he would have told her had he known they were on their way. "I wasn't expecting them so soon."

"And the soldiers with them?"

"I'm sure it's just an honour guard." He lofted his eyebrows, so she added, "He's the Wolf of Craeick. He's probably got more enemies than the rest of the kingdoms put together, so it's only natural he'd take extra precautions with his mother."

The reasoning rang false, even as she tried to convince herself of its truth—who would dare attack the Wolf's kin?—but their kingdoms were bound now, by treaty and marriage. It mattered not how many troops they brought with them.

"Never mind," Tristan said. "I'll sort something out. Ma'am." He brought his heels together, nodded his head, and strode away, muttering about needing to be prepared for anything with Craeick involved.

While she was debating whether to follow him or not, Hodges arrived with her morning correspondence. A letter from Lord Elland sat at the top of the pile, and she broke the seal and opened it straight away, devouring the contents almost faster than her eyes could take it in.

He would be home soon. Maddie's muscles relaxed, and she started walking again as she opened the next missive—which confirmed Tristan's intelligence.

She sighed. "Hodges?"

"Yes, Ma'am?"

"Make the guest rooms in the private wing ready, and I'll need to review the menus for next week..." She caught her lip between her teeth. What else?

There were so many things to attend to before her in-laws' arrival, it would take every minute she had left to get through them all. She walked to her office at as swift a pace as decorum allowed and sent instructions for her current plans to be postponed.

By the time she finished all the items on her list for the day, exhaustion dragged at her limbs, and all she wanted was to eat and climb into bed. The thought reminded her of Lucas's kiss that morning and sent a zing of energy through her body.

It carried her to their room, where she washed, devoured a bowl of stew and suet dumplings fast enough to give her indigestion, and paced the rug by the fire while she waited for him to join her. The longer he took to return, the more knotted her insides became until she was soon a bundle of nerves wrapped around a lump of congealed meat.

She straightened the covers for the fourth—or was it the fifth—time and checked her appearance in the mirror. No stray hair escaped her braid, and her dress lay smoothly over her chemise.

Footsteps outside drew her head around, but they passed the door and receded. Not Lucas. Where was he? Surely whatever business had kept him busy throughout the day should be concluded by now. She glanced at the window, the curtains long pulled shut against the chill that fell outside with the descent of the sun.

Would he have taken his solitary walk as usual? She could not fathom doing so with the weight of what lay between them on her mind, the fluttering in her stomach that accompanied every thought of him. But she was far less experienced.

She stilled. Maybe that was the cause of his delay. Maybe her inexperience had gnawed at him throughout the day, making him regret his suggestion of more. Had her kiss been lacking in some way? The possibility worked its way into her thoughts like a splinter beneath her skin.

Dropping into her favourite chair, she stared down at her hands as she absently picked at the edge of her thumbnail. Could it have been so bad for him? It had felt wonderful to her—impossible, magical, breathtaking. But she knew nothing of marriage aside from what she had observed between her parents and the other couples at court.

On the whole, they had seemed to enjoy each other's company, her parents especially. They would often hold hands or kiss each other, and spent many evenings snuggled together in the library while she and Joss played at their feet.

Maddie's eyes stung, and she blinked against it. If she was no good at kissing, what would that mean for her and Lucas? Would he prefer to keep to the original terms of their agreement after all?

No! She scrubbed her palms down her face. He had been the one to suggest they amend it, and that had been after their kiss. Something else must be keeping him, some emergency, though she could think of nothing so serious that she would not have heard of by now.

And so her thoughts went, round and round, until she finally dozed off in the chair by the fireplace, where she dreamed of being lost in a maze, alternately chasing and being chased by a fierce wolf.

Chapter 16
Maddie

Maddie dropped her quill to the desk the next day and stretched her arm. It had itched all morning, almost enough to distract her from the fact that Lucas never returned to their room the previous night.

She clenched her fist against the memory of waking in the chair to find the bed empty and undisturbed, and returned her attention to the figures Hodges was showing her.

"Should I order more tisane, Ma'am?" he asked, frowning at her arm.

"No. I can manage. Thank you." She needed to be clear-headed over the coming days, and the pain in her arm had receded to a dull throb she could ignore.

His pursed lips suggested he thought otherwise, but he tipped her a nod and slid the next page in front of her. The amounts seemed reasonable, so she signed at the bottom without checking the total, trusting him to have added it correctly, and pretended she did not see his disapproving look.

He gathered the records together and picked up their notes for the banquet that would honour the arrival of Lucas's mother. "I'll get these ordered this afternoon, Ma'am."

"Thank you, Hodges."

He left, and she sat back in her chair, her mind wandering to her husband's whereabouts once more.

According to Parker, who was on duty that morning, he had ridden out with some of his men an hour before dawn, but Maddie could not understand why. Or why he had not told her. She had kept half an ear out for his return during every meeting she had sat through, but it neared lunchtime, and concern was beginning to seep into her thoughts.

A clatter of hoof beats in the courtyard set her heart galloping. Was that him? She peered through the window but could not see anything from that angle. "Drat."

With barely a thought for decorum, she flew across the room, flung the door open and hurried around to the courtyard entrance, where Lucas and his men were indeed dismounting. She descended the steps, eyes glued to her husband, searching him for obvious signs of injury or distress.

"Lucas. There you are. I was—"

"Can I help you, Princess?"

It was not his choice of words that punched the air from her lungs so much as the cold indifference in his tone. She froze as he turned and cast an equally bored glance up and down her. What was happening? Why was he being like that?

She looked around his men for an explanation, but they all ignored her. Except for the red-haired woman, whose sneer sent a shiver down Maddie's spine.

Dragging her gaze back to her husband, she tried again. "I was worried about you. After yesterday, I thought…"

"You thought what?" His features may as well have been made of stone when he looked at her. "There's nothing between us. You're a means to an end, a convenience that allowed me to speed my plans. Nothing more."

Nothing more. The words chipped at her heart, flinging shards through her chest that bit far deeper than any sword's edge. Could it be true? Had he changed his mind about them—or never been in earnest in the first place?

But how could that be? He had made her want him, had made her care. Why, if it was all for naught? Here was confirmation of her worst fears from the previous night, those that had seemed so absurd in the light of day. Yet what other reason could there be for his cold dismissal?

Her hands stroked the sides of her skirt of their own accord, the sensation providing a small anchor for thoughts cast adrift by his rejection. She grasped it, clearing her throat and forcing herself to meet his eyes. She even managed a smile, brittle and small though it was.

"Then I bid you good day."

How she turned and walked inside without stumbling, she could not say, but she did. She walked all the way back to her study and only when the door was firmly closed behind her and she was alone did she crumple to the nearest chair and allow her hope to shatter.

When the door opened sometime later, she half expected it to be Lucas come to tell her that he had made a mistake and wanted to pick up where they had left off the day before, but it was not.

Tristan stormed in, brandishing a scrap of paper like a weapon, a dangerous light in his eyes that she had only seen twice before. "That Wolf has betrayed us."

Maddie blinked at him. "What?"

"He's betrayed us—betrayed Tyrrath. He's chopping down half the forest around Hawkesden and building a fortress large enough to house a sizeable army, and his soldiers are pouring over the border and taking provisions from the local settlements again."

"That can't be right. Are you sure?"

He held the paper out to her. "Lieutenant Wash sent this by carrier pigeon. Came in just now, so the news can't be more than an hour or two old."

She scanned the contents of the brief note, then read it again more slowly. Bile rose in her throat, and the paper slipped from her fingers. It was true. Lucas had betrayed her.

"We can't let him get away with it," Tristan said. "This is not what we agreed."

Maddie mentally scrolled through the terms of the treaty. Technically, they had not set a limit on the size of the fort as long as the entire settlement remained within the bounds of Hawkesden valley, and the number of troops it accommodated ‘could be increased in extenuating circumstances’.

She closed her eyes as the truth wormed deep inside her core. Lucas—the Wolf King—had been manipulating her all along.

It was not her kiss that had pushed him away. He had simply been distracting her, biding his time until he had his men in position and it was too late for her to do anything to stop him. The terms of their agreement had given him just enough leeway to get a foothold in her kingdom, and their marriage gave him the legitimacy to take more.

What a fool she had been!

Pain seared through her chest, and she bent low, hiding her face in her hands. The Wolf was not the only one at fault. She had done this. She had let her people down. Her father would be so ashamed of her.

“I’m sorry,” she mumbled into her fingers. “So, so sorry.”

Gentle hands lifted her shoulders. A solid chest lent her strength, absorbed her tears. Tristan’s voice soothed her panicked thoughts, and his hands rubbed warmth back into her arms. She sank into the familiar comfort of her oldest friend until despair burned away, leaving a nugget of pure, brilliant anger behind.

She might not be able to remove the Wolf from her kingdom, but she could remove him from her presence and make it abundantly clear that his games had been found out and she was not so easily beaten. Straightening, she met Tristan’s worried gaze and asked, “Where is he?”

"In the forest, hunting with his second-in-command. Should I summon the guard?"

"No. Much as I hate to admit it, he's broken no law. Yet." She stood and paced, chewing on her bottom lip. "Put a watch on his men here. I want to know the moment they do anything that could constitute breaking the treaty. And send word back to Lieutenant Wash to stay in Hawkesden and monitor the situation there. Lord Elland will ensure the Craeickish army makes reparations for the provisions they've stolen." That, at least, was a violation they could tackle directly, though relatively minor in relation to the whole.

She paused at the prospect of being without her most trusted political advisor even longer, but it could not be helped.

"And their leader?" Tristan asked.

Their leader. The Wolf. Her husband, albeit in name only. If the previous day was anything to go by, he would likely stay in the forest until he thought the rest of the palace asleep. They could search for hours and never find him—Joss had proven that enough times.

Maddie started pacing again, the space in front of her desk feeling more cramped than usual. When she headed to the window to let in some fresh air, the answer struck her. She might not know where the Wolf was now, but there was one place she knew he would be later—his nightly walk around the grounds. He never missed it.

She smoothed her features into a blank mask before turning back to Tristan. This was one confrontation she intended to have alone. Whether Lucas Sinclair liked it or not, she was going to look him in the eye and get some answers. Tristan could have his turn afterwards.

Chapter 17

Luc

Luc eased out from behind the tree he was using as cover, careful to avoid snapping any twigs, and brought his bow up. Sighting along the arrow, he relaxed, held his breath, and released. The arrow flew true, but his aim was slightly off. It passed the buck by a whisper, setting it running deeper into the forest.

His third miss of the day. He scratched his neck, the scruff rasping against his fingernails, and set off after his quarry. It was that dragon-cursed woman's fault, invading his mind like a disease. He had come to Tyrrath with a plan, and it was time he stuck to it. He needed to stay away from her.

"Love is a weakness," he told himself, "and you're not weak."

Aiden appeared beside him, a throwing dagger in hand. "Nothing weak about you, my friend." He clapped Luc's shoulder. "Slow, maybe, but not weak."

Luc shoved him off and would have taught him just how fast he could be, but the bushes ahead rustled, bringing his focus back to the hunt. He signalled for Aiden to move around to the left and closed in on the sound.

A brace of blackbirds winged up from the foliage, directly in front of his face, and into the branches overhead. He straightened and met Aiden's lopsided grin with a shrug. Another false alarm.

They stalked the deer, following its tracks along a thin trail through the underbrush. It would not have run far.

"Looking forward to your mother arriving?" Aiden whispered.

"Yes. I'll be able to hand Flynn back to her."

They shared a grin, but Luc had spoken true. He needed her here, needed all of his family. When they were together, he was at ease, balanced. They gave him strength, unlike the soft princess who muddled his purpose. He should view her like he did everyone else—profit or prey.

The buck stepped out from behind a large oak ahead, and he and Aiden melted into the trees around them. He waited while the animal nibbled some grass and took another step away from its cover, then nocked an arrow.

Before he or Aiden could move in or take the shot, an arrow whizzed through the air and struck the deer cleanly behind its shoulder. It dropped to the ground, and Rhee emerged from a thicket off to their right.

"Nice shooting," Aiden said.

"You drove him straight to me." She reached the downed animal and bent to check for a pulse.

Luc returned his arrow to its quiver and joined the others. Up close, the buck was even more impressive—strong and healthy, not like the mountain deer at home. Its antlers were already half regrown after winter, and there was enough meat on it to keep them fed for several days should they remain in the woods.

"We should send you out on your own," he said to Rhee. "You'd catch enough to feed the whole unit with some to spare."

"Not for long," she said, using her belt knife to gut the carcass. "Aren't the rest arriving soon?"

"Mm." Many more of his troops were travelling with his mother, but most would be diverted before they reached Tyrrath's capital. "Angus and Rory will be with them. They can help."

Rhee snorted. "Get in the way, more like. At least you move silently, even if you do shoot like a bairn on its first dragon run."

Luc chuckled absently at the ribbing, twisting the signet ring around his finger as his mind turned towards weightier matters. A sizeable fortress at Hawkesden had not been part of his initial plan, but it was too good an opportunity to miss. Surrounded by readily available supplies, within easy reach of Craeick, and not far from the Brunland border, it made the ideal staging ground for what would come next.

When the bulk of his army arrived, he could probe the fat neighbouring kingdom and then…

"Daydreaming?" Aiden's voice broke into Luc's calculations, along with a few twigs hitting him. He looked over at his friend, who was stripping a branch to carry the buck back to the palace and tossing bits of debris at him.

"No. Just thinking."

But Aiden had a point. For now, it was a dream, and Luc must not get ahead of himself. He helped Rhee tie the buck's legs to the rough pole. First, build the fortress, which meant more wood and more labourers. And in the meantime, hunt and avoid the troublesome princess.

Chapter 18
Maddie

Maddie crept through the palace garden by the thin light of the cloud-covered moon, searching the shadows for the Wolf. The luminous faces of night blooms that Olivia had trained over a series of arches cast pools of brighter light along the main paths, their sweet scent at odds with the acid churning in Maddie's gut. She tightened her grip on the dagger she carried unsheathed and swung around at the sound of gravel crunching behind her.

A peacock strutted out from behind an ornamental urn, its colourful feathers muted to varying shades of grey in the darkness. Ridiculous bird. It had nearly given her a heart attack.

She walked on, moving to the grass at the side of the path to quiet her movements. At the hedge between the formal and rose gardens, she paused and looked around. Which way would the Wolf pass? And how might she best confront him?

The dagger caught in the dense foliage of the hedge, and she yanked it free, raining leaf fragments down onto her skirt. She stared at the bared blade, struck by the absurdity of carrying it. What had she been thinking? She could not use it as a weapon, and even if she could, she was no match for the Wolf.

The sense of security it had given her evaporated, leaving cold reality behind. She was alone in the garden at night, waiting to confront a man who was known for his ruthlessness and had clearly turned against her. This was not like her. She was careful, measured—responsible—not impulsive or ruled by her emotions. At least, not normally.

She sheathed the dagger, pulled her cloak close, and headed back to the palace. A good night's sleep and time to calm down and weigh her options would serve her much better than running around the garden in the dark. "Use your brain, Maddie. You're a ruler, not a silly girl jilted by her first…"

Her first what? She shook free of the thought. That did not matter. What did was—

A shadow moved ahead, and she froze.

The Wolf walked through the formal gardens, his features momentarily lit by the night blooms as he passed under an arch. He reached the small pond in the centre and stopped, facing the water, not twenty feet from her.

If she continued forwards, he would see her, and there was no easy way past him. Slowly, she backed away, edging behind one of the large topiary bordering the square as quietly as possible. The kitchen garden had an entrance she could use, though it would mean taking the long way around.

She took a last peek to make sure he had not moved, and her gaze caught and held. A strange glow emanated from his hand—no, his signet ring—painting his face and the night-darkened plants around him in shades of deep red. Her breath stalled. What was that? Was it magic?

No, it could not be. Every fibre of her being rejected the notion, and yet… Her mouth dried. Was he using magic against her? She could not recall any mages in his ancestry, but she had hardly made careful study of the subject.

The ring glowed brighter, its unnatural light swirling like blood over his features, and a moment later, he spoke. The flat monotone carried across the silent flowerbeds and still pond and rooted her in place.

"I do not love the princess. She is nothing to me. Only my true family matters." The ring flared again, and he continued. "I will expand the fortress at Hawkesden, and when my army arrives, I will secure Craeick's future." Another flare. "Until then, I will get close to the Brunnish ambassador and discover all I can about their relationship with Tyrrath."

Maddie pulled back, cold sweat sticking her chemise to her spine. He was not using magic—he was being controlled by it.

Her husband was under some sort of curse.

Her mind spun, faster and faster as implication after implication, question after question buffeted her thoughts. It was too much to untangle, but one thing settled in the eye of the maelstrom—a curse explained everything.

Relief and outrage chased the revelation, burning and soothing at the same time. If he was cursed, then he was not the one betraying her. But someone else was, and it seemed their sights were set on more than just Tyrrath. Whoever it was must be found and stopped.

She needed to get back to the palace, to think. As she eased away from the giant ball of fragrant bay, something crunched beneath her foot, and she let out a small cry, clamping her hands over her mouth too late to stifle the sound.

Was that a snail? Eww! Her legs jiggled, torn between jumping aside and throwing her shoe as far from her as possible and remaining still to avoid discovery.

"Who's there?"

She squeezed her eyes shut, praying it was some other snail-crunching interloper Lucas had heard, but the rasp of a sword being drawn forced her to face reality. Lowering her hands, she blew out a long, slow breath, wiped the bottom of her shoe on the grass, and darted a glance around the bush.

Darkness shrouded the garden once more. The ring no longer held him in its grip. She had little choice but to show herself or risk him running her through—she doubted she could escape before he caught her.

Counting on his continued need to maintain the pretence of their marriage, she stepped out onto the path. Her heart pounded against her ribs, and she wiped her palms down her skirts as she walked forwards.

"It's me. Princess Madeline."

"What are you doing here?"

In her own gardens? She bristled at the question but tamped it down. A clear head was vital now. Instinct warned her not to reveal her newfound knowledge, so she scrambled for an excuse for her intrusion on his walk.

"I needed to see you, and you've been avoiding me all day. Why? What did I do wrong?"

He sheathed his sword and sauntered closer. "Nothing. We had some fun, and now I've got other things to do."

"Was that kiss just to distract me from whatever you're doing?" Tears were surprisingly easy to conjure, but she would deal with that later.

"You found it distracting? Well, I am a good kisser."

An easy grin stretched across his lips, and he reached out to touch her face, but she batted his hand away. "You can't toy with my affections like this. I'm your wife."

He flinched, confusion flitting through his eyes so fast she might have missed it had they not been standing so close. Then the cool mask dropped into place and any emotion was snuffed out.

Was that how it worked? Was the real Lucas trapped inside the curse, waiting to be freed? Hope bloomed, but she slammed her own armour in place, reverting just in time to playing the crushed, besotted fool he had intended to make of her. Covering her face with her hands, she heaved an exaggerated sob and ran from the garden as fast as her legs could carry her.

Only when she was well beyond his sight and within view of the entrance did she slow her pace and drop her arms. Resolve hardened her steps.

Her husband was cursed. And to save them all, she needed to save him.

Chapter 19

Maddie

Maddie returned to her room and, after dragging a chest across the doorway and lighting every candle she could find, spent the rest of the night alternating between pacing and sitting in the middle of her bed facing the door. Her mind continued to churn through what she had witnessed, devising and rejecting stratagems, listing questions with no apparent answers, and circling always back to relief-tinged outrage.

When the first rays of sunlight finally broke night's hold on the sky outside, she pulled the chest aside and made her way to Joss's room. She rapped three times and was immediately rewarded by the sound of footsteps approaching from within.

Joss yanked the door open, fully dressed in trousers and a tunic, and stalled. "Maddie. What're you doing here?" She looked Maddie over, and her forehead pinched. "What's happened?"

"Come with me?" Maddie asked, tipping her head in the direction of Olivia's room. "I don't want to have to repeat myself."

"Of course." Joss stepped outside, closed the door behind her, and walked with Maddie to the next door along the hallway.

It took more than three quick knocks to rouse their youngest sister, and when she let them in, her hair was sleep-ruffled and the pattern embroidered on her cuff was imprinted on her cheek. "Wha'd'you want, Joss? It's still early."

She clambered into the bed, but Joss threw the covers off her. "Uh-uh. Wake up. Maddie needs us."

With a groan that spoke of far too little sleep, Olivia scooted up to the headboard and sat with her feet tucked inside her nightdress, glaring blearily at her sister. Joss, meanwhile, flung the east-facing curtains wide to let in the light now bathing that side of the palace. Then she dropped onto the edge of the mattress and gestured for Maddie to start talking.

Maddie glanced around the room and tutted. She picked up a couple of books from the chair between the window and fireplace and added them to the nearest stack on the table. Then she folded one of the blankets that formed a nest on the seat.

She could feel her sisters' eyes on her, but Olivia's room was too cluttered for her to think straight, and now that she was here, her lips refused to open. After folding the rest of the blankets and placing them on the chest at the end of Olivia's bed, she sank onto the chair and faced them.

"Let me finish before you say anything. All right?" she asked.

"Yes," Olivia said at the same time Joss murmured an 'mm-hm.'

"Swear it, Joss."

"Fine. Done."

At first, Maddie had no idea where to begin or how to explain everything, but once she got past the first few halting words, the rest flowed out. Her sisters both stiffened as she outlined Lucas's cold behaviour the previous day, sharing a glance that Maddie tried not to interpret as pity. But at the first mention of the ring glowing, any traces of sleep vanished from Olivia's features and Joss leapt to her feet.

"Glowing? Are you sure?" she asked.

"You said you wouldn't interrupt."

"Yes, but I thought you were going to tell us you were pregnant or something, not that he has a magical ring."

Maddie stared at her, mouth gaping. Pregnant? They weren't even— "That's ridiculous. Why would you think that?"

"Is he a mage then?" Olivia asked before Joss could reply.

Tearing her focus from Joss, Maddie looked at their youngest sister. "No. I don't think so…"

She told them the rest as succinctly as possible while Joss paced the rug and Olivia's eyes grew to the size of dinner plates. The moment she finished, they asked so many questions, so quickly, that they bled together and she could not tell who had said what.

Hands raised in front of her, she said, “One at a time, please.” Their voices trailed off, and she lowered her arms. “How do you expect me to answer you when you talk over each other and don’t give me time to speak?”

“Sorry,” they both said at the same time.

“It’s just so hard to believe,” Joss said. “Lucas Sinclair—cursed.”

“I know.” Maddie looked down at her hands. She had seen it with her own eyes and still struggled to accept it.

Joss resumed her pacing. “How do you think it works? Could we break it somehow? What happens when he takes it off?”

“I don’t know. I—”

“A red glow, you said?” Olivia scrambled from the other side of her bed and rummaged through one of her chests, mumbling under her breath. Maddie caught Joss’s eye, but she only shrugged.

“Ah. Here it is.”

Olivia held up a worn, leather-bound book and grinned at them over her shoulder. She snatched up some paper and an ink pot and quill as well and carried it all over to the table beside Maddie, where she knelt on the rug and nudged enough books aside to set down her load. The ancient volume landed on top of the rest, and Olivia flicked through it, stopping at a drawing of a large black stone.

“Look. I knew I’d heard of something like that before. It’s right here.” She read from the text beside the image, “…she used a dragon stone to defeat him. It was the largest in the land, and when she accessed its power, the red glow could be seen for miles around.”

"Dragon stone," Maddie whispered. Could that be what Lucas's ring was made from? "Does it say anything else?"

Olivia scanned the next page and slumped back onto her heels. "No. Sorry. But I can keep looking."

She slipped a piece of paper into the page and let the book fall shut. While she opened the ink pot and scribbled a few notes on another sheet, Joss drummed her fingers on her thigh.

"So there's a dragon stone in the king of Craeick's signet ring instead of obsidian," she said. "Has it always had one, or was it added more recently? And how is someone using it? I didn't think mages had that much power anymore."

"Good questions," Olivia said. "I'll make a note of them."

Maddie leaned back in the chair. "I've been trying to work out who it could be."

Joss snorted. "Someone who hates the king of Craeick enough to curse him? Might need more paper for that list, Mouse."

"No." Maddie fiddled with the ends of her hair, staring at nothing in particular. "I don't think that's it."

"What isn't?" Joss asked.

Maddie met her gaze. "Whoever's doing this isn't targeting Lucas because they hate him. If that were the case, they'd tell him to fight poorly, or—"

"Or jump off a mountain ledge," Joss suggested.

"Exactly. But they're not. They're using him to target us, and maybe the rest of Egrea."

Olivia looked up, a sheen of moisture in her eyes. "Does that mean he's been cursed the whole time?"

Swallowing the nausea welling up her throat, Maddie clasped her hands together on her lap. "I don't know."

"When did you first notice a difference in him?" Joss asked her.

Another question that had kept Maddie awake all night. He had changed so much since their wedding, the cold, ruthless Wolf King appearing to slowly melt with the spring to reveal a charming, warm man. And they had grown close, had begun to care for each other, had—

She slammed a lid on the memory of their kiss and said, "There's no way to tell. We don't know what he was like before he got here."

Arms akimbo, Joss narrowed her eyes. "So, what are we going to do about it?"

A soft smile nudged Maddie's lips. *We*. That was why she had come to her sisters. She could not face something so overwhelming, so heinous, without their support.

Before she could respond, Joss asked the one thing Maddie had hoped to avoid. "Have you told Tristan yet?"

Maddie grimaced. "No. And I don't think we should."

Joss and Olivia both started to object, so she rushed on before they could. "It's not that we can't trust him or that he wouldn't believe us or anything like that. It's that..." How to explain? She filled her lungs with air and calmed her racing thoughts. "Tristan's highest duty is to protect us. If we told him, his position would demand he act on the information, but we have no idea what impact that would have.

"We know Lucas is cursed but not how to break it, who's behind it, what their true goal is, or what they might do if they realise we're aware of the curse. We don't even know if he's the only one under their control.

"If we make a move now, our chances of stopping them will be ruined, and it might just drive them to more desperate or dangerous measures. I trust Tristan with my life, but we can't tell him about this. Not yet. Not until we know more."

"Like a game of Knights," Olivia said.

"Yes." Except in this match, the stakes were so much higher.

"Do you think Lucas knows he's cursed?" she asked, her face crumpling.

Maddie picked up the ends of her hair again, seeing an image of his eyes flickering with emotion before cooling to silver in the weak moonlight. "I don't know. But I think the real Lucas Sinclair is still in there somewhere."

"Maybe that's the answer." Joss perched on the arm of the chair opposite Maddie, resting her elbow on her knee as she gesticulated. "Maybe you can help him break it from the inside? Get him to take the ring off and work with us?"

"I'm not sure it'll be that simple, but I'll try."

Joss jumped up again. "In the meantime, I can go to the guild, see if any of the mages know anything about cursed rings or who might be powerful enough to control one."

A groan almost escaped Maddie, but she swallowed it. Joss was only trying to help, and she could never tolerate doing nothing while others risked themselves. "Just be careful, all right? And try asking Nessa Rhyll." If any of the mages could help them, it would be the fifth-level leader of the new Tyrrathian guildhalls, and Maddie trusted her discretion should Joss reveal too much.

"I'll search the library," Olivia said. "Try to find out more about dragon stones and how they work."

And Maddie would search for her husband.

Chapter 20
Maddie

Maddie glanced at Lucas, standing opposite her on the steps outside the palace's main entrance. Sunlight glinted off the silver adorning his all-black outfit and the wolf-headed pommel of his sword. His face could have been set in stone, the scar a vein of calcite down his left cheek. He had not looked at her once since they assembled to greet his mother.

She held back a sigh. This was the first time she had seen more than a passing glimpse of him since their encounter in the garden two nights prior. Though she had sought him out more than once, preparations for the coming visit had kept them both busy, especially after news arrived that the Craeickish party had made good time and would arrive earlier than expected.

Beside him, Flynn bounced on his toes, eyes fixed on the open gates, and on Flynn's other side, Aiden Munroe stood with Rheann Braydeson, both wearing dragonhide armour and double sword belts.

Maddie studied them from the corner of her eye. Could one of them be responsible for the curse?

General Munroe had only ever appeared devoted to Lucas, guarding his flank as steadfastly as Tristan protected her. Surely he was far too loyal to use his king so horrifically. She turned her attention to the third of their group, catching a sneer of disdain cross Rheann's features as she scanned the courtyard.

Animosity had shadowed the quiet redhead whenever Maddie had encountered her, but like her superior, she followed Lucas's every word. Would she be willing to compromise him to wipe her enemies from the face of the continent? Maddie's gut said no.

Which left her where she had started, with a short list of possible suspects, none of whom made complete sense. She needed to get Lucas alone to find out more about that ring.

Cheering beyond the palace gates pulled her focus to the wide avenue that wound through Faerstolmere and into the palace grounds. Hoof beats and marching feet mingled with the crowd's shouts, and a few moments later, a pair of mounted soldiers appeared around the bend.

Behind them, the carriage bearing Lucas's mother and stepfather rolled into view, its large body covered in a light purple-grey dragon hide with a row of claws edging the roof like a razor-sharp crown. It swept around in front of the palace steps, and precious gems winked from the crest adorning the door.

Maddie patted her hair for loose strands and straightened to her full height. With a glance at her sisters, standing to her left in their finest dresses, she descended the steps and waited for the groomsman to open the carriage door.

Lucas did not. He walked forwards, threw the door open, and held his hand out to his mother.

She scooted to the edge of her seat, ducked through the opening, and allowed Lucas to lift her down. He spun her around first, squeezing her tightly before setting her on the ground and giving her a brilliant smile.

Maddie stared at her husband, whatever he was saying muffled by the shock pounding her senses. He was behaving so… normally. How could he be so warm towards his mother when the curse had made him so cold around everyone else? Unless Maddie had mistaken the cause of his indifference. But that meant—

"Mama." Flynn flew down the palace steps and into his mother's arms, clutching her waist and burying his head in her embrace.

"Flynn. There you are. Let me look at you." She pulled away and looked him over, then her gentle smile flattened as she gave him a warning look to rival Tabitha's best. "We'll talk about how you got here later, young man. Now, where's my daughter-in-law?"

Her eyes found Maddie's, and warmth flooded Maddie at the welcome in her pale blue gaze. Deep red hair threaded with grey framed her heart-shaped face, and the soft rose-coloured dress she wore hugged a lithe figure. Everything about her spoke of kindness and confidence.

"Lucas," she said without turning, "Are you going to introduce us?"

“Mother, this is Princess Madeline of Tyrrath. Princess, my mother, Catriona, the Queen Mother of Craeick.”

Maddie bowed her head. “A pleasure to meet you, Your Majesty.”

“And you, my dear.” Lucas’s mother did likewise, then smiled brightly enough to crinkle the fine lines around her eyes. “But please, call me Tria.”

The familial offer hit Maddie in her most vulnerable spot, and a pang of longing for her own mother shot through her. She pushed it aside and said, “And I’m Maddie.”

Movement behind the queen caught Maddie off guard. She had been so focused on greeting her mother-in-law that she had not noticed the man stepping down from the carriage behind her. He matched the queen’s medium height but held more weight on his stocky frame, and the hair and short, neat beard framing his ruddy face was fully grey.

“It’s good to see you, Sire.” He bowed to Lucas and ruffled Flynn’s hair. “And how are you, my boy? Keeping up with your brother?”

“I’m well. Lucas has been training me to fight.” Flynn smoothed his hair down and copied Lucas’s stance, causing his father to chuckle.

“He has, has he? Are you any good?”

“Good enough to begin sparring soon,” Lucas said with an affectionate grin.

Again, the ease with which he spoke to his family struck Maddie, offering a glimpse of the man he could be without the curse. She fisted her hands, more determined than ever to free him from it.

The man, who could only be Lord Ross, clapped Lucas's shoulder and joined his wife. Green eyes the same hue as Flynn's fixed on Maddie, assessing behind the twinkle.

"Your Highness, may I introduce my husband, Lord Gabriel Ross," Catriona said. "Gabriel, this is Princess Madeline of Tyrrath, Lucas's bride."

'Bride' seemed such a gracious term, given the situation. Did Lucas's family truly not know the circumstances of the marriage treaty? The question almost caused Maddie to stumble over her greeting to Lord Ross.

Confirming her suspicions, Catriona touched her arm and said, "You must tell me how you two met. When Lucas set out, he only mentioned a training exercise. I never expected him to find a wife while he was gone."

"Nor did I," Lord Ross said.

Lucas remained silent, so Maddie scrambled for an appropriate response—would her mother-in-law be as affable when she discovered the truth? She settled on, "He made me an offer I couldn't refuse."

The rattle of another carriage entering the courtyard interrupted her thoughts. She looked up and sucked in a breath. Soldiers filled the area, fifty or sixty at least, standing to attention as more filed through the palace gates behind the royal party.

She shot a glance at Tristan, who gave her a reassuring nod. Aware of the curse or not, he had anticipated a show of force and had made additional arrangements for her defence. He would not allow so many of Craeick's forces within the palace walls if that were not the case, no matter how ominous they appeared to Maddie.

A hinge creaked, and someone stepped down from the second carriage, which was much simpler in design and drawn by two instead of four horses. His belted green robes immediately marked him as a friar of the Creator's Way, and Maddie winced internally that she had not thought to include Faerstolmere's abbot in the welcoming party. But royalty rarely travelled with a cleric in tow.

He inspected the area around him like someone finding too many bones in his fish stew, his sharp gaze taking in the palace, the guards and officials flanking the entrance, and finally, Maddie and her sisters.

"You brought Utham?" Lucas asked his mother in an undertone.

"Yes, he's delivering a thesis to the monastic conclave in the White City next month, so he travelled down with us."

The friar walked towards them, gave the shallowest bow courtesy demanded, and said, "Do you have somewhere quiet I can pray? The noise of your city made it impossible to complete my morning devotions in the carriage."

"Please, come inside." Maddie said with a tight smile. She turned to address Catriona. "You'll be staying in the east wing, and I've arranged a light luncheon to be served in our private solar at noon. Hodges will see to your things and send a maid to assist you should you wish to bathe or change before we eat. I do hope your stay with us will be comfortable."

"That's very kind of you. Thank you." Catriona followed her up the sun-drenched steps and into the shade of the entrance hall.

"As for your men…" Maddie pressed her lips together as she surveyed the troops still standing to attention outside, a hundred in total. "You brought an impressive contingent with you."

"When Tria's safety is at stake, I never underestimate numbers." Lord Ross cast an affectionate glance at his wife. "Besides, a company is the minimum honour guard Craeick would countenance for the royal family. Anything less would denigrate our kingdom's status."

"Indeed. Well, Captain Kaar will see to their lodgings, but I'm afraid we can only accommodate so many inside the palace."

"Not to worry," Lord Ross said. "Lucas sent word for the majority to make camp outside the city now we've been safely delivered. That way, they won't be underfoot."

Maddie said nothing further, though through the lens of Lucas's curse, it sounded more like strategic placement of his army about her kingdom than relieving the barracks of cramped conditions. She could only trust the counter-measures Tristan had put in place should Craeick prove false, and focus her energies on finding a way to break the curse.

Chapter 21
Maddie

Maddie pulled the door to her father's room closed with a quiet click. She did not know whether he could hear her in his perpetual sleep, but she took strength from the memories of his steady council. He had always believed in her, so she would not let him down.

She mulled over her options as she descended the stairs and turned towards her study. It had been four days since she had discovered the curse, two since Lucas's family had arrived. He could not hide from her forever.

As she passed the room provided for his personal use, the rumble of male voices made her pause. Maybe this was her opportunity to talk to him. She stopped outside, debating whether to knock or wait for whoever it was to finish.

Before she could decide, the volume of one of the voices increased, anger spilling through the door, though the words remained muffled. Footsteps stomped towards her, and the door flew open to reveal Friar Utham.

He started, his glare faltering, then he turned back to the room and said, "Just do it."

Lucas's voice replied in a monotone that grated at Maddie's ears. "I will, of course."

"Your Highness," Friar Utham said, his sharp gaze on her. He gave a perfunctory nod and swept past her in the direction of the chapel.

What in the world was that about? She stared after him for a moment but shook off the questions scratching at the corners of her mind and stepped inside. This was too good an opportunity to miss.

Lucas sat behind a large desk, twisting the ring around his finger. His sword, a couple of small pots, and some cleaning rags sat in front of him, and she tried not to look too closely at the dried brown stains on the nearest cloth. Or at the stand against the far wall, where his dragonhide armour glimmered in the firelight. Had he turned the room into his personal armoury? She suppressed a shudder at the thought.

"Good evening, Lucas. I hope I find you well."

"Princess." He picked up a small box from the corner of the desk and held it out. "As you're here, you can have this. My mother brought it for you."

Maddie walked forwards, her attention on the box. What could his mother possibly wish to gift her? When she reached for it, he dropped it into her palm as if he were discarding leftover bones from a meal.

It was heavier than she had expected. She opened the lid and sucked in a breath. Inside, cushioned by a silk cloth, lay an ornate gold ring with a black stone in the centre.

Her entire body froze, her mouth drying. *Say something*, she mentally screamed at herself.

"Um, thank you, but—"

"It's the ring worn by the queens of Craeick. Mother assumed it would pass to you, and I didn't want to disappoint her. You can wear it—for her."

Maddie could not take her eyes from the stone, a match to the one in Lucas's ring. Was it cursed as well? Fingers trembling, she picked the ring up by the band, careful not to touch the stone. Nothing appeared to happen, but she dared not slide it on her finger.

Wetting her dry lips, she pretended to inspect it. "It would be my honour, but I'll need to have it resized first. It's a little large for my hand, and I wouldn't want it to fall off and be lost."

She would send it to Nessa and see if the mage could discern whether it was cursed. If so, maybe it would provide a clue as to how to break the magic's hold on Lucas.

"As you wish." He dismissed her with a bored wave of his hand and leaned back in his seat.

Maddie sealed the ring within its box and slipped it into her waist pouch. Thrown by the unexpected gift and its potential implications, she hovered while Lucas dipped a cloth into one of the pots on his desk, then rubbed it along the length of his sword.

The rasp of sand on metal filled the space between them until she stepped closer and cleared her throat. "I'm glad I found you today. I've wanted to see you."

“Oh.” He continued cleaning his weapon without looking up.

“I’ve just come from my father. He’s no better, unfortunately, but no worse either. I’m hoping one of the healing mages might be able to help him now that their powers seem to be growing.”

Was he even listening to her?

“Your mother mentioned your father earlier.”

Finally, he stilled, though the intensity of his expression rivalled the sharpness of his sword.

“Will you tell me about him? Please? I don’t want to accidentally say something that would upset her.”

His muscles eased a fraction, and he laid the sword down on the desk. “He died when I was twelve, along with my older brother. We were hunting in the northern Balewicks, and I wanted to make them proud, so I rushed ahead, not realising I was close to a dragon’s nest.”

He rubbed his jaw, his fingers pausing on his scar, and an idea began to form that caused Maddie’s stomach to twist.

“They saved me from the beast but were both killed in the attack. My father was thrown from the ledge and fell to his death, and my brother died from a chest wound. I was made king the same week.”

His voice was not cold, or mechanical, which would have been understandable when recalling a difficult memory. He spoke with casual indifference, as if relating the state of the weather beyond the window. Nevertheless, her heart ached for him, for the boy who had lost his father and had so much responsibility foisted on him in the same instant.

"Is that when you got that scar?"

"Yes."

No wonder he hated to talk about it so much. It was a permanent reminder of the worst day of his life.

"I'm so sorry."

"Why? You weren't there."

She eased closer, an arm's length from him. "But what impacts you impacts me. I'm your wife."

He looked up at 'wife', meeting her gaze at last.

"And family is important," she continued. "You've been a true comfort to my sisters and me since we returned, taking our minds off Father's condition. You and Flynn, both. I want to be able to do the same for you, as any wife would for her husband."

His brows scrunched as if struggling to remember, and she closed the gap between them. Standing so close her skirts grazed his legs, she reached towards him. "I've missed you these last few days. It's not good for husbands and wives to be apart for so long."

A tingle coursed through her as her fingers trailed down his cheek. Whether from the smooth warmth of his skin, their proximity, or the danger not fully banished from his eyes, she could not tell, but she could not stop now.

Slowly, as he had done with her less than a week prior, she bent and kissed him. She poured all her love into the kiss, begging him to break free from the curse and kiss her back. His lips moved against hers, and thrilled, she pulled away.

"Lucas?"

His eyes flickered, confusion swimming in their depths, but the blank mask slammed down, and his lips twisted into a sneer. "Well, well, well. It seems the princess isn't so high and mighty after all." He relaxed into his seat and scanned her lazily from head to toe. "But if you're trying to seduce me, I'm afraid I'll have to decline. Wouldn't want you getting any romantic ideas about us."

He may as well have slapped her. Her hand fisted, and quick as lightning, he grabbed her wrist, his gaze turned deadly. "And we'll have none of that either. I've enough scars from real warriors."

Yanking her arm free, she backed up out of his reach. How had their encounter gone so horribly wrong? She had hoped that reminding him of their love would break the curse's hold. "I-I'll leave you to your work then."

She all but ran from the room, swinging the door closed behind her on the way out, and bumping straight into a solid chest when she turned in the direction of her study.

"Easy there," Tristan said, catching her arms to steady her.

"Oh. Apologies. I didn't see you." She stepped away, keeping her gaze lowered. Tristan had always been able to read her too well, and the last thing she needed was an interrogation.

"Are you well?" he asked.

"Yes. Fine. I was just in a hurry. Olivia wants to talk about the spring festival before she retires."

It was only a partial lie. Her sisters loved planning the annual event. She peeked up at him, but he was frowning at the door. Thank the Creator she had shut it. Touching his arm to regain his attention, she donned a bright smile and forced herself to meet his gaze. "Apologies again, Tristan."

"Don't think of it. When will Joss be back?"

"Hm?" Her brain scrambled towards the new topic. "Oh, in a few days, I expect."

He rubbed his jaw. "I still can't believe you sent her to check the progress of the guildhalls. Are you sure she's up to the task?"

"Possibly not, but the activities Catriona prefers were beginning to stifle her." Another half-truth.

He snorted a laugh, no doubt imagining Joss trying to embroider. "Maybe I should've sent more men with Parker. They might need to drag her back."

"I hope not." Stomach sour from keeping the truth from him, she could only add, "Goodnight."

With that, she sidestepped him and walked away as quickly as decorum would allow. What a mess she had made of everything.

Chapter 22

Luc

Luc raced along the upper palace hallway, flung open the door to the solar his family had been using, and came to an abrupt halt. His mother sat on the lounger with Flynn tucked against her side and worry lines creasing her face. From her tight expression, and the fact that she had sent for him, the situation must have been bad.

"I got here as fast as I could," he said. "What happened?"

She started to speak, but Flynn lifted his head from her shoulder and pointed at his left arm, where a wad of blood-soaked cloth wrapped his forearm. "I hurt my arm."

He moved it only a fraction, then paled and let out a pitiful moan.

Luc strode forwards and crouched in front of him.

"I'm sorry, Luc," their mother said. "Gabriel's out riding, and it's…"

"It's fine. I was only training. Let me see, Flynn." He held Flynn's arm as carefully as if it were one of their mother's delicate glass hair pins and lifted one side of the bandaging.

Flynn sucked in a sharp breath, so to distract him, Luc asked, "What were you doing?"

Flynn lifted his chin, but a couple of fat tears rolled down his cheeks before he could swipe them away with his uninjured hand. "I was practicing being a knight."

"Go on," Luc said.

"Well, I was acting out killing a dragon, only…" He ducked his head, and Luc took the opportunity to peel the bandage farther back, wincing at the raw, angry wound. Serious, indeed. Masking his dismay, he shifted his head into Flynn's line of sight, and the boy continued in a small voice. "I fell off the chair and landed on the corner of the fire grate."

Luc glanced across at the grate's decorative twisted metal points and grimaced. With a practice sword involved as well, no wonder Flynn was so badly hurt. "Why were you playing with your sword inside? Weapons aren't toys, Flynn."

His brother's eyes welled again, and their mother tucked him closer into her side. "There's no point lecturing him now, Luc, and as I recall, you were just as bad at his age."

Luc scraped a hand over his face. "Sorry. Where's the healer?"

"She should be here soon," she said. "I sent for—"

The door swung wide, and a woman in a healer's apron bustled into the room, a bag of supplies slung over one shoulder and a small medallion around her neck. A mage healer. Good.

Luc pushed up to his feet.

Dipping into a brief curtsey, she said, "Your Majesty. I'm Bronwen. You sent for a healer?"

He waved her forward. "My mother did, yes. For my brother."

Her gaze swung to Flynn, and she walked to the lounger, already lowering her bag. Luc started to move out of the way, but Flynn gripped his sleeve with his good hand and refused to let go. Their mother met Luc's eyes over the lad's head and gave a subtle shake of her head, so Luc sat down on Flynn's other side.

The healer—Bronwen—knelt on the thick rug at their feet and said, "Flynn, isn't it?"

Flynn nodded.

"I thought so. I've seen you around the palace. Can I see your arm?"

He nodded again, lifting it slightly towards her.

Bronwen rewarded him with a bright smile. "This might hurt a little, but I need to see what you've done."

Luc squeezed his brother's knee as she set about inspecting his arm.

She hummed once or twice to herself while she worked and murmured encouragement when Flynn cried out. Amazingly, the wound did not bleed as she probed it—one of the benefits of having magic, Luc supposed. If only he could have employed such a mage to work with his men, they might have suffered fewer losses over the years.

After a thorough examination, she sat back on her heels, a frown squeezing her features briefly before she adopted a pleasant smile.

"Flynn, I just need to talk to your…" She looked between Luc and his mother, and at a tilt of his mother's head, continued, "…brother for a moment. I'll be right back."

Luc patted Flynn's knee and joined Bronwen at the far side of the room.

"The bone's broken," she said. "My power's grown much stronger recently, so I can probably fix that as well as the flesh wound, but I'll need to set it first…" She did not need to tell him that doing so would be excruciating. "I'll give him something to dull the pain, but will you be able to hold him down if I tell you when?"

If it would save his brother's arm, Luc would pin him down for a week. "Yes."

"Well, then. I'll get started."

She returned to the lounger and gave Flynn a small vial of liquid to drink. Then she helped him to lie down, his head on his mother's lap and his injured arm stretched out across a chair she dragged across for the purpose.

When he was settled, she directed Luc to kneel by his brother's side and took her place by Flynn's head. She stretched her shoulders and hands, stilled, and took two deep breaths with her eyes closed.

Finally, lips pressed into a firm line, she removed the cloth covering his arm and was about to start when the door opened again and Gabriel strode in.

“I heard Flynn was hurt.” He cast a frantic glance around the room, locked onto his son and rushed forwards, agony etching his features. “What happened?

Luc’s mother answered him. “He hurt his arm playing. But Bronwen’s a mage healer, so she’s going to fix it. Aren’t you?” She directed the question at Bronwen, though her tone made it more of a statement.

“Yes, Ma’am. I’ll do my best.”

Gabriel walked to the end of the lounger where Luc’s mother sat and stroked his son’s hair. “Please. Do everything you can.”

Bronwen nodded and bent over Flynn’s arm, her hands covering the wound at first, then moving to either side. Luc waited for her to tell him to hold his brother down, but instead, her eyes flew wide, and she gasped.

“What is it?” Gabriel asked.

She looked up, directly at Luc, and said, “I’m holding him on my own.”

“How?” he asked. “I thought—”

“I don’t know.” She frowned down at her hands, then shook her head. “I’ll figure it out later. For now...”

She gave both ends of Flynn’s forearm a quick yank, then covered the wound with her palms again and stilled. Her eyes closed, and her lips moved silently. A few tense heartbeats later, the flesh knitted together, and the edges of the gash closed and smoothed out before Luc’s astonished gaze.

Though it felt like an eternity, barely ten minutes passed before she sagged back onto her heels and dropped her hands from Flynn’s arm. “I’m done.”

All that was left of his mishap was a thin pink line and a few smears of half-dried blood.

"Oh." Their mother ran her hand over the area, glancing up at Gabriel, then raised teary eyes to the healer. "Thank you. Thank you so much."

"Yes, thank you," Gabriel said.

"You're welcome, Ma'am, Milord," Bronwen said, her voice weaker than it had been moments earlier.

Sweat beaded her temples, and her eyelids drooped with fatigue. Using magic to heal clearly took its toll on the mage.

Nevertheless, she straightened and glanced between them, a vee forming between her brows. "That was the strangest thing. I've never felt so much power before, like a wave rolling over me."

She got to her feet, holding onto the back of the chair, and Luc felt a fleeting urge to steady her.

"Thank you. For healing Flynn," he said. "You should get some rest."

"I will, Sire. If you'll excuse me." With a bobbed curtsey, she picked up her bag and left.

Luc crouched down again and ruffled Flynn's hair. Whatever Bronwen had given him must have been potent, for he barely stirred. Luc slid his arm under his brother's shoulders and sat him upright, and a few moments later his brother's eyelids fluttered open.

He squinted as if thinking hard about something, then looked at his arm, turning it this way and that to inspect it from every angle.

"It doesn't hurt anymore," he said.

Luc couldn't help but chuckle at his incredulous tone.

"Maybe it should," their mother said, "so you don't do anything so foolish again." She raised one brow in a way that said he would have little opportunity for at least a week, but the colour had returned to her cheeks.

"All is well, my dear," Gabriel said, patting her shoulder. "Shall we dine here tonight? It's been a long time since we ate together as a family."

"All four of us?" Flynn asked.

"Why not?" Gabriel looked to Luc for confirmation.

Given the circumstances, Luc did not have the heart to refuse. He eyed his brother, whose head bounced up and down, and let out a longsuffering sigh, followed by a wink. "I'll make the arrangements."

Then he walked to the door, where he asked a passing servant to request a platter from the kitchen.

After a simple meal, during which they talked and laughed like old times, Luc relaxed on the lounger and watched his mother and brother set up a game of pick-up sticks. The warmer climate of Tyrrath suited her—she had not mentioned the aches that plagued her joints in winter since she had arrived. And—that afternoon aside—now that she was here, Flynn was far less underfoot, which meant Luc had more time to devote to his plans.

He popped a piece of leftover pork pie into his mouth and reviewed his strategy, testing it for weaknesses or flaws. He had already put the next phase in motion, sending Rhee off before sunrise with specific orders for the men camped outside Faerstolmere's walls.

They would need to follow his instructions to the letter, or everything could fall apart and leave him in a tricky situation, but he trusted each of them implicitly. Gabriel had brought the best of Craeick's elite troops.

A satisfied grin tugged at the scar on Luc's cheek—everything was lining up perfectly. With free access to Tyrrath as the princess's husband, what could he not achieve? She had proven no match against him, and once his men had finished their task and the spring markets lowered vigilance along the borders, the other kingdoms would fall like untrained squires against a dragon—or in this case, a wolf.

"Are you well, Luc?" his mother asked.

"Couldn't be better. Why?"

"You seem lost in your thoughts." She gave him a sly smile. "Will Maddie be joining us tonight?"

A lump of meat stuck in his throat, and he coughed and thumped his chest. "No. She's busy with her father and sisters." Or so he assumed.

"What a pity. I've barely seen you together since we arrived. She's a lovely girl—a perfect match for you." The knowing grin slid across her face again, chased by an overly innocent expression. "We spent a lovely afternoon together yesterday…"

He tuned her out. Why did she insist on throwing the princess at him at every opportunity? He rubbed the pad of his finger across his lips, recalling her kiss the previous evening. Why had it felt so—

“Are you listening to me?” His mother stared at him through narrowed eyes.

“Of course.”

She harrumphed, then pointed to the pile of sticks on the table between her and Flynn. “You're sure you don’t want to join us?”

His nose wrinkled. Pick-up sticks was his least favourite game. “Maybe for a round of stones.”

Flynn’s head jerked up. “It was my turn to choose.”

“Yes, it was, dear.” Their mother patted Flynn’s arm, gave Luc a stern look, and turned to her husband, who was sitting by the fire reading a history of Brunland’s dragons. “What about you, Gabriel?”

“What’s that?” He lifted his gaze, his features softening as they did each time he looked on Luc’s mother. “No, thank you, dear. Did you know Brunnish even use dragons for fishing? They take them out in skiffs off their southern coast.” He shook his head at the book. “Fascinating.”

Having spent half his life fending off wild dragons, the concept of domesticating the beasts made Luc’s scars itch, but the westerners’ control of them was impressive. The benefits of having such a wealthy kingdom under his influence would easily outweigh his aversion to their practices.

His mother went back to her game, his stepfather went back to his book, and Luc set aside the empty plate and returned to his thoughts.

He was calculating how quickly his army could be made battle ready when a small body landed across his chest, knocking the air from his lungs. Curling his torso inwards, he grinned at the mop of deep red hair bouncing by his elbow but affected a pained tone. "Oof! What's this? A dragon whelp attacking me? Begone, foul beast."

He poked Flynn in the ribs, producing cries fit to wake the dead. The squeals dissolved into giggles as he switched to tickling his brother's sides, and Flynn slid off his lap onto the floor, wriggling to escape his clutches.

"That's enough, Lucas," their mother said. "He'll never sleep if you make him so excited like that."

Luc sat back, allowing Flynn to sit upright and straighten his tunic. He looked up at Luc and asked, "Will you come play sticks with us?"

"Haven't you had enough of them? You've played three times this evening."

"Not with you."

Unable to resist the hope shining in his brother's big, green eyes, Luc sighed and walked over to the games table. Flynn raced back to his seat, and their mother collected the sticks into a tight bundle.

An image of squeezing around a similar table with Flynn and three sisters floated through his mind, their laughter echoing in his ears. He gritted his teeth against it. This was the only family he needed—the one in front of him—not the whisper of a dream that was not real.

A voice in the depths of his soul, the one that guided him whenever doubts assailed, reminded him of that truth. In rare moments of whimsy, he liked to think it was the voice of his father, but he knew it was only his conscience, his way of assessing information and making sound, logical decisions.

He slammed a mental door on any thoughts of the princess, locked it securely, and studied the pile of sticks his mother dropped for one he could safely remove.

Chapter 23
Maddie

Maddie stepped out of her room two days after her aborted attempt to break the curse at the same time as Lord Ross emerged from his room farther along the hallway. He bowed as she walked towards him, heading for the main staircase and the council chamber.

"Your Highness. I didn't expect to see you this morning."

She lifted the stack of papers and the latest letter from Lord Elland she had come upstairs to retrieve. "I left these behind. But it gave me a reason to call a recess and think through some issues."

He nodded slowly. "Ah, the pressures of rule."

Of course, he would know it well. He had advised Lucas since the start of his reign. They rounded the corner from the east wing into the upper gallery, and the row of windows fronting the palace cast a chequerboard of light on the thick, central runner and opposite wall.

"Have you always worked in the royal court?" she asked.

A vee furrowed between his brows. "No. My family tended goats, in a small village high in the mountains."

"Oh. I had no idea." Before Lucas had fallen under the influence of the curse, he had told her stories of life in the mountains, of dragon attacks and avalanches and many other perils. "That's a dangerous occupation in Craeick…"

"Yes." The vee deepened, and his hand went to the pouch at his waist. "I lost my first wife and son when a landslide destroyed half our village. Not in the disaster itself—in the time it took for aid to arrive."

Maddie's chest ached for his loss, and she paused at the top of the staircase that led down to the main entrance hall. "I'm so sorry."

He gave her a brittle smile and descended the steps. "I worked my way to the position of king's councillor to make sure it never happened again. Lucas's father—"

A door slammed off to their left on the lower level, and Friar Utham stomped into view. He pulled up short when he saw them, then changed direction and met them at the bottom of the stairs.

"Something must be done about the spring festival," he said with the briefest of nods to Maddie.

She blinked at him. "The spring festival…?"

"Yes. I've been told you light candles and set them adrift on the lake."

They did, and it was a mesmerising sight—thousands of tiny flames lighting up the night sky as they floated out on the water. "Yes."

He frowned. "And people often pray when they release them."

"Yes?" What was he saying?

His eyes widened and he reared back as if scalded. "But that is intolerable. I knew the lowland kingdoms were corrupted, but I had no idea the influence of heathen rituals had spread so far. I must pray for your souls."

He pulled the token of his faith from the neck of his robes—a small obsidian stone on a simple leather cord—and clutched it like a shield. Then he stalked away, muttering about affronts to the Creator and even the chapel being overly ornate.

Maddie eyed Lord Ross, who grimaced.

"My apologies, Ma'am. Friar Utham can be a little…zealous in his fervour, but he means well."

"So I see." She mustered a reassuring smile. "I'm sure all will be well. The abbot has never had an issue with the festival's arrangements, and nor did the White City's bishop when he visited two years ago. Maybe one of them can assuage the friar's concerns."

Another set of footsteps tapped across the marble floor at the other side of the entrance hall, and Maddie looked in their direction. Tristan strode towards them, his face thunderous, hand balled around a scrunched-up piece of paper. What could have happened now?

She turned to Lord Ross and said, "If you'll excuse me, it seems I'm needed."

"Of course." He tore his gaze from Tristan's ill-treated missive and fingered the pouch at his waist. "I must be on my way as well. Much to see today."

With a tilt of her head in acknowledgement, she met Tristan, who said only, "We need to talk, Your Highness."

He kept walking, bypassing the council chamber where her advisors waited, and she fell into step beside him, her insides knotting. When they reached her study, he held the door for her, followed her inside, and shut it behind them with an ominous click.

Safe from listening ears behind the solid walls and thick oak door, he flattened the paper on her desk beneath his spread hand and said, "He's up to something again. Wash sent word this morning that several youths have gone missing from Lord Greyston's land and there's increased activity around the Craeickish fortress building site."

"All ri—"

"There's more." He straightened, sucking in a breath. "I checked the camp outside the city, and as many as half of them are missing." A disgusted sound rasped in the back of his throat. "They must've slipped out in small groups disguised as commoners. I don't know what he's planning, but I don't like it. Not one bit."

Maddie set the papers she had collected from her room aside and stared at the report. So this was it, this was the first step of Lucas's plan to take her kingdom—no, the ring—the person behind the curse—she rubbed her temple. Was he stealing her people to bolster his army? The knots in her stomach writhed at the possibility, but even Craeick must lose foot soldiers in battle.

"Maddie? Did you hear me?"

Tristan leaned over the desk, ducking his head into her line of sight. She gave herself a mental shake and met his worried gaze. "Yes. Of course."

"We need to work out what he's planning and stop him before it's too late."

A knock at the door pulled both their heads around. It opened, and Hodges slipped inside, lips pursed tighter than if he had sucked a lemon. "There's a woman here, Your Highness. Quite hysterical. I would have had her thrown out, but she had this on her."

He walked over and placed a small brooch on the desk. It took Maddie a moment to recognise it as the token she had given Bronwen in Northold and insisted she keep should she ever need Maddie's help.

"She's here?" And hysterical, Hodges had said. Whatever had brought her to the palace must be serious. Sara? "Bring her in."

Hodges jerked, clearly having assumed his distaste would have proven justified. He fumbled the door handle on his way out and reappeared within the space of five breaths with Bronwen in tow.

Tears streaked her blotchy face, her eyes red rimmed and raw. She twisted a handkerchief in a white-knuckled grip, and her whole body shuddered with each attempt to draw air into her lungs. As soon as she saw Maddie, she lurched forwards and dropped to her knees in front of the desk, causing cold dread to pool in Maddie's gut.

"O-oh, You-your Highness. I'm s-so sorry to both-b-bother you."

"Think nothing of it," Maddie said, already rounding the table. "But you must calm yourself. Hodges. Fetch some brandy. And a tisane."

She helped Bronwen into a chair, sitting beside her and meeting Tristan's eyes over the mage's head. He shook his head but crouched at Bronwen's other side, giving her forearm a gentle squeeze and whispering that she was safe.

"Is it Sara?" Maddie made herself ask.

A shake of Bronwen's head eased Maddie's racing heart.

"Finley, then?"

Bronwen moaned, fresh tears coursing down her cheeks. Fortunately, Hodges arrived with a cup of brandy, and after choking down a sip or two, she collapsed back into the chair, spent. Maddie set the cup on the desk and rubbed the poor woman's hand until she straightened and wiped her face with her palms.

She looked around and started, straightening her shawl and skirts as she tried to back away from Maddie.

"Bronwen, look at me," Maddie said in the voice she used to calm Olivia after a nightmare. "You're safe, and you're fine. I'm glad you came to me. But I need to know what happened. Can you tell me? From the beginning?"

With a glance at Tristan, Bronwen nodded and settled, folding her hands together on her lap. Then she breathed in and out, slow and steady, and began.

"I was out in Mochynden Forest, taking Finley his lunch—he forgets it sometimes, so I leave it in a hollowed-out tree by the stream for him—when I saw a group of men with swords pushing Finley and a few of the others into a clearing—the one by the big oak?"

Maddie knew the one and hummed for Bronwen to continue.

"They didn't say much, just made signs to each other with their hands, so I wasn't sure what they were after at first. I figured if it were money, they'd see my Finley didn't have any and let him be as long as he didn't cause a fuss. But the men never searched them. Well, only to prod their muscles.

"The one in charge asked if any of them had used a sword before. Then he handed them one, one at a time, and told them to show him what they could do." She sniffed, her eyes watering again. "Finley's a truffle hunter. He rears pigs. I don't think he'd ever touched a sword in his life before today."

Maddie recalled his aversion to violence, his devotion to his family, and swallowed back tears of her own. He must have been terrified.

"When the strangers started to tie them together, one of the men who works with Finley—a gamekeeper, I think—fought back." Bronwen squeezed her eyes closed for several moments, crushing her skirt in her fists.

"He said he wouldn't let them take him anywhere, got real panicked, and tried to run. And they—they killed him. Caught him within a few paces and slit his throat in front of the others. I barely stopped myself from screaming. The leader said the same would happen to anyone else who tried to run, so the rest stopped struggling."

She turned to Maddie, waterlogged eyes so full of anguish it pierced straight through Maddie's chest. "They took them. I don't know where, couldn't follow without being seen. But they took my Finley, and Creator knows what they're going to do with him."

Maddie stared blankly as Bronwen dissolved into tears once more, seeing a line of captives being stolen away, men it was her duty to protect. A bone-deep wail of grief dragged her focus back to the present, and she clenched her jaw, steadying her own nerves before attempting to soothe the mage's.

She spun to the desk to pour some of the tisane, but Hodges hovered beside her, a cup already in his hand. With a flashed smile that felt more like a grimace, she handed the brew to Bronwen and rubbed her back as she drank it down.

When Bronwen was calm again, Tristan pulled up another chair and sat facing her. "You said they used hand signals to communicate. Like this?"

He made a couple of vaguely familiar gestures, and she pointed at the third. "That one. They used that one a few times. What is it?"

"Just a signal to move," he said. "The one who spoke, did he have an accent at all?"

She scrunched her face. "Not that I could tell. I was hiding a ways back in the trees, so I couldn't hear well. Sorry."

"Don't be, you're doing well." He smiled, a genuine one that crinkled the corners of his eyes. "Just a couple more questions. Was there anything you can remember that could identify them? Any armour or an insignia, or a distinctive weapon?"

"No."

"And they were wearing normal clothes? Not all the same colour?"

"Yes, no. I mean"—she shrugged, spreading her hands—"they looked like anyone else—trousers, tunics, a couple in shirts and jackets, and browns, blues, one in green."

By the time she had answered Tristan's questions, her eyes had dried and her breathing returned to normal. Maddie squeezed her hand and addressed Hodges.

"Bronwen will be staying here until this is resolved. Please arrange a room for her and Sara upstairs."

"Oh, Your Highness I couldn't—"

"You can and you will," Maddie told the other woman. It was the least she could do after bringing the family to Faerstolmere and into more danger than if they had remained in the north. Besides, it was something tangible, and Maddie needed that when so much else was uncertain. "Now, if you're ready, Hodges will get you settled."

"Yes, Ma'am," Hodges said. He offered Bronwen his arm and a surprisingly gentle smile.

"Thank you, Your Highness." Bronwen bobbed a curtsey, then opened her mouth but closed it again.

She shuffled out with Hodges, and when the door closed behind them, Maddie looked to Tristan. He stood, hands fisted, eyes trained on the door. "Those were Craeickish soldiers. I'd stake my life on it."

Gall rose in Maddie's throat. "But we can't prove it."

Lucas had used her own tactic against her, disguising his soldiers as common labourers just as she had in the trap where he was captured. Was this her fault? If she had broken the curse the other day, could she have stopped it from happening?

"Proof? Those were military hand signals they were using. And where would a group of peasants find so many swords?"

Maddie stood, her fingers itching for something to do. "But there was nothing tying them specifically to Craeick." She straightened the stack of papers on her desk. "They could even argue they were recruiting for Tyrrath's defences, which would technically be within the bounds of the treaty." Another hole her enemy had exploited. "Besides, we'd have to capture them first, and if they've made their way to the fortress already, we stand little chance against it."

Tristan's jaw tightened. "Then what do you suggest? We can't just sit here and let them do this."

"No." Returning to her seat, she picked up the report and smoothed the creases from it. "But we're not going to win by brute strength, not against Craeick. We need to be smart, use guile…"

She had played Lucas at Knights, outwitted him at the border. She knew how he thought. But this time, he was not her true opponent. The best way to stop him was to break the curse and stop whoever was controlling him.

"Send reinforcements to Lieutenant Wash. He can't attack the fortress"—Craeick's troops would wipe him out without breaking a sweat, much as she hated to admit it—"but a show of force will hopefully make them think twice, and he can stop them from bringing in more people. And alert the local militias across the north of the kingdom to be on the lookout for bands of men dressed as commoners who can't prove their identities. Regular patrols should reduce their ability to… recruit." The word tasted sour in her mouth.

"We need to catch them in the act before we can do anything more, but tell the lords to be careful. I don't want anyone else being killed for resisting."

Had she forgotten anything? Was the response enough? She worried her lower lip between her teeth and looked up at Tristan, who had straightened and was nodding slowly.

"What about the Wolf?" he asked.

Maddie winced. Should she tell him about the curse?

He folded his arms across his chest. "I wish we could toss him in the deepest cell in the dungeon and throw away the key."

No. She could not say anything, not yet. Even if he believed her, he would simply remove Lucas from the palace, and then they might never find their true enemy—and she might never get her husband back.

"I'll deal with him." She raised a hand when he made to protest. "Please. Trust me."

He worked his jaw, scrutinising her with an intense, narrow-eyed gaze, but eventually, he gave a single, tight nod.

Rather than feeling relieved, pressure bore down on her. She had taken on so much responsibility. Was it too much? And how would she accomplish what she had promised to do? The questions ate at her like a canker. Shoving them to the back of her mind, she gave him a tight smile and stood to return to the council meeting.

At least Joss should be back soon, and hopefully with information they could use.

Chapter 24

Maddie

After a few hours of not being able to focus on anything else, Maddie concluded that it might be best to send her sisters somewhere safe. Her father, she could protect with additional guards, but her sisters would be better off far away from Redcairn Palace. She could not bear the thought of them suffering for the mistakes she had made.

She hurried over to the great hall at lunchtime and scanned the high table, relaxing when she spotted Joss sitting at the far end. Bless her for not absconding to the forest when Maddie desperately needed to speak to her.

Olivia gave Maddie a timid wave, and Maddie squeezed her shoulder on the way to her seat. "How go your studies, Mouse?"

Eyes darting around their audience—Lucas's family and the disgruntled friar, plus some minor lords at one of the lower tables—Olivia ducked her head and said, "Well. I, um, I learned some interesting things about mages this morning."

Maddie started. Had Olivia discovered something about the curse? She had all but given up hope after nearly a week with no new information. She speared a piece of the chicken the serving maid placed in front of her and dipped it into the bowl of aromatic sauce. "You did? That's wonderful. You'll have to tell me all about it this evening when my head's less full of land disputes."

"Problems among the gentry?" Lord Ross asked from farther along the table as he dug into his own portion.

She grimaced, and he offered a sympathetic smile.

"Actually," she said, piercing Joss with a loaded stare, "I was hoping you might be able to help me with one of them, Joss. Lord Huntley's having some issues with poachers along the Iskarian border. A royal visit might soothe his ruffled feathers and ease tensions with them." She gestured to their youngest sister. "You could take Olivia with you if you want the company."

Joss's forehead wrinkled, but she followed Maddie's lead. "Of course, if that would help. When would we leave?"

The tension in Maddie's shoulders eased. "As soon as possible."

"What about the spring festival?" Lord Ross asked.

"Oh, yes," Catriona said, her words tripping over her husband's question. "You must wait until after the festival. I've been looking forward to the procession of lights since we set out from home, and it wouldn't be the same without the three of you leading the way."

"Heathen ritual," Friar Utham muttered, touching the stone hanging around his neck, but no one else paid him any heed.

Maddie pasted on a smile for her mother-in-law. "In that case, I wouldn't dream of disappointing you."

Truthfully, the prospect of heading the procession without her sisters curdled the meat in her stomach, and sending them away beforehand would disappoint more than just her guests. She resigned herself to worrying over them instead and picked at the chicken on her plate.

The maid brought more dishes out, rousing Maddie's appetite with the scents of herb-baked fowl and apricot stew. The rest of their meal passed in amiable conversation, and before long, people drifted out of the hall in ones and twos until only Maddie, the friar, and Catriona remained.

Friar Utham stood and, with a respectful bow to his queen and one slightly less so for Maddie, excused himself from the table. The echo of his clipped footsteps followed him out, and Maddie stood to leave as well.

"Sit with me for a moment? Please," Catriona said.

Maddie sank back into her seat. "Of course."

Catriona scooted her chair closer, eliciting a squeak that made them both flinch and then chuckle. But the older woman's mirth soon faded, replaced by a slight frown. She met Maddie's gaze with saddened eyes and said, "I hope Lucas will join you for the festival."

Maddie's mouth opened, but no words came out.

"I don't mean to pry, and please tell me if I overstep, but it pains me that the two of you don't spend more time together. I know your marriage began as a treaty, but I know my son, and from the time I've spent with you, I'm convinced you'd make a fine couple, given the chance."

Memories of riding through the woods with Lucas, playing games in the library with their siblings, talking through the long hours of the night, and falling asleep in his arms danced through Maddie's mind. She bit back the desire to admit how true Catriona's words were. It would only lead to more questions that she could not answer.

"I—" She cleared her throat and tried again. "I'll do my best to get to know the real him."

Though her true meaning was lost on Catriona, she made it a promise between them.

"Thank you, my dear." Catriona leaned across Lucas's empty chair and squeezed Maddie's forearm. "You won't regret the effort. Now, are we still touring the gardens this afternoon?"

"Yes. Olivia's been wanting to plant some new seedlings since we got back from Northold. I told her you mentioned an interest in seeing them."

A grin crinkled the corners of Catriona's eyes. "Then I'll fetch my cloak and meet you by the rear entrance?"

"Yes."

She stood to leave but turned back and said, "It's so lovely spending time with you young women. I love my boys, but I always wanted a daughter."

Maddie's eyes prickled. "We miss having a mother sometimes too."

With a final smile, Catriona swept from the room, leaving Maddie to contemplate their conversation. She liked her mother-in-law and would consider her approval a blessing if there were not so many insurmountable problems to overcome.

As things stood, Catriona was one more person counting on her, and Maddie was close to buckling under the strain. Pressure tightened the muscles in her neck and sucked the moisture from her mouth. How was she to accomplish all she must do?

If only Lord Elland could return or her father wake from his long slumber—or Tristan abandon his hatred of Lucas for long enough to help him. But none of those was going to happen. Her sisters aside—and she would protect them with her life—she was on her own.

Chapter 25

Maddie

That evening, Maddie stood with her sisters by their father's bed while Parker, disguised as a maid, deposited a tray of hot dakka on the side table. Darkness shrouded most of the room, the candles at the head of the bed unable to dispel the shadows looming around them, and the usually peaceful space felt ominous for the first time.

"I'll be just through there if you need me, Ma'am." The guard pointed to the door in the corner of the room, bobbed a quick curtsey, and slipped into the adjoining solar, taking a single candle with her.

Olivia sat on the bed and picked up their father's hand. "Would Lucas really come after Papa?" she whispered.

"No. I'm sure he wouldn't." Maddie wrapped an arm around her sister's shoulders. "Tristan only replaced the servants in this wing with guards as a precaution. He takes his responsibilities seriously, so he wanted to guarantee nothing could happen. That's all."

"It's almost worth it to see Parker cleaning," Joss said with a chuckle.

"Joss!"

She sobered and joined Maddie and Olivia, picking up a cup of dakka. When she offered the others around, Olivia shook her head, but Maddie accepted. Warmth seeped into her fingers, and the rich, creamy scent curled inside her nostrils, soothing her jagged thoughts.

"I wonder what Papa would think of all this," Joss said.

So did Maddie, but she had no wish to dwell on how many times she had failed him in the last months. Turning from his peaceful countenance, she looked at each of her sisters in turn. "Are you sure you both want to stay here? I can make your excuses for missing the spring festival."

"But then you'll be on your own," Olivia said, her brows tugged together.

"Hardly." Maddie sat in the chair that had been placed by her father's bedside for visitors and met Olivia's gaze. "I have Tristan and his best guards around me all day."

Joss dragged another chair over from the fireplace and dropped onto it. "But they don't know what's really going on. You need us."

"Yes, and we're not leaving you."

Olivia lifted her chin into a stubborn tilt, and though it quivered slightly, Maddie raised her hands in defeat.

"All right. Fine. But promise me you'll both be careful."

They glanced at each other and said in unison, “We promise.”

Maddie shook her head—so much for protecting her sisters—but a secret corner of her heart warmed at their determination to face the curse together. She had always drawn strength from their presence.

“I found something today.” Olivia slid off the bed and fetched a scroll from the table where she had left it when they arrived. “I’d almost given up, but then I remembered that chest of old documents Hodges moved upstairs when he was first appointed and decided to clean everywhere.”

She handed it to Maddie and settled back on the bed, tucking her feet up onto the side panel and wrapping her arms around her knees. Maddie took a sip of her dakka, placed her cup on the floor, and unwound the scroll’s leather bindings.

When she spread it out on her lap, it revealed a drawing of two dragon stones carved with the same pattern. The inscription was written in Dracestian, the ancient language of the mages, but someone had scribbled a note beside it.

“Power stones and control stones—made from the same dragon stone, must bear the same mark,” Maddie read aloud. Her eyes jumped to Olivia. “So whoever’s controlling Lucas must have one of these, a control stone.”

Olivia nodded. “I think so.”

“Then we know what to look for.” Joss set her dakka aside and pulled the scroll across to read it for herself.

Maddie glanced at her. "They're not going to leave it around for anyone to find. They'll have it hidden away somewhere."

Joss shrugged and gave the scroll back. "We could always search their rooms while they're out. Do you have any idea who it might be?"

"Search their—?" The desire to send Joss away after all clogged Maddie's throat. She slowly released the air in her lungs through her nose and pierced her sister with a stern look. "You will do no such thing. As for who could be behind all this…"

She pursed her lips to the side, staring down at the twin stones in the picture. "If the curse had been activated later, I might have a few suspicions. The only person I can think of who was here at the time and seems to hate Tyrrath enough to want to destroy us is Rheann Braydeson, but I doubt she'd use Lucas like that to do it."

"What if the stones work over a distance?" Joss mused.

Maddie's head snapped up. "Did Nessa say something when you saw her?"

"Not about that, but I could go back and ask. Oh—" She rummaged in her waist pouch and pulled out a box that she held out to Maddie. "She did say this was safe, though. There's not a trace of magic on it, and she spent half a day examining the thing."

Maddie took the box, unsure whether the fluttering in her chest was caused by relief or something else. The reaction was silly, she knew. Lucas had not given her the ring inside—his mother had. Still, she opened the lid and removed the ring with care. It was a Sinclair heirloom, passed down through the generations from queen to queen and now to her.

Could she truly wear it? She dropped it back inside the box and snapped the lid shut. Not while her marriage was in name only, not while she was at odds with her husband, not until she had freed him, and her kingdom, from the curse.

"Thanks, Joss."

"You're welcome." Joss glanced at the box in Maddie's lap but, thankfully, said nothing further.

Maddie retrieved her cup from the floor and sipped her drink, grimacing at how much it had cooled. "Where were we?"

"The stones working from a distance," Olivia said.

Of course. Maddie stared down into the dark brown liquid and tapped the cup's rim with her finger. Something tugged at her mind, a memory of…

She stilled. Friar Utham wore a black stone around his neck. She shook the thought loose. No, it could not be him. Why would a man of faith wish to curse Craeick's king? "If the ring can be controlled from far away, it could be anyone. We might never discover who's behind it."

"Maybe we should just focus on breaking its hold?" Joss said. "When Lucas is free, he can track them down himself. He is the Wolf King, after all."

"All right, but how?"

Olivia shifted on the bed. "Wouldn't the best way be to get the ring away from him? If he's not wearing it, it can't control him."

There was only one problem with that. "He never takes it off."

"Oh." Olivia dropped her legs to the ground, a worried frown creasing her forehead.

"Then we'll have to do it when he's sleeping." Joss straightened. "Or unconscious."

She sprang to her feet before Maddie could ask what she was thinking, and paced the length of the bed, muttering under her breath. Whatever she was planning, Maddie was fairly certain she would want no part in it. She sighed and looked to Olivia, who lifted one shoulder and glanced at the candle flames Joss's movements had set flickering.

"I've got it," Joss said, dropping her hands down on the back of the chair she had vacated, a familiar twinkle in her eyes. Shadows loomed around her, reminding Maddie of the danger they all faced should whatever scheme Joss had concocted go wrong.

As if reading her mind, Joss faced her directly and said, "Trust me, please? I know what we need to do."

Chapter 26

Maddie

Maddie walked along the city's main cobbled street at dusk three days later, flanked by her sisters at the head of the procession of lights. This was her first time leading it—her father fell ill not long after the last—and her body thrummed with nervous anticipation, her skin pebbling in the cool evening air.

Lucas walked directly behind her, his looming presence stealing some of the joy from the event, but Tristan and the rest of the guards around them offered some comfort. She tried to focus on the festival she usually adored. There would be plenty of time later to worry about her husband.

The candle she carried flickered, and she cupped her hand around the flame, protecting it from a gust of wind. The urge to check her hair for loose strands tightened her muscles, but tonight, her utmost priority was the tiny light she carried in its oiled-paper boat.

More and more people fell in behind her as she passed, snatches of songs riding the wave of excited murmurs that lined her route. A glance over her shoulder revealed the long stream of lights weaving through Faerstolmere and down to the lakeshore.

As they left the last of the buildings behind, the scent of roasting meat wafted from ahead, making her mouth water. The boars the palace provided for the occasion always tasted better outdoors. She quickened her pace, her feet pounding the dirt path and then sinking into soft sand.

When she reached the waterline, she slipped off her shoes, hitched her skirts with one hand, and stepped into the water. Icy cold stole her breath as droplets splashed up her ankles, but she pushed on until it reached her mid-calves, where she stopped on a large, flattish stone.

Eyes on the candle's flame, she prayed the only thing she could—that her father would wake from his sleep, and that she could break the curse and free her husband, and thus her people, from its evil hold.

Then she placed the boat on the surface of the water and gently pushed it out into the lake. It joined the last rays of sunlight glinting on the wind-rippled surface, a pale, yellow spot among streamers of deep orange and red.

Olivia and Joss waited behind her, and she stepped aside to allow them to release theirs. Soon, more people joined them, their paper- or bark-borne candles floating out from the shore until the whole near side of the lake appeared to be on fire.

Maddie lifted her face to the sky and drew in a deep lungful of cool evening air. Then she turned and made her way to the royal pavilion, Tristan acting as her shadow. From there, they would be able to watch the lights drift across the lake into the distance and enjoy the remainder of the festival.

They stopped to watch a trio of jugglers performing in front of a wagon with 'The Three Stifados' emblazoned across the side in peeling red and gold lettering. The men, whose matching bulbous noses alone would have identified them as brothers, had evidently lost some of their talent to age and pained joints, but they still drew a crowd among the revellers.

They were taking a bow to rapturous applause when Joss bounded up to Maddie and Tristan, her own guard in tow. "Are you two coming?" she asked. "I'm starving."

Maddie looped her arm through her sister's and set off again along the shore. They passed numerous craftspeople who had laid out their wares on blankets to get an early start on the markets and headed to the small, cleared area beyond, where the royal pavilion stood surrounded by torches and a handful of guards.

Beneath the canopy, Tabitha waited beside an array of plump cushions and a low table. "There you are, Your Highness. Let's get you seated so the feast can begin." She searched behind them. "Where's Olivia?"

Joss groaned. "She stopped to talk to an Iskarian bookseller. Please say we can start without her."

Tabitha hummed, her lips flattening into a straight line as she narrowed her eyes at Joss. Either oblivious to her displeasure or too hungry to pay it heed, Joss plopped down onto one of the cushions and scanned the bowls of nuts and berries already on the table.

With an apologetic shrug, Maddie sat as well and arranged her skirts so they would not become overly creased. She looked up as three servants arrived bearing platters of food—roasted boar drizzled with truffle oil, braised vegetables, and a whole trout on a bed of spring greens.

The sight made her mouth water, and while she had planned to wait for the others, she unsheathed the dagger Lucas had given her and speared a piece of meat to try. Succulent and rich, bordering on nutty with a hint of earthiness from the truffles, it should have been delicious, but the flavour only reminded her of Finley, the truffle hunter and one-time military messenger.

He might have found the truffles used in the evening's meal, but he would not gather more, or return to his wife and daughter, unless Maddie could save him from the clutches of the Craeickish army. The pork she had eaten turned sour, sticking in her throat and curdling her stomach as she forced it down.

She looked over at Joss, who had already loaded her plate and was stuffing a chunk of bread-wrapped fish into her mouth. Joss gave her a subtle nod before jerking her chin in the direction of the general merriment.

Olivia and Flynn walked towards them, Parker one step behind Olivia. They were followed closely by Lucas and the rest of his family, flanked by Aiden and two other Craeickish soldiers. Fortunately, Rheann was nowhere in sight, and Friar Utham had chosen to remain at the palace.

The latecomers took their seats, Olivia choosing a place near Catriona, and Flynn sitting on his mother's other side. Lucas sank into the space reserved for him beside Maddie but angled himself to face Lord Ross.

"Now that everyone's here, shall we have some wine?" Maddie asked.

"I'll pour," Joss said. "To make up for starting without you all."

Maddie watched carefully while her sister poured the wine yet was unable to catch her adding anything to Lucas's goblet. Unsure whether to worry about Joss's talent for subterfuge or simply appreciate the opportunity it afforded, Maddie licked her dry lips and accepted the wine her sister handed her. She passed Lucas his, making sure not to spill any, and raised hers in a toast.

"To the Creator's bounteous light and the first markets of the new season."

They drank, and Maddie focused anywhere but on her husband. How long would the soporific take to work? What if they could not get him back to the palace before he succumbed to its effects? Would he realise what they had done, and if so, what would he do?

The questions destroyed the last of her appetite and soured the sweetness of the wine on her tongue. Despite her efforts, her eyes found Lucas, who drained his goblet without mentioning anything amiss. He dug into the roasted boar, and she resigned herself to wait.

It took an interminable time for him to slump back on the cushions, mumbling incoherently. He scratched his jaw, and his head drooped onto his chest.

"Maybe someone should take Lucas back to the palace," Joss said. "It looks like he's had quite a bit to drink."

He swung his head towards her. "Is fine. M perfe'ly fine."

"I'll go with him," Maddie said. "I'm quite tired anyway."

Lord Ross frowned down at his wine, swirled it around, and peered at Lucas. "It's not like him to overindulge."

"No." Catriona touched her husband's hand. "But he's young. It's good to see him relaxing once in a while."

"You're right, of course, my dear." Lord Ross gave her an adoring smile and sipped his drink.

Maddie finished the meat on her knife, brushed a few crumbs from her skirts, and stood. When she looked up, she found Catriona's gaze on her, the older woman's eyes sparkling in the torchlight. Why was she so happy?

"Aiden. Take Lucas back to his room," Catriona said before Maddie could ask Tristan to help her.

"Aye, Your Majesty."

As Aiden hoisted Lucas to his feet, Catriona stood and walked over to them. She cupped her son's face for a moment, then stepped closer to Aiden and said something Maddie could not hear. He nodded once and secured his grip around Lucas's waist.

Lucas grumbled a little under his breath but allowed Aiden to guide him from the pavilion, and with a quick 'goodnight', Maddie followed them out into the cool night air.

Tristan fell into step beside her, and they walked back to the palace in relative quiet.

They took a more direct route back, past the empty market that would open in the morning. Pigs snuffled on the far side, herded into pens over the last few days ready to be sold, and a waft of their urine made her nose wrinkle.

"Stinks. 'S whole kindom stinks," Lucas slurred, flinging his arm around them. "Pigs…"

Aiden steadied him. "Aye, Sire. They do at that. Let's get up to the palace and away from them, yes?"

"Do you need any help?" Maddie asked.

"No, Your Highness. I can manage."

She glanced at Tristan, who only shrugged, and kept walking.

By the time they reached the palace, Lucas's feet dragged, and Tristan ducked under his other arm to keep him upright as they half carried him up the stairs and around to his and Maddie's rooms. She darted ahead and opened the door, and they shuffled him sideways through the opening and across to the bed.

He made a weak protest when they lowered him onto it but did nothing to stop Aiden lifting his feet onto the mattress, only flopped back against the pillows. Maddie lit a candle and studied him from the foot of the bed, hands clasped together at her waist. Joss's scheme had gone without a hitch so far. Now all she needed to do was get rid of his guard and get the ring off his finger.

She turned to Aiden, but before she could speak, he frowned down at Lucas and said, "I'm not sure about leaving him like this, but Her Majesty asked me to bring her a couple of blankets."

"Is she well?" The possibility of Catriona becoming ill interrupted Maddie's thoughts and carried her a step towards him.

Aiden shook his head. "She'll be fine, Ma'am. She never likes to make a fuss, just doesn't do well in the cold. It's far better here than at home."

"Oh. As long as you're sure."

"Aye, Ma'am."

Her concerns assuaged, Maddie hid a swell of pleasure—returning to the lake would take him far longer than fetching a tonic from the kitchens. "Then go, please. Lucas will be perfectly safe with Tristan on guard."

The two men eyed each other for a moment before Aiden nodded, cast a glance at Lucas, and walked from the room. He closed the door behind him with a soft click, leaving Maddie and Tristan alone with his king.

Maddie waited until his footsteps had faded, then set about removing Lucas's boots. She peered at Tristan over her shoulder and said, "You don't have to stay. He's not exactly dangerous in this state."

The look he gave her made it clear her attempt at humour had fallen flat, but all he said was, "I'll be inspecting the night watch," and he left.

Finally alone with Lucas, she sat on the edge of the bed and stroked the hair from his forehead. He murmured at her touch, a grimace stealing over his face that pierced her heart.

"I'm sorry," she whispered. "This was the only way to save you and bring you back to me."

He stilled, his breathing deepening, and she gently nudged his shoulder. When he did not respond, she took a steadying breath and eased his hand away from his body. The ring, warmed by his skin, slipped easily over the first knuckle of his little finger. But as she tried to tug it past the second, it stuck.

She pulled with more force, to no avail, and examined it more closely, trying to discover how it was caught. There was nothing she could see that prevented the ring from sliding off his hand, but no matter how hard she yanked at it, it refused to shift farther than the base of his fingernail.

Was this part of the magic? Had it latched onto his body somehow like a parasite, preventing anyone from tampering with the curse? Panic surged through her limbs, and she paced the length of the dim chamber. What should she do now?

When Lucas woke, the aftertaste of the garricon root would tell him he had been drugged. He was supposed to have been freed of the curse when that happened, allowing her to explain, but if he stirred before she could break its hold… How would he react?

That could not happen. She could not let it. Returning to his side, she gripped the ring and pulled with all her might. It crept over the second knuckle and as far as his cuticle, but again, nothing she did could coax it beyond that point.

She sank to the floor beside the bed, dropping her forehead to his hand. "Please. Please let it come off."

One last try… and she gave up. They were not going to be able to break the curse. Not like that, anyway.

Lucas moaned, twisting his head on the pillow, and she jerked her eyes to his. They were still closed—the concoction Joss had poured into his wine should hold him in a deep sleep for several more hours—but the fine hairs on her arms rose. They had made a terrible mistake.

She leapt to her feet and hurried to the door, desperate to get away. Her mind raced, circling back to the same questions over and over again. How could they possibly break the curse now? And what would happen when Lucas woke up?

Chapter 27

Luc

Luc climbed up through the dark recesses of his mind into consciousness, his limbs leaden and his head throbbing. Grit scraped his eyes as he opened them, and a bitter film coated his tongue. He tried to work moisture into his mouth and groped for the edge of the bed, rolling himself upright.

The room spun, shadows blurring together in the dim candlelight, and he clutched his head in a futile attempt to make it stop. How could he feel so hungover when he had only had a couple of cups of wine the previous night?

He rubbed his tongue over his teeth, testing the bitterness. This was no mere hangover—it tasted of garricon root. He had been poisoned.

He surged to his feet, only to sink back onto the mattress, his legs wobbly as a newborn colt. His fingers curled into fists, his brain caught between returning to sleep and making someone pay.

Who had done this to him?

The princess's face swam behind his closed eyelids, watching him drink, and he had his answer. His fists tightened, causing a twinge in the little finger on his left hand. He glanced down and brought it closer to his face. The skin around his knuckle was chafed and red, though nothing else appeared amiss. What had she been trying to do?

Carefully, he stood again, took a step, then another. He staggered towards the door but missed his goal, bumping into a chair instead. It barked across the floor, and something fell with a loud clatter that set his head thumping more violently.

"Shhh," he told it, and kept going.

The hallway outside was empty and dark, the torches not yet lit. He had not realised it was so early, but that would make finding his quarry that much easier. But first... Using the wall for support, he made his way to his parents' room and banged on the door.

It opened almost instantly, and Gabriel's face appeared in the gap, lit from below by a candle he carried. He blinked at Luc and stepped into the hallway, a robe haphazardly tied around his sizeable waist.

"Lucas? What's wrong? I heard a noise."

That must have been the chair. Luc winced. "Never mind that. Are Mother and Flynn safe?"

Gabriel's forehead wrinkled as he glanced back into the darkened room. "They're asleep. Why?"

Luc slumped against the doorframe, still a little sluggish from the garricon root. "The princess poisoned me," he blurted.

Gabriel started. He looked both ways along the hallway. "You can't say that here. Come, tell me what happened."

Luc's instincts screamed to go after the princess, but he valued Gabriel's advice, so he allowed his stepfather to usher him inside. He dropped onto a chair and rubbed his temples while Gabriel closed the door to the adjoining bedchamber where Luc's mother slept.

"Now, what's all this about the princess?" Gabriel asked, setting the candle on the table and sitting opposite Luc.

"She poisoned me, last night at the festival. Tried to steal my signet ring too—must've wanted to use the seal for something." She must have discovered his plan and decided to act first.

Luc looked up as Gabriel sat back, his expression stunned. The older man blinked, scratched at his beard, and frowned down at the candle. "Are you sure?" he asked.

"I can still taste the garricon root. And who else would dare poison me?"

"Hmm."

Gabriel stood and paced, hands thrust deep into his pockets, and Luc slumped into the chair. Sleep still called to him, but he refused to give in to its demands. He needed to find the princess and make her pay for what she had done. He needed to…

"Lucas?"

Gabriel's voice brought Luc back to himself. Damn that garricon root. He scrubbed a hand over his face and looked up at his stepfather. "What was that?"

"What are you going to do?"

Luc pushed himself to his feet. "I'm going to find the princess."

He headed for the door but turned when Gabriel said, "Be careful, Luc. She's the crown princess of Tyrrath, and we're in their capital."

"I will."

He left Gabriel standing in the middle of his solar and walked into the hallway, straight into Friar Utham.

"Friar. What are you doing here?" Luc steadied himself against the wall, his head woozy.

"Are you well, Sire?" The friar's brows gathered like storm clouds above a mountain peak. "It seems you imbibed overmuch at the festival." He pulled out the stone from around his neck. "I will pray for your soul."

Luc closed his eyes, cursing his misfortune. Of all the people…

When he opened his eyes, his head felt even worse. He peered up at the peevish friar, only to find him no longer there, already striding away in the direction of his room.

Luc turned in the opposite direction. What had he been doing? Oh, yes. The princess. He could not barge into her sisters' rooms, so he would search the other places she might be first—her study, the library, the empty guest rooms in the north corridor.

The more he thought about it, the more certain he was that she had discovered his plans and tried to kill him before he could act. Fortunately, she must have underestimated his size and strength for the dose, but he would not make the same mistake.

He descended the stairs, his head clearing with each beat of his heart. Killing her would not only assuage his need for revenge. If he blamed it on rebels—or better yet, a neighbouring kingdom—it would give him the perfect reason to invade. No one would argue with a man set on avenging his wife's death.

"My wife—hah." Now there was a joke.

Something niggled at the back of his mind, something important, and he paused at the bottom of the stairs, his forehead pulling tight. What was it? A memory of words whispered to him as he fell asleep danced just beyond his reach, fuzzy and indistinct.

He shook his head, desperate to clear the last vestiges of the poison from his body. The princess would pay for what she had done to him. As soon as he found her, she would pay.

Chapter 28
Maddie

Maddie waited in Joss's room for her sisters to return from the festival, nausea eating her insides at how badly their plan had failed. No matter how she thought about it, she could not see a clear path out of the mess she had plunged them into, and her eyes burned with tears whenever she considered the ramifications for her people—for innocents like Finley.

She must have fallen asleep at some point, for a hand shaking her shoulder startled her awake. She jerked upright, rubbed the grit from her eyes, and looked up at Joss, who lofted her brows.

"Why are you here? Where's Lucas?"

Her brain slowly caught up with Joss's questions, and her eyes shot to the door, half expecting to see him there, sword drawn. She focused back on her sister and swallowed. "It didn't work."

Joss's expression shifted to one of horror. "What?"

"The ring wouldn't come off his finger. It must be held on by magic."

"He's going to know…"

She backed away, and Maddie scrambled off the bed. She gripped Joss's shoulders and forced her to meet her gaze. "He'll come after me, not you. I'm his main threat. But that's not going to be a problem because I'm telling Tristan—right now—everything."

Joss threw her arms around Maddie, and they held each other for an endless moment. "He's going to be so angry about this," Joss eventually whispered, and Maddie let go with a wince.

"I know. But that can't be helped. I don't have a choice anymore."

"You mean we don't. I'm going with you." Joss offered a smile that looked more like a grimace and headed for the door.

They did not have to search far. Tristan stood outside their father's room at the end of the hallway, talking to a sharp-eyed maid with a rather large dagger at her waist. He looked up at their approach, and Maddie gestured for him to join them.

With a nod to the maid, he followed them inside Joss's room, where his eyes bounced between them when they did not immediately speak.

"What is it? Did Lucas do something?" He scanned Maddie as if searching for injuries.

"Nothing like that," she said at the same time as Joss muttered, "Not on his own."

Maddie glared at her sister and raised her hands before Tristan reached the wrong conclusion and stormed out after Lucas. "He's cursed," she said.

His face scrunched. "What?"

"He's cursed. His ring is." She took a deep breath and tried again. "Someone's controlling him through his signet ring."

Tristan stared at her. "How do you know?"

"I saw it myself. It's a dragon stone. It glowed red and put him in some sort of trance. He spoke like he was repeating something he'd been told and then acted like nothing had happened afterwards."

He rubbed his jaw, shifting his scrutiny to the floor. After a long moment, his eyes popped back up to hers, and he asked, "When was this?"

Maddie winced, muscles tensing in anticipation of his reaction, and whispered, "Ten days ago."

"Ten—" He threw his arms in the air and spun away from them, pressing a fist over his mouth.

She shrank back, glancing at Joss, who had also retreated a few steps. Joss met her gaze, lifted her hands in a helpless gesture, and eyed Tristan, remaining quiet for once.

When he twisted back around, the veins at his temples bulged, and his expression rooted Maddie to the spot. "You and I are going to have a long conversation later, but right now, tell me everything. From the beginning."

She did, and he listened in silence, barely moving until she finished. Then he scrubbed a hand over his scalp and pierced them both with a glare. "You should've told me sooner."

"I know. I'm sorry," Maddie said. "What do we do now?"

"*We* do nothing. I need to get you somewhere safe while I take him prisoner, secure the city, and investigate."

"But whoever—"

He snapped his gaze back to her, and she closed her mouth on the rest. "Maddie, you need to trust me."

"I do."

A snort escaped him. "Evidently." He blew out a deep breath and stepped closer to her, his expression finally softening. "I can't focus on protecting you and capturing whoever's behind this at the same time. They won't be able to do anything if the entire palace is under guard and the city gates are barred, but we need to move fast, preferably before Lucas wakes up. Then we can question him and hopefully find out who we need to take prisoner.

"Until then, I need you far away where no one can reach you. Understand?"

She nodded.

"Good." He glanced at Joss. "Block the door, and don't let anyone in until I get back. I'm going to arrange a guard and get the horses saddled."

"Oslengil," Joss blurted as he reached the door. "No one would think to look there."

He paused, said, "Good idea," over his shoulder, and walked out.

Maddie considered the suggestion while she and Joss pushed a heavy chest across the doorway. The stone castle at Oslengil had been abandoned since before their grandfather became king. It would be the perfect place to hide, but it was a hard day's ride from Faerstolmere. Olivia would struggle to make it.

Joss raced over to her wardrobe and started flinging dresses aside, muttering, "I'm sure I had a spare in here. Aha. This should fit."

She pulled out a riding skirt, scattering a quiver of arrows across the floor, and held it out to Maddie.

Caught off guard, Maddie looked down at the wrinkled gown she had worn for the festival the evening before. She had not thought to change earlier, but something more practical would be necessary if they were to make Oslengil by nightfall. She accepted the skirt and untied the laces on her gown, saying, "What are we going to do about Olivia?"

Joss tossed her hunting pack onto her bed and added a water skin. "I'll stay here with her. We'll hide in the north tower." She tucked a couple of pine nut rolls into the bag and faced Maddie. "But you need to go. Tristan's right. Of all of us, you're the one Lucas and whoever's controlling him will come after. I'm so sorry, Maddie."

Her face crumpled, and Maddie wrapped her in a firm embrace. "Don't blame yourself. This is my fault, no one else's."

"But drugging him with garricon root was my idea. If I hadn't—"

"No." Maddie stepped back and wiped a tear from Joss's cheek with her thumb. "If I'd done things differently, made better decisions from the start, you never would've been in that situation."

Joss shook her head, opening her mouth to reply, but a rap at the door halted their discussion. Breaths held, they exchanged a look and listened for more. Three came in quick succession followed by one on its own—Tristan's code. Maddie finished changing out of her gown as quickly as she could while Joss told him to wait for a moment and shoved the chest out of the way.

When Maddie was decent, her sister opened the door, and Tristan slipped inside. "Are you ready?" he asked.

"Joss is going to stay here with Olivia," Maddie said. "They can hide in the north tower. Tabitha too."

"All right. I'll put a guard detail on the stairwell."

Maddie blinked. She had expected to have to convince him, yet he had agreed so readily. Had that been his plan all along?

She had no time to worry about it. Within a handful of heartbeats, she was hurrying along one of the hidden passageways that riddled the palace walls, her sisters headed in the opposite direction. It let out into the servants' staircase, where she descended to the side entrance between Tristan and another guard, Joss's provisions in hand.

They reached the door, and he made her wait while he looked outside. Then they slipped like shadows around to where three more of his best men stood with the horses. She took Midnight's reins and rested her forehead against his soft nose, the familiar scent of him steadying her jittery nerves.

Tristan touched her shoulder, and his eyes told her without a single word spoken between them that she was forgiven, that she would be safe, and that he would do everything in his power to stop the threat to Tyrrath and to her. She gave him a quick, tight hug and followed the lead guard down the narrow passage and through the gate into Mochynden Forest, mounting as soon as they were clear of the brambles on the other side.

They rode south through the forest in silence, the four guards flanking Maddie front and rear where able and riding single file when the track narrowed. They made good time and were soon racing across fields dotted with pig sties towards the rolling hills of the southwest and Oslengil, the stone castle of her forefathers.

The farther they travelled from Faerstolmere, the darker Maddie's thoughts became, no amount of fresh air or bright sunlight able to break their hold. Even flying through the countryside astride Midnight brought no relief.

Visions of Tristan cut down by Lucas's sword, her sisters held captive by the vicious monster behind him, or worse, enthralled by more rings, shredded her heart. In her mind, her husband razed Redcairn Palace to the ground in search of her, the dust around him glowing eerily red as he turned curse-deadened eyes on the city.

She had failed. Her people, her sisters, her husband—a sob escaped—her father. She had failed them all, and so many innocents were paying the price for it.

There was nothing she could do for them now. She knew that. But she was running away and leaving those she loved to face the consequences of her mistakes. Wind-whipped tears lashed her face, their sting no match for the pain lodged in her chest as the truth settled there like a burning rock. She would never live up to her father's legacy. She had failed.

Chapter 29
Maddie

They arrived at Oslengil as the sun was setting, the castle and surrounding woods silhouetted against ribbons of orange and purple. The outer walls had crumbled in places, and nature had reclaimed most of the inner bailey, but the keep itself appeared intact. Forgotten yet sound, it would be a good place to await news of her husband's capture—or hide from his wrath.

Maddie and one of the guards, a tall man called Marsh, climbed up to the keep's entrance while the others saw to the horses and scouted the perimeter. The doors groaned when Marsh pushed them open, and a waft of musty air hit them, tickling Maddie's nostrils.

Darkness shrouded the interior, so Marsh lit a torch and lofted it overhead as they stepped inside. A thick layer of dust softened the sound of their footsteps and painted everything grey. That it was undisturbed confirmed no one had visited the site for years—a perfect place to hide.

The dim outline of a great hall slowly resolved around them, tables and benches arrayed down either side, the high table on a raised dais at the far end. According to legend, Oslengil had been abandoned when a mage lost control of his magic more than a century earlier. Half the residents had vanished in an expanding bubble of light, and the rest had fled, leaving virtually everything behind.

Maddie had not believed it until now. Even the stories of the mage's voice whispering through the castle on dark nights seemed suddenly plausible. She looked up at the cobweb-strewn rafters high above them, half expecting to see his shadow lurking there, but they were alone.

Marsh set the torch in a wall sconce, walked over to the nearest set of window shutters, and, with some difficulty, managed to yank them open. A few tendrils of ivy came with them, stuck to the wooden boards, and more filled the space beyond, blocking out what waning sunlight remained.

"Where d'you want this?" One of the other guards appeared in the doorway with an armful of firewood, and Marsh pointed to the fireplace opposite.

"Over there."

While the guard set about building a fire and Marsh fetched an axe and cut the ivy away from the window, Maddie searched for a task to occupy her hands. She spotted a stout branch on the pile of firewood and gathered some of the ivy to tie into a makeshift broom.

Her tool complete, she was about to start sweeping when Marsh grasped it, stopping her. "Begging your pardon, Ma'am, but you should let one of us do that. There may be vermin."

Her eyes darted around the floor, at all the nooks and crannies beneath the furniture, and she relinquished the broom. "Very well, but there must be something I can do."

She winced at the desperation in her tone and peeked up at him. His expression held no trace of pity, and the tension in her muscles eased a fraction. He jerked a thumb over his shoulder and said, "Seaburn brought a couple of carrier birds if you want to let the captain know we made it."

By the time she finished writing a short message to Tristan and sent it off with a pigeon Seaburn called Lady Grey, Marsh had a simple soup ready. It bubbled in a pot above the fire, releasing wafts of herb-laced steam that made Maddie's mouth water despite everything.

He and the others kept up a steady chatter while they ate, and when she had drained her bowl, he showed her to a side chamber where she could sleep. A bedroll covered most of the cleared floor space, and a candle stub burned in a tin dish beside it. Her eyes stung at his thoughtfulness.

"Goodnight, Your Highness," he said, ducking his head in a quick bow. "I'll be right outside if you need anything."

She slept fitfully, stalked by nightmares of wolves and shadowy figures with glowing dragon stones for eyes, and woke at daybreak with a throbbing headache. Her muscles also protested the night spent on the cold, hard ground, but she bit back a groan of complaint. She could endure a few bruises, given the circumstances.

Seaburn scrambled to his feet as she stepped into the great hall. He must have replaced Marsh at some point during the night. "Morning, Your Highness," he said. "Can I get you some breakfast?"

"No, thank you. I don't think I could eat anything yet."

With a glance around the otherwise empty hall, Maddie headed towards the stairwell. Maybe a little exploring would help her appetite. At the very least, the view from the battlements should prove a welcome distraction.

She wandered the upper floors, Seaburn trailing in her wake. Her mind returned again and again to Redcairn Palace and her sisters, and from there to Lucas. The solar conjured memories of quiet evenings with him in front of the fire. A table in one corner revived their last game of Knights. The bedchamber held ghosts too—his arms wrapped around her, his lips on hers.

Everywhere she roamed, she saw his face, his eyes crinkling with laughter, his brows lowered in thought. The good times they had enjoyed together overlaid Oslengil like a rich tapestry over an old chest, interspersed with flashes of him being interrogated in the palace dungeon.

Her hands fisted in her skirts. Why was she thinking about him when everyone she loved was in danger? And why did her stomach revolt at the notion of his capture and questioning?

With a growl that brought Seaburn's head up, she sought out the fresh air of the rooftop battlements. But even there, she saw herself and Lucas riding across the undulating landscape, the wind whipping their cloaks out behind them as they raced through the fields. Her fingers curled into the moss-covered wall. Why could she not escape him?

She emptied her lungs and tipped her face to the sky, only for his eyes to appear before her, brimming with confusion behind the curse. None of this was truly his fault, but he would suffer for it. Again, the notion sickened her, and this time she chased the feeling, trying to pin down why.

Her eyes popped open, and she stepped back from the wall. It could not be. Surely, she did not… But she could no more escape the truth than she could fly from the parapet. Somewhere between being blackmailed by a wolf and being betrayed by his curse, she had fallen for her husband.

A laugh bubbled up her throat. Of all the times to make such a realisation, she had to do so hiding halfway across the kingdom while her sisters cowered in fear, her people faced an unknown yet deadly threat, and her closest friend imprisoned the man she loved in hopes he would reveal the source of all their troubles. There must be something wrong with her.

She walked along the battlements, her thoughts turning in time with her steps. What in the world was she supposed to do now? How did this revelation fit with everything that had happened, was still happening?

The view before her changed as she rounded the castle, open plains giving way to forested hills and the mountains of Garellion rising from the treetops in the distance like rows of jagged teeth. She stopped walking and leaned against the wall, letting their rugged beauty clear her mind.

When a bird cawed overhead, she shielded her eyes and watched it circle the sun in a lazy arc. If only she could be as free. Responsibility. Expectation. Duty. The weight of rule drove her every decision, fuelled her fear of making a mistake. Gutted her to the core now that she had failed.

The bird swooped down into the canopy and rose with something in its talons. It carried its kill to the peak of a nearby hill, where it dropped it into a nest at the top of a tall tree. A rueful smile tugged at Maddie's cheeks. It seemed even birds bore certain responsibilities that could not be ignored.

Footsteps pounded behind her, and she turned to find Marsh jogging towards them.

"Your Highness. I need you to come inside now."

All thoughts of anything else scattered as her stomach dropped at the seriousness of his tone. "What is it? Have you had news from Redcairn?"

"No, Ma'am." He glanced at Seaburn and held an arm out to her. "Someone's here. We need to get you secure while we find out who it is."

"Oh. O-of course." She hurried to the stairwell entrance, a chill of gooseflesh racing across her skin. Marsh went down first, and Seaburn brought up the rear.

"Winslow's doing a sweep of the perimeter, and Danielson's standing watch downstairs," Marsh said as they reached the first landing. He looked over his shoulder at Seaburn. "You're with the princess until you hear the all clear. Got it?"

"Yessir," Seaburn said.

They arrived at the solar, and Marsh flung the door open. He scanned the room, nodded to Seaburn, and left them to it, clattering down the stairs to the great hall.

Maddie looped a few stray hairs behind her ear and walked inside. Seaburn shut the door behind them, and she started at the sound of the bolt sliding home.

"Just a precaution, Ma'am," he said.

He looked through both windows, easing ivy aside in the second for a better view, and took up position by the door, between her and any possible threat.

She swallowed at the thought and wiped damp palms down her skirt. Her ears strained for the slightest sound, but all was quiet, not even the birds twittering in the trees outside.

"Would you like something to eat, Ma'am?" Seaburn asked, startling her from her vigil.

"No, thank you." Her stomach still protested the mere thought of eating.

He shifted his weight, eyeing her as if trying to think of an alternative distraction, so she dusted off the nearest chair, sat, and set about tucking her windswept hair back into place.

Some time later, after she had drawn a Knights board in the dust on the table and started playing an imaginary opponent, raised voices drifted up to them. She jerked her head to Seaburn, who stiffened, his hand going to the sword at his hip.

The clash of swords rang out, and she sprang to her feet, knocking her chair back. A few steps carried her to the centre of the room, where she paused, torn between finding out what was happening and hiding from the violence below. Her hand rose to her arm where Lucas's blade had scored her flesh, too aware of the pain a sword could inflict.

"Steady, Ma'am," Seaburn said, his calm voice anchoring her storm-tossed thoughts. "Marsh and the others know what they're doing."

The battle raging below seemed to last for an eternity, but the sun had not moved outside the window when silence descended. Maddie took another step forwards. How soon would Marsh knock at the door?

Something rasped against stone—the metal tips of a gauntlet?—and a voice that sent a tremor through Maddie called out. "I know you're here, Princess."

Seaburn backed away from the door, motioning for her to be quiet.

The warning was not necessary. She could not have made a sound had she tried. Cold sweat stuck her dress to her back, and her heartbeat thundered in her ears. How was Lucas here?

She cut off any further questions, refusing to allow herself to fear the worst. Instead, she listened to the scrape of Lucas's gauntlet draw closer and scrambled for a way out.

The solar had only one entrance, but the bolt was solid and would hold against a single man. The windows? Under normal circumstances, they would be too high to use as an escape without ropes, but could the overgrowth that had reclaimed so much of the castle prove their solution?

She ran over to the nearest, throwing herself across the wide ledge to inspect the wall outside. Only a few stems climbed to their level, none of which would bear her weight, never mind Seaburn's.

A rattle at the door made her jump, and she spun, eyes glued to the handle.

"Open up, Princess. You can't hide in there forever."

The thud of something—someone—hitting the wooden panel followed, another landing a heartbeat after the first. At the third, one of the ancient hinges gave, a piece pinging across the floor, and Lucas let out a dark chuckle from the other side.

Maddie looked to Seaburn, whose expression hardened, though his throat bobbed and sweat darkened his hairline. He drew his sword and planted himself between her and the door.

Lucas slammed into it again, and a second hinge gave way. One more and he would be inside.

"Stand aside, Princess Madeline," Seaburn said, hefting his weapon.

She backed up, bumping into the table, her breath caught in her chest. There was no doubt in her mind who would win the impending fight, and then what? Would Lucas kill her too?

The door crashed inwards, and she closed her eyes against a billow of dust, covering her face with her arm.

Lucas surged forwards before it cleared, a growl vibrating through the air around her. His sword met Seaburn's, the rasp of metal grating her raw nerves. They clashed twice more and then a wet thrunk overtaken by a pained grunt told her it was over.

She looked up in time to see Seaburn's body slump to the ground, his knees hitting the floor first and his torso following a moment later. Her husband stood over her guard, his sword stained red, his chest heaving beneath his dragonhide armour.

He scanned the room, and when his eyes found hers, he eased his hold on the deadly blade and straightened. He sauntered forwards, and the nonchalance with which he stepped over Seaburn's legs brought a surge of bile to Maddie's throat. She scrambled away from him, putting the table between them.

"Please, Lucas. Don't do this. This isn't what you want."

"No?" He cocked his head to the side, appearing in no rush now they were alone. "Then what do I want?"

She wanted to say peace—from the burdens of his rule, from the guilt of his brother's and father's deaths, from the torment of the curse—but the words refused to form. Did he really want those things, or did she only wish that was the case?

In truth, they had spent such a short time together, she did not know. Was he the infamous Wolf who cut down his enemies without a moment's thought, or was he the man who hated to lose at Knights, apologised all afternoon for hurting her, and curled around her in his sleep? She stared into his cold eyes, begging that man to come back to her.

"Ah. You thought you could get close to me?" He sneered. "That we'd fall in love and rule together?"

She shook her head, though that was exactly what she had hoped.

"Or did you always intend to betray me?" He ran his tongue across his teeth. "Garricon root wasn't the wisest choice of drug."

Her back hit the wall. "It's not like that. I was—"

"You were stealing my signet ring. To do what? Take over my realm as revenge for taking yours?" His tone still bordered on conversational, but a sharp edge lurked beneath the casual veneer.

"No. I..." How could she explain? How could she get through to him when every time she tried, she failed?

"Well, now I have what I want." A wicked gleam turned the silver in his eyes molten. "So, thank you for that."

He shoved the table aside and moved in, leaving nowhere for her to retreat. The thought of dying at his hand was worse than the prospect of death itself. Would he regret slaying her? Would he even remember it?

She wished she could hug her sisters one last time and tell them how much she loved them. She wished she could have found a way to break the curse. But she could not bring herself to wish she had never met the Wolf, even now.

Tears blurred her vision, but she lifted her chin. If this was her fate, she would meet it head on. There was little else she could do.

"I'm not afraid of you," she whispered.

He raised his arm, sword steady in his grip, and growled, "You should be."

Her heart squeezed, and she closed her eyes, waiting for the blow that would end her life. *Goodbye, Lucas*, she thought. *I love you*.

Chapter 30

Maddie

Something whistled through the air, and Lucas hissed sharply, but nothing pierced Maddie's flesh. She opened one eye and peeked up at him, then straightened, the other popping open too.

A line of blood welled across the curve of his bicep below his shoulder armour, and he no longer faced her. She followed his gaze to the doorway, where Joss stood with an arrow nocked and pointed at him. Maddie's heart tripped over itself—what was she doing there?

"Get away from my sister," Joss said.

Lucas glanced down at his arm. "Or what? You'll scratch me with more arrows? I doubt you have it in you to kill me."

"No, but I do." Tristan pushed past Joss into the room, sword drawn, expression grim. "I told you to wait for me," he said over his shoulder, not taking his eyes from Lucas.

"It's a good thing I didn't. He was going to kill Maddie."

"I still am," Lucas said, transferring his sword to his other hand. "Only now I'll have to kill you too."

Tristan snorted. "No, you won't."

As he stalked forwards, Joss skirted the wall, her bow at the ready. Maddie's feet turned to stone, her legs to jelly, and her stomach to a sea of acid. Three of the people she loved most in the world were in danger because of her. It was her worst nightmare brought to life.

She clenched her hands so tightly her fingernails dug into her palms, and her eyes flicked between the men and her sister, unable to decide where to land.

Blades swung, met, pivoted, and swung again. The clangs and rasps reverberated around the room, ringing in Maddie's ears and echoing through her core as Tristan circled around and pushed Lucas away from her.

Her heart stuttered with each grunt of pain, and though she could not see any of the wounds inflicted, occasional splashes of crimson drew her eyes to the floor where the evidence of the fight stained the dust. She looked back up and prayed for it to end before either of them was seriously injured.

Lucas's strikes lost some of their precision and power as blood soaked his right sleeve, and Tristan took full advantage. He attacked Lucas's weakened side with a barrage of blows, forcing him towards Seaburn's body at the same time.

Swords flashed. Lucas stumbled. And within a heartbeat, Tristan had his blade to Lucas's neck.

"Drop your sword," he growled.

Joss sprang forwards, bow aimed at Lucas from the other side, and though a snarl curled his lips, he threw his weapon to the ground.

Maddie sagged against the wall and heaved in a breath. Her chest ached, and her brain refused to function, but none of that mattered. It was over.

"Maddie." Tristan called her name as if not for the first time. "Are you well?"

She looked up, stunned to find Parker binding Lucas's hands. When had she arrived? Lucas pinned Maddie with a malicious smirk and said, "This won't hold me forever, Princess."

A shiver coursed over her skin as Tristan shoved Lucas into the nearest wall and trained his sword on the hollow at the base of Lucas's neck. "Try it."

Lucas chuckled, his throat bobbing against the blade pressed to it. "You must be enjoying this, Captain." He eyed his wounded arm. "That's the only reason you beat me, you know."

They stared at each other for a moment, tension thickening the air around them. Then Tristan leaned forwards and said, "Make one move towards her and I'll cut your throat, curse or not."

Lucas's entire face wrinkled. "Curse? What curse?"

Maddie started. He truly was not aware of it? She stepped closer to ask, but Joss tackled her in a hug so fierce it drove all else from her mind.

"I was so worried about you," Joss said into her hair. "Lucas had already gone when Tristan got to your room. We didn't think he'd be able to track you so fast, but—"

"We?" Tristan made a disgusted sound. "If I'd seen you sneaking out, you'd be back in the north tower with your sister."

Joss pulled out of the hug. "Someone had to warn Maddie he escaped the palace."

One hand on her sister's arm, Maddie placed herself between them and asked, "Is Olivia safe?"

His expression softened. "Of course she is. I've got guards posted throughout the palace, and every entrance is locked down. But what about you?" He scanned her from head to toe. "Are you well?"

"Yes." Her eyes landed on Seaburn's body. "I'm unharmed."

Tristan moved to block her view, and blood on his right trouser leg caught her attention.

"Oh. You're not, though." She tried to inspect the rest of him, but he fended her off.

"I'm fine. It's just a couple of scratches."

She studied him through narrowed eyes but knew well enough that he would never let her tend him, no matter how grave his wounds. Still, he appeared to be able to walk and use his arms, so the cuts could not be too deep.

But Lucas's injury had been more severe. She sidestepped Tristan to get a closer look at her husband's arm, halting at pressure on her elbow.

"I need to talk to him," she said.

Tristan worked his jaw for a long moment, then let go. "Be careful."

She crept towards Lucas, who sat propped against the wall and followed her movements like a predator watched prey.

"What are you going to do now, Princess?" He lifted his bound hands, causing Parker to ready her sword. "We've been here before, and as I recall, it didn't end well for you."

Smoothing a hand down the front of her skirt, she straightened and said, "I didn't know about the curse then."

"Curse," he spat. "You'll say anything to win."

"You don't believe us?" Joss stepped up beside Maddie. "Wait till your ring starts glowing and talks to you." To Maddie, she added in an undertone, "Are you sure it won't come off?"

Maddie knelt next to him and reached for his left hand. He jerked it away from her, only to find bare steel pressed to his neck.

"Give the princess your hand," Parker told him. "Slowly."

He did, and Maddie gripped his finger and began to remove the ring. Bound and held at knife point as he was, he still put up a struggle, curling his fingers into a fist. "You'll never get away with stealing this. At least when I strip my enemies of their possessions, I kill them first."

"Don't tempt me," Tristan mumbled.

Holding Lucas's finger straight with one hand, Maddie tugged the ring with the other. It stopped after the second knuckle again. "See?" she said, showing them all.

She was about to release it when something strange happened. One of her fingers touched the tip of his, and the ring slid a fraction closer to the end. She dropped his hand and sat back, her eyes jumping to his. Had he noticed the additional movement?

He stared at his ring as if it had turned into a snake. "What is this?" he asked. "What've you done to my ring?"

While Tristan fired questions at him and Joss paced, Maddie tended her husband's wounds as best she could, doing her utmost to ignore the venomous looks he cast her way. When she was finished, she stood and stared down at the dragon stone. What if…?

Her mind circled the spark of an idea, nothing quite catching light until suddenly, it did. It seemed ridiculous, preposterous even, but as the solution settled in her mind, it burned through the tangle of her fears and doubts, leaving behind a clear path and a sense of calm she had not felt for a long time.

"I can transfer the ring," she said. "Take the curse from him."

"What?" several voices said at once.

She looked around. Horror etched Joss's features, confusion Tristan's, and suspicion marked Lucas's stony countenance. With a beckoning gesture for her sister and friend to follow, Maddie walked past the broken door and out to the landing, where they could talk with a little more privacy. But where to start? She gazed through the window at the treetops surrounding the castle, the sun dappling their upper leaves in lighter shades of green.

"When Papa first fell ill, I was terrified of taking over. I thought ruling well meant being perfect—staying in control, not making any mistakes, fixing every problem myself—but it doesn't. I know that now." She turned to face them. "It's about being willing to make sacrifices for the sake of the whole."

Joss narrowed her eyes. "What does that mean?"

"It means our people are the most important thing, and to save them, we need Lucas—the real Lucas." Maddie glanced through the doorway at her husband, hands bound, head bowed low. "So I'm going to make sure he's free to help us."

"How?" Tristan asked.

Straightening, she took a steadying breath. "By transferring the ring to me."

The silence that greeted her statement lasted a single heartbeat.

"Have you lost your mind?" Joss cried a fraction ahead of Tristan saying, "Then let me do it."

Maddie shook her head. "I know exactly what I'm doing, and it has to be me. The two of you know the palace better than anyone, and you can both fight if it comes to that. I can't. But I *can* distract whoever's behind all this while you find a way to stop them." She clenched her hands around the fabric of her skirts. "I'm trusting you to help me save our kingdom. If you work with Lucas, I know you can find out who cursed him and catch them before they do any more damage."

Tristan's jaw tightened. "I don't know, Maddie," he said, his voice low and serious. "What if they hurt you?"

"Or make you do something terrible?" Joss added, her brows bunching together. "How can you even think about giving up your freedom, control of your own body?"

"Because it's the best way to save our people." Maddie lifted her chin. "Besides, I don't think they'll hurt me. More likely they'll try to use me as they have Lucas, which is why I can't rule."

She faced Joss and raised her voice for all to hear. "Jocelyn Dalbot, I'm passing the authority of our father, King Johnathan the Second, to you. From this point on, you stand as his proxy, and your word supersedes any orders I may issue. Creator and all who can hear, bear witness to my vow."

Joss backed away, face blanching, eyes wild, but Maddie grasped her hands and gave them a squeeze. "I know you can do this, Joss. I need to know the kingdom's safe from the curse, and I trust you to do the right thing."

Before anyone could stop her or try to change her mind, she walked back into the solar, knelt beside Lucas, and reached for his hands. She could feel his eyes on her as she slid the ring over his first knuckle, but she dared not look up. He allowed her to touch the tip of her finger to his, and with a tremulous breath and damp palms, she pushed the ring off his hand and onto hers.

Chapter 31

Maddie

As soon as the ring left Lucas's finger, he slumped forwards, his head lolling on his chest. Maddie stilled, half expecting… what? She had no idea what to expect, aside from the ring to glow red at some point and the curse to force her to its will. In the meantime, she felt nothing.

No tingling, no wash of power, no voice in her head—no change whatsoever as far as she was aware.

"Lucas?" She touched his shoulder, gave it a little shake, but he made no response. An icy shiver ran down her spine. Had removing the ring hurt him? She placed her hand on his chest and relaxed when it rose and fell in a steady rhythm under her palm. Asleep, not dead. Hopefully, he would wake soon, free of the curse.

She looked down at the ring. The wolf's head engraved on the dragon stone stared back at her from her fourth finger. It was heavier than the simple band below it that she had donned on her wedding day, and the metal was warm. Was the heat from Lucas's finger or the curse? She was about to try removing it when Joss appeared at her shoulder.

"Oh, Maddie," she said, tears in her voice. "What did you do? Will it come off?"

She tried to grab Maddie's hand, and Maddie batted her away. "Stop it. You're knocking me over." She held out her other arm. "Here. Help me up."

Joss pulled her to her feet and immediately reached for her hand again. Twisting away from her, Maddie held it out of reach but slid the ring up her finger in full view of everyone. It stopped at her second knuckle.

She swallowed.

When she gave it a little yank, her finger twinged as if she had pulled it instead. Had Lucas felt that when she had tried to tug it from his hand? She glanced down at his still form, glad that he was free of it. Then she pushed the ring back into place and pasted a smile on her face.

"All is well, Joss. I feel no different than before."

Joss eyed her dubiously. "Maybe it takes a while to take effect."

"Or it only works on Lucas," Tristan said from the doorway.

"Or it doesn't fully activate until the person uses the control stone?" Maddie offered. "We might catch them before then."

"Do you think they know it's changed hands?"

Joss pointed between Maddie and Lucas, and Maddie paused. She had not thought of that. Still, Tristan had the entire palace under guard, preventing whoever was behind the curse from acting on the knowledge, and it was too late to undo it now.

He walked over from the doorway and nudged Lucas's leg with the toe of his boot. "What now?"

Maddie fought the urge to get between the two men. "We wait for Lucas to wake up and find out what he knows about the curse and the person behind it. He must know something that can help us. Then we go back to Faerstolmere, capture them, and make them undo it."

"That simple, eh?"

She cringed at the doubt in his voice but lifted her chin to look him squarely in the eye. "That simple. I'm sure I'm far enough away to be safe for now, and if the curse activates before we get back, I have every faith you'll save me from it. It just means working together."

He let out a long sigh, cast a glance at Lucas, and nodded. "We'd better get settled then. Parker."

"Yessir."

"Take the princesses up to the roof for some fresh air."

Maddie frowned. "But we—"

"There are bodies downstairs—and here"—he flicked his eyes in the direction of Seaburn's body—"that we need to deal with. Best you not be around to see any of that."

Her stomach flipped over on itself. "O-of course."

The sight of one guard's corpse had been bad enough, and she had tried not to look too closely at his remains. She could not bring herself to imagine the scene that awaited them in the great hall.

"Are you coming, Joss?" she said.

"If I must," Joss said. "I'd rather spend the time hunting, but the roof's better than being cooped up in here."

Parker snorted. "Not using your new position to force our hands then?"

Joss visibly shuddered. "Don't even jest about that." She jerked a finger at Maddie. "Maddie's still in charge, unless the curse gets her."

Unless. Maddie chewed her lower lip. Something told her the more appropriate word might be 'until'.

They shared a simple meal of grouse and bread in the great hall, studiously ignoring the grass-covered stains on the floor. Despite the horrific events of the day and the emotional toll they had taken, Maddie ate her fill, picking the bones clean and licking the juice from her fingers. She briefly wondered whether the curse had increased her appetite but shied away from thinking too deeply in that direction.

When the remains had been cleared and guards chosen for the first watch of the evening, she retired to the room where she had slept the previous night and made space for Joss to join her.

"How long d'you think it'll be before he's awake?" Joss asked, exploring a few nooks and crannies along one wall.

Maddie lifted her eyes to the ceiling. "I don't know."

"What if he never wakes up?" Her sister's voice dipped to a whisper. "Like Papa?"

Heart clenching, Maddie tugged her sister down onto her bedroll and wrapped her in a hug. "I don't know," she admitted. "But he's strong—and stubborn. If anyone can recover from being cursed, it's the Wolf of Craeick."

"I suppose so." Joss's lips quirked to the side. "I wouldn't want to be whoever did it when he catches them."

Maddie grimaced. "Neither would I."

Joss leaned back against the outer wall and closed her eyes, pushing some ivy away from her face. It sprang back into place, so she straightened and gave it a tug, but it still did not come free. With a muttered curse that Maddie pretended not to hear, she twisted around and yanked on it with more force, and a stone shifted in the wall. "What in the..."

Turning onto her knees, Joss used her dagger to cut back the ivy and started working the stone loose.

"What are you doing?"

"There's something here."

Maddie frowned at her sister's back. "Yes, the outside. This place is covered with ivy that's grown through the walls. Leave it alone."

"No, this is something else... Aha." She pulled the stone free, bringing a small shower of crumbled mortar with it, and dropped it to the floor with a dull thud.

One of the guards rapped on the door. "Are you well, Your Highness?"

"Oh, yes," Maddie called out. "No need for alarm."

"We're just looking around." Joss waved dust away from her face. Then she peered into the gap she had made and sat back with a triumphant smile. "See?"

Maddie leaned closer, and sure enough, there was a dark hole where the solid outer layer should have been. Someone had built a hidden compartment into the wall.

Joss got to work on the adjacent stone, which came away much more easily, and she soon cleared an area the size of a small chest. Maddie held the candle nearer, and almost dropped it when she spotted a leather-wrapped bundle hidden amongst a few more strands of ivy and enough cobwebs to make a silk handkerchief.

Joss brushed them away, carefully lifted the bundle out, and set it on the floor between them. "Do you want to open it?" she asked.

And discover the nest of spiders whose webs they had just destroyed? "Go ahead."

The leather was stiff with age and covered with a thick layer of dust, but Joss managed to peel it back without damaging it or setting them both sneezing. A surprisingly well-preserved cloth came next, tied with a leather thong, and within that sat a stack of three ancient books.

Joss picked up the one on top and squinted at the remnants of gold lettering on the cover. "I can't read this."

She laid it aside as Maddie reached for the next. Its title, too, was illegible, so she eased open the cover and studied the first page. Was that the old tongue? Dracestian? She had only studied enough of the archaic languages to understand the history of her kingdom, and never that of the mages.

"What a waste," Joss said, closing the third book with a grimace. "Still, Mouse will love them."

She would. The thought made Maddie smile, despite everything. "Let's take them back for her."

She rewrapped them and set the bundle by the door while Joss replaced the stones and swept the scattering of mortar away from their sleeping mats with her foot. Then they finished readying for bed and crawled under their blankets.

Maddie blew out the candle and closed her eyes, but sleep refused to allow her the comfort of its mindless embrace. A different position offered no relief. Nor did the third or fourth or fifth.

Eventually, she gave up and lay on her back, counting Joss's soft snores and letting her gaze wander the confines of their small room. Silvery moonlight painted silhouettes of the trees outside the window across the opposite wall, and she watched their contours fade and brighten as clouds passed across the moon's face.

She lifted her hand into the light and stared at the cursed ring, ran her finger over the engraved surface. So many questions tumbled through her mind that she could not choose one on which to focus. She needed sleep. Dropping her arm, she shifted onto her right side, facing the wall, closed her eyes again, and imagined a blank void behind her eyelids.

Red seeped through, and they sprang open as she bolted upright.

The ring was glowing.

Her body stilled, invisible fingers of ice sliding under her skin and wrapping around her heart. Then a voice that was not her own crawled into the recesses of her mind, insidious and irresistible.

"Return to the palace as soon as possible after you have finished with the princess."

Something compelled her to repeat the instructions, scoring them into the very fibres of her being. "I will return to the palace as soon as possible after I have finished with the princess."

"Go straight to your rooms when you arrive, and do not let anyone see you on the way back."

"I will go straight to my rooms when I arrive, and I will not let anyone see me on the way back."

The ring's glow faded, leaving the room washed in shadows and moonlight once more. While the voice no longer spoke inside her head, a portion of Maddie's own thoughts echoed it, and a sense of urgency thrummed through her, the cold threads tugging her body to obey. She had nothing to finish with either of her sisters, so she needed to leave.

But how without being seen?

An owl hooted outside, drawing her eye to the window. She crept over to it, careful not to wake Joss or alert the guard at the door, and peered around the immediate area. Silent. Still. She could fit through the opening and make her way to the horses without the guards outside seeing her.

She tied her dagger to her waist, snatched her cloak from the head of her bedroll, and clambered up onto the deep window ledge, cracking her knee on the corner and holding in a cry of pain. A small part of her, the part that was still her, wondered how Joss did these kinds of things, but she managed to swing her legs over the other side and use the overgrowth to shimmy down to the ground.

Her sister still slept soundly inside the room, her light snores carrying through the quiet. What would she think when she woke to find Maddie gone? The thought caused a pang in Maddie's chest, but she had no choice. She needed to get to the palace as soon as possible.

Her legs moved almost of their own volition, taking her into the darkness of the surrounding vegetation and around the castle to the clearing where Midnight and the other horses had been tied. She hid behind a tumbled section of the outer wall until she was certain no guards would see her, then padded over to Midnight and rested her forehead against his muzzle.

"Shhh," she whispered. "We need to go now."

She slipped his lead rope loose and led him away from the castle, down an embankment, and into the night. When they were far enough away that the torches of the perimeter guards were mere pinpricks in the fabric of the forest, she mounted Midnight's bare back and guided him along the moonlit trail that would take them home.

Once they were on their way, she found herself able to think more clearly again, and she tried to resist, to turn back. But it was futile. The full ramifications of her decision to take on the curse struck hard. It had complete control over her and was impossible to deny, taking over her body and planting thoughts as if they were her own, though she knew they were not.

She shuddered as she recalled the cold that had gripped her heart as the voice invaded her mind. Was that what Lucas had experienced each time the ring activated? Her eyes stung at what he must have endured, how he must have railed against it.

Then again, he had not appeared aware of the curse, even immediately after it bent him to another's will. Strange, when she recalled every moment of the encounter, was fully aware of the voice's command. Would she forget over time too? Or had he been compelled to erase it from his mind to protect the person behind it all?

She pondered who would do such a thing to him until the trail ahead stole her attention. It had grown dark, the thick canopy and a mass of clouds overhead conspiring to smother the moon's light. She peered into the inky depths of the forest, grateful for Midnight's superior vision as they picked their way across the unfamiliar terrain.

By the time they emerged into open countryside, fatigue weighed on her limbs as emphatically as the curse, and Midnight's steady gait soon lulled her eyelids closed. He shook his body, and she jerked upright, tightening her grip on his lead rope. Curse or not, if she did not stop to rest soon, she could fall from his back and hurt herself.

A tug at her core urged her to keep going, and she clenched her jaw. Did 'as soon as possible' really mean putting herself in danger? She fought against it, mentally screaming that it was madness to ride when she was so weary.

And the impossible happened.

Something gave way in the darkness of her mind, as if in pushing against the hard surface of the curse, she had finally found its edge. Though it still urged her onwards, the insistence dulled enough that she was able to dismount and find a place to sleep for a while.

She tied Midnight to a nearby tree and curled up on the grass at its base. At first light, she would resume her journey and reach the palace by mid-afternoon. Then she would finally come face to face with her enemy—one who had complete control over her.

With that thought hounding her mind, she huddled into the folds of her cloak and fell into an exhausted, nightmare-filled sleep.

Chapter 32

Luc

Luc woke to a headache the size of a mountain and a pain in his chest that made him question whether he had been skewered on said mountain by the sharp talons of a dragon. Why did everything hurt so much? He had been…

What had he been doing? Fuzzy bits and pieces came to him—a castle, a swordfight, flashes of dark brown hair, and the scent of sandalwood mixed with a coppery tang. Nothing that formed a complete or sensible picture.

He shifted, peeling his eyes open and focusing them on the moonlit outline of a dusty wooden floorboard an inch from his nose. Another twist of his body told him his wrists were bound, the hemp rope taut against his skin, and his right arm and left leg throbbed independently of his head.

Voices drifted from somewhere beyond his feet, and he shut his eyes, pouring what little focus he had into making them out.

"I still think we should go straight after her," a familiar female voice said, drawing nearer.

"And I said we need to know what we're riding into. Bad enough she was able to leave because I made assumptions and didn't guard her properly. We'll never catch her before she reaches the palace, so we need to find out as much as we can before we do anything rash. Look at me."

There was a pause before the deep, male voice spoke again. "I hate it too, but we can't help her if we don't know all the facts. They won't hurt her before we get there."

"You really believe that?"

"I have to."

Another pause, and the young woman said, "Come on, then."

Footsteps approached as Luc finally placed the voices. The man was Tristan Kaar, Captain of Tyrrath's royal guard, and the woman was one of the princesses, though which one eluded him. Now he only needed to determine where the three of them were and what they were all doing there.

A hand shook his shoulder, causing him to tense, as light bled through his eyelids and warmed the side of his face.

"Good, you're awake," the princess said from just above his head.

He opened his eyes again, wincing at the increased pressure in his brain. The captain lit more torches, brightening the area to a painful degree, as she stepped away and folded her arms.

"Are you yourself?" she asked.

Luc looked between them, pushed himself upright, and took a moment to lean his battered skull against the cool wall behind him. "Who else would I be?" he rasped.

"An evil monster?" the princess—Jocelyn—muttered.

When he looked up at her, brow furrowed, she rolled her eyes and said, "You betrayed us, broke the treaty, stole our people for your army—"

"I did?" He thought back, but his head buzzed, and large sections of his memory were blurred.

"Yes," the captain said. "And you tried to kill Princess Madeline."

He had?

Luc searched the recesses of his mind, and the weeks and months came rushing back in a flood. The invasion, his capture, their bargain, his wife—so many good memories of her—his betrayal. He closed his eyes. He *had* tried to kill her. But why? His stomach recoiled as the rest of the night's events slotted into place, and he forced his gaze to his left hand, to his naked little finger.

"You remember," Jocelyn said.

He had been cursed? He swallowed hard. What had he been forced to do? How many of his decisions as king had been at the behest of another? Acid boiled up his throat. Had he endangered his people because of it?

"How long?" he whispered.

"What?"

He caught and held her eyes. "How long was I cursed?"

She winced but did not look away. “We don’t know. At least a week before the spring festival.” Her voice dropped low. “Probably a lot longer.”

A chasm opened in his gut, but he nodded. He glanced back at his finger. Madeline had freed him. He had betrayed her, tried to kill her, and in return, she had taken the ring, placing herself under the curse to free him from its clutches.

The hole tore through his chest, decimating his heart. Why would she do that? And how could he ever repay her?

Reluctantly, he met her sister’s gaze. He would not blame her for seeking revenge, would gladly accept whatever she did to him if it would end the agonising nightmare he had woken into.

She stared down at him, hands on hips, lips pursed for a single, agonising heartbeat. Then she lashed him with questions, speaking so fast they landed on top of each other with no time for him to think between one and the next.

Captain Kaar placed a hand on her shoulder and said, “Slow down, Joss. Let him answer.”

Rather than thank his erstwhile adversary, Luc forced his mind to focus on her initial questions. “I don’t remember much about the curse, and I have no idea who’s behind it.”

“Well, who’s had access to your ring?” she asked.

“No one.”

She opened her mouth, but again, the captain stopped her, allowing Luc to explain.

"I've had that ring since I was twelve years old. After—" He swallowed, his mouth dry. "After the accident, Gabriel—Lord Ross—had the ring retrieved from my father's body. I think Rhee was the one to find it. She was always one of our best climbers.

"Anyway, they brought it back to Lochanack, and Friar Utham put it on my finger as part of the coronation ceremony. I've not taken it off since, so I don't understand how anyone could have cursed it."

Jocelyn flung her hands up. "Then we're just wasting time here."

"No." The captain scratched his jaw. "Maybe we're going about it the wrong way. Do you remember talking to anyone before you followed Madeline here?"

Luc thought back, ignoring the pain that stabbed between his temples. "The last person I remember was Rhee. I bumped into her on my way out."

He had told her to find Aiden and prepare to leave for the border, but given the way the captain's jaw ticced, Luc did not deem it wise to share that information.

"Rheann Braydeson." Jocelyn faced the captain. "It could be her. She was on our list of suspects."

"No." Luc shook his head despite the pain. "I don't believe it. I've known Rhee since we were children. Aiden and I saved her from— Well, a bad situation. She'd never hurt either of us."

Jocelyn spun on him, her eyes sharp as daggers. "But she'd hurt us. Would she use you to do it?"

He paused, just for a moment. "No. It must be someone else."

"Who else did you see yesterday?" Captain Kaar asked.

"Gabriel, I think. A couple of servants… I don't really remember."

His interrogators exchanged looks.

"Did any of them have a black stone like the one in your ring?" Jocelyn asked. "With the same engraving?"

Luc glanced down at his left hand, half expecting to see his ring there. Another one like it? Surely not. It had passed through twelve generations of his family. He shook his head, and she dismissed him with a click of her tongue.

"Never mind. We'll find out which one of them's behind it when we find Maddie."

His head snapped up. "What do you mean, 'when you find her'? Where is she?"

Captain Kaar answered, his tone dripping with displeasure. "She took her horse and snuck out in the middle of the night. We assume she's been summoned back to the palace by the curse."

"She what? How did she get past you? Did you not have a guard on her?"

The captain ground his jaw. "I don't answer to you. The only reason I'm still here is because I needed to see what you know before I set out."

Luc was too concerned about his wife to take umbrage. "Then what are we waiting for? We need to go after her."

He attempted to rise, the feat made more difficult by his bonds, the injuries to his leg and shoulder, and the dragon-spawned weakness pervading his body. But he could not sit still and do nothing, not while his wife—his brave, reckless Madeline—was riding into danger. The thought of her suffering for his sake sickened him.

He stilled at the rasp of a knife being drawn, looked up at Jocelyn stalking towards him. He would not blame her if she wanted to vent her rage on him. It was his fault her sister was in this mess, his fault so many of her people were dead. But he was the Wolf of Craeick. He lifted his head and met her gaze unflinchingly as she dropped to a crouch by his knees.

She pointed the knife at him, and said, "If you hadn't been cursed at the time, I'd hate you for everything you've done."

Then she cut his bonds.

Slowly, he gained his feet and tested his injured leg, which complained when he put weight on it but would hold. He glanced at the captain, who smirked, though bandages poked out from the top of his left gauntlet and through a slice in his trouser leg.

"We should get Bronwen to heal your wounds when we reach the palace." Jocelyn looked between them. "I have a feeling you'll both need to be at full strength if we're going to get Maddie back."

The captain nodded and left the room, calling for his subordinates to break camp, but instead of following him out, Jocelyn stepped into Luc's path. She studied his face so intently it would have made a lesser man flinch.

Eventually, she spoke, and the amusement lacing her question suggested she already had her answer. "You care about my sister, don't you?"

Mention of Madeline brought with it images of an insidious voice bending her to its will, and he clenched his jaw. The thought of her being in danger sent a shard of ice through his chest, but the memory of holding her in his arms, fuzzy as it was, melted him.

He met her sister's eyes. Dragons take him if he was going to discuss his feelings with a slip of a girl who enjoyed taunting him at every turn. Especially not before he had fully examined them himself. "That's between me and my wife."

"Thought so." A grin slid across her face as she spun around and walked out. Before he could catch up, she threw over her shoulder, "And you'd better send a message to your second to stand down the invasion of Brunland too."

He fisted his hands at the reminder of what he had done while under the curse's influence. Yes, he would do that. And he would find whoever had set him on this course and make them pay with their lives.

Chapter 33

Maddie

Maddie set out at daybreak the next morning and reached Faerstolmere not long after noon. She managed to remain unseen until she arrived at the hidden gate to the palace, where she encountered two of the additional guards Tristan had posted. They let her straight through, and as she made her way into the main building, past two more guards, and up to her chambers, she wondered why the curse had not compelled her to avoid them.

Was it because she was no longer 'on the way' but had arrived? If the wording of the instructions allowed room for interpretation, had Lucas been able to work around the ring's compulsion as well? And if so, how much of what he had done was the curse and how much was simply the Wolf of Craeick?

She put the questions aside as she approached the door to her room. She had more urgent things to worry about, such as how long it would take for the person behind the curse to come for her, who it might be, and how they might react to finding her instead of her husband. Sucking in a deep breath, she reminded herself to trust the others. They would save Tyrrath, no matter what happened next. That was why she had sacrificed herself for Lucas.

Fingers trembling despite the curse, she twisted the handle, pushed the door open, and walked inside.

"Lucas. There you are. I've been wai—"

Lord Ross turned from the window and froze. He recovered quickly and, with a glance behind her, bowed low. When he rose, a smile lifted his bearded cheeks. "Apologies, Your Highness. I was looking for Lucas."

Her body stilled, the curse no longer urging her forwards, but her skin prickled as she stared at him. Why was he here? And why had he assumed she was Lucas?

"You were expecting him." All at once, the pieces fell into place, and she gasped. "It's you. You're the one behind all of this."

"All of what?" He spread his hands. "I'm certainly not the one who locked us inside the palace."

She walked farther into the room and lifted her left hand.

His eyes trailed from hers to the ring, and his jaw fell slack. He stepped forwards, his arm rising, but stopped by the farthest fireside chair and gripped the backrest. "What did you do?"

"I transferred the curse to me."

Several emotions flitted across his features too fast for her to follow. His fingers tightened on the chair, the knuckles turning white, and Maddie shrank back from the darkness in his eyes. After an endless moment, he scraped a hand across his bearded jaw and blew out a breath, his expression restored to his usual pleasant mask.

"Well, my dear. It seems we have much to discuss, starting with how you came by Lucas's signet ring."

He reached into his waist pouch and removed a small black stone, rubbing it between his fingers. Her ring started to glow, and she swallowed as a frisson of fear coursed through her. Before he could invade her mind and force her to his bidding, she asked, "Why? Why would you do this? Were you trying to take the throne for yourself?"

His fingers stilled, and the glow around her hand dimmed. "Creator's breath, no. I'm just ensuring Lucas does what's best for Craeick."

"Best for Craeick?"

"Yes." His voice hardened. "For centuries, my people have bled and died defending the other realms from the dangers of the northern dragons, and in return, we were given scraps while you grew rich and fat, and left to fend for ourselves when things got too hard. Well, no more. Thanks to me, Lucas has made Craeick stronger and more powerful than any of you, and we can take what we're owed without begging from anyone."

Pummelled by his vitriol, she backed up a step. "But to curse your king, your own stepson? How could—"

"It isn't a *curse*," he spat. "It helps me guide him, ensures he listens to my advice. And now, thanks to you, our connection's broken."

He spun away from her, and she remained silent while he paced, afraid of his reaction should she attempt to speak again. He had revealed far more than she had expected, far more than she could take in.

When he turned back to her, a dangerous gleam lit his eyes, though he shook a playful finger at her. “I admit this is a surprise. But I think that together, we can make it work even better than my original plan.”

He offered her a wide smile and activated his stone.

Red washed the room as cold hands gripped her body and held it in place, and his voice slid inside her head. She heard it through her ears at the same time as it echoed through her mind, and as before, she was powerless to disobey.

“Tell me everything you know about Lucas and the curse, including who else is aware of it and any plans they might have to thwart my goals.”

“I will tell you everything I know about Lucas and the curse…” Time stood still while she did. She left nothing out, even the details of her and Lucas’s time together and the fact that she loved him. The voice wanted it all.

“Answer me. Does he love you as well?”

“I thought so, but I am not certain.”

The voice was silent for some time, and the hold on her body and mind loosened enough for horror to seep through. She had told him everything, putting Lucas, Tristan—her sisters—in danger. Her vision swam, and salty tears rolled down her face, past the corners of her mouth, and gathered at her jaw.

“Stop that, now,” the voice demanded.

"I will stop that now." She blinked away the moisture in her eyes, swiping a hand over her chin to collect those droplets already spent.

The voice's grip on her tightened again as a whisper slithered through her mind that it was pleased, that it could use what she had told it.

"Come with me, and tell any guards we meet to let us pass."

"I will come with you and tell any guards we meet to let us pass."

He walked towards the door, and her legs followed of their own accord.

"Good. You will follow every instruction I give you without hesitation."

"I will follow every instruction you give me without hesitation."

He pocketed the control stone, and the red light winked out. She waited for his command, ready to do whatever he asked, her body tensing with the need to obey.

"Come," he said, opening the door and ushering her through.

She walked along the corridor beside him, past the two guards at the end, whom she told to stand down, and around to the main staircase. When they reached the bottom, Lord Ross led her past several more guards to the council chamber and opened the door for her to precede him inside. She stepped into the spacious room and waited at the near end of the long table where she met with the great lords of the land.

"Bring your father's signet ring to me," Lord Ross said. "And some paper, quills, and ink."

Maddie hurried to the cabinet hidden behind a tapestry in the corner of the room. She had not been able to bring herself to wear her father's ring while he lay in his sick bed upstairs, so she had kept it there, along with a few other valuable items, ready to seal official documents when necessary.

"This is so much easier than the way I've had to deal with Lucas," Lord Ross said conversationally as he rounded the table and pulled out her seat. "I could never be so direct with him, but there's no need to hide anything from you, and I find I rather like it."

Inside her head, part of her screamed that this was wrong, that she should not be at his beck and call, but the rest of her, the part that controlled her actions and speech, cared not. There was no alternative but to obey his directives. Her body hummed with the need to comply.

She placed the ring on the table before Lord Ross and gathered the writing implements.

"Sit," he said when she returned, and she did. "Now, we're going to create some binding documents together. I will write them, and you will sign and seal each one, passing those that require urgent action to the guards outside. Do you understand?"

"Yes, Lord Ross."

He sat beside her, his lips pressed together. "I think you should call me Gabriel, seeing as we'll be working closely together from now on."

"Very well, Gabriel."

"Good. Now, let's begin."

He opened the ink pot and started writing, his hand neat and precise. The words flowed across the page, and he soon handed her the first sheet to sign. It was an edict ceding control of Tyrrath's forces to Lucas.

She did not understand why Gabriel would make her sign such a thing when he knew she had passed her rule to Joss. Her sister would be able to undo it within a day. Still, she moved automatically, adding her name, then dripping wax at the bottom and pressing her father's signet into it.

Setting it aside to give to Lucas later, she picked up the next document—an order for the capture of Jocelyn Dalbot and Tristan Kaar for the act of treason. She scanned the page even as her hand signed her name and reached for the wax to seal it, and what she read made the part of her that was still aware want to weep.

Gabriel had blamed her flight from the palace on them, had claimed—in her name—that they had conspired to take the throne from her, backed in their attempt by a Brunnish faction, because they did not approve of her alliance with Craeick. He had even included the 'preposterous' claim they were spreading that she wore a cursed ring and had freely given control of Tyrrath to Joss to prevent the kingdom falling into an evil mage's hands. If either of them recounted that story, the edict stated, it should be taken as a sign of their guilt by anyone who doubted the charges.

They were to be captured on sight and taken to the palace dungeon to await punishment. Their hostage,

Lucas, who had set out after them to free his beloved bride, was to be brought to the great hall.

She rose to deliver the decree to the nearest guard, but Gabriel stopped her with a hand on her forearm. He passed her two more notes, and she sank back onto her seat to sign them. One was a simple note requesting Olivia's presence. The other was a summons from him for some of his men, with an addendum from her instructing the palace guard to allow them through.

"That's all for now," Gabriel said. "When you've dealt with those, ask for a light meal to be served in the great hall and join me there."

"Yes, Gabriel."

Rising once more, she walked to the door leading to the entrance hall and reached for the handle.

"Oh, and Madeline…"

She stopped at his voice, and the ring glowed, painting the oak door the colour of new wine, pinning her in place, and pushing his next instructions straight into her head.

"Make the guards believe this version of events. Do not contradict anything you have signed."

"I will make the guards believe this version of events. I will not contradict anything I have signed," she repeated, the words becoming true as they seeped into her mind and body.

"Good."

The glow faded, and the ring's hold on her muscles loosened. She slumped forwards, catching herself against the solid door, then opened it and walked over to the nearest guard.

"I need these missives delivering."

"I'll see to it, Your Highness."

She handed him the papers, the proclamation of her sister's treason on top. He gave it a cursory glance, looked again, and gaped at her.

"Are you certain, Ma'am?"

Her face crumpled into a pained expression. "I'm afraid so. I wish it weren't true, but Joss and Tristan deceived us all. They're most likely on their way back here and must be captured at once, before they can cause any more harm."

The guard straightened. "Yes, Ma'am. I'll see the watch commander gets this at once."

"Thank you. And when you've done that, please ask one of the kitchen maids to bring a cold platter to the great hall, and some soup if they have any on hand. I've not yet broken my fast."

"Right away, Ma'am."

He jogged across the entrance hall, his boots thudding against the marble and his scabbard jangling at his side. The guard that had been on duty with him stood to attention, jaw set, lips pressed into a grim line. She gave a curt nod as Maddie turned and headed for the great hall, and Maddie could only reciprocate.

Gabriel waited for her at the high table. "Join me."

He gestured towards her usual place, and her legs took her across the hall, up onto the dais, and around to the decoratively carved chair. She slid onto the padded seat as bid, sitting stiffly upright, fingers clutched together in her lap.

"Don't worry, my dear," he said, his gaze dropping to her hands. "We'll get rid of those troublesome elements soon enough, and when Lucas returns, everything can go back to normal.

"I admit, I worried about your influence on him when I first heard of your marriage—that's why I suggested he avoid you as soon as I was within range—but there's no need for that now. The two of you can live happily together for the rest of your lives if that's what he wishes."

The part of Maddie that could think for herself wondered how, when only one of them could be controlled? Surely Gabriel knew she would never stop fighting him unless he took her memory of the curse.

He must have read her thoughts, for he fished in his pouch and pulled out a second ring, holding the dragon stone up to the light. Crimson threads swirled beneath the surface, and her stomach turned to lead.

"You didn't think I'd come all this way without a backup, did you?"

Chapter 34

Maddie

Two rings. Gabriel had two cursed rings. Maddie closed her eyes as he tucked the second back inside his pouch. How could they ever defeat him now? The others were walking into a trap, and there was nothing she could do to stop it. She would have cried had the curse not been preventing her from shedding any more tears.

She sat beside him, powerless to even move without his say so, her conscious mind flitting about its cage. Her only hope, slim though it was, was that Lucas would refuse to submit and would choose to save them as well as himself.

The servants' door opened, interrupting her spiralling thoughts, and a couple of kitchen maids entered bearing a platter of cold meats, cheese, bread, and preserved ryllfruits, a tureen of vegetable soup, and a carafe of wine with two goblets. Maddie pushed a smile onto her face lest they notice something amiss and Gabriel punish them for it.

They set the food on the table and poured a goblet of wine each for her and Gabriel, then stepped back and bobbed matching curtseys. "Would you like anything else, Your Highness?" the taller girl asked.

"No, that will be all, thank you," Maddie said.

Despite having missed breakfast and lunch, she only picked at the platter, her appetite non-existent, but as soon as they had gone, Gabriel said, "Eat your fill. You should be grateful for the food you have in Tyrrath."

She immediately unsheathed the dagger Lucas had gifted her and speared a piece of pork, dipping it in the fruit juices before taking a large bite. Inside, her soul cried yet again for her loss of control.

A short while later, when her stomach was full and only a few scraps of the food remained, she sat back in her chair and returned her dagger to its sheath at her waist. Gabriel drained the last of his soup and smacked his lips as he plonked the bowl on the table.

"Delicious. I'm going to enjoy living in the lowlands."

Maddie had no chance to respond, for the doors at the end of the hall swung open and a group of six Craeickish soldiers walked in, hardened warriors all. They strode down the centre of the room to the high table and stopped a few paces away from the dais, giving Gabriel a smart salute, their right fists thudding against the left breasts of their leather armour.

"You sent for us, milord," the one at the front said. Battle scars criss-crossed his hands, and the lower portion of his right ear was missing.

"Yes. I need you to make sure Lucas comes directly to me as soon as he arrives."

The soldier's thick brows lowered, and he flicked a glance at Maddie.

"Speak freely," Gabriel told him. "She's under my influence."

A smirk flashed across the man's face and was gone. He knew about the curse? "Is the king not also under your control?"

Gabriel made a disgusted sound. "The princess here managed to take his ring, but he'll be with us again soon enough. Go. Keep watch for him, and bring him here the moment he returns."

"Aye, my Lord."

The men turned on their heels and marched from the hall, leaving Maddie's mind racing. How could they know about the curse and do nothing? Were they not loyal to their king?

"I pay them handsomely for their allegiance, and every one of them has benefitted under Lucas's rule," Gabriel said as if discussing the weather. He winked at her. "Another insurance against failure. Just in case he doesn't want to come willingly."

"I—"

He held up a hand, and her mouth closed, though her brain continued to boil at the sheer audacity of his actions.

A short while later, the curtain across the archway to the royal apartments swished aside, and Olivia stepped through, accompanied by Tabitha. Maddie's heart skipped a beat at the sight of her sister, and she pressed damp palms into her skirts beneath the cover of the table, vowing to do all she could to protect her, little though it might be.

"You're back." Olivia surged forwards but faltered as she glanced around. "Where are the others?"

Since Gabriel had not given Maddie leave to speak, her mouth stayed stubbornly shut, but she poured all the assurances she could into her gaze—I'm here. You're not alone. All will be well.

"We have no need of your maid, little one." Gabriel dismissed Tabitha with a wave of his hand, but she looked to Maddie for confirmation.

Maddie nodded her assent. The fewer people caught up in his schemes, the better. She only wished she could shield her sisters from his attention as well.

Tabitha touched Olivia's shoulder and said, "When you've finished with your sister, I'll show you that new embroidery stitch. We can work it into the border on your sage dress."

With a sharp look at Gabriel and a deep curtsey to Maddie, she strode from the room, letting the curtain fall back into place behind her.

"Come, Olivia:" Gabriel stood and rounded the table, beckoning Olivia to join him. "There's no need to be shy."

She glanced at Maddie before walking forwards, arms wrapped around her middle. "What's happening?" she asked, her voice small.

"Exciting things," he replied. "Your sister's going to join Craeick in uniting the kingdoms of Egrea under one banner. Aren't you, my dear?"

"Yes," Maddie said.

Olivia's head whipped around. "What? Why?"

He gestured for Maddie to lift her hand above the table. She did so, and Olivia's eyes bulged when they locked on the signet ring on Maddie's finger. She looked up, the anguish in her gaze turning to horror as the full implications broke over her.

Mouth open, body trembling, she backed away from Gabriel. "You control the ring," she whispered. "You're behind everything."

"That's right. From now on, I'll be able to talk to Lucas *and* Madeline while we carry out our plan." He frowned. "I'm sorry I don't have a ring for you as well, but you'll have to keep our secret without one. Can you do that? Or will I need to make alternative arrangements for you?"

Chapter 35

Luc

Luc rode through the quiet streets of Faerstolmere beside Jocelyn and the captain, the rest of their small company some distance behind. The absence of the city's usual bustle sped their progress but cast an ominous pall over the place, as if the locals knew what stirred in the palace and hid in fear.

Not him. He would ride into the jaws of death and back to save the stubborn, infuriating, reckless woman he was honoured to call his wife. How could she have taken a curse on herself like that? When he found her, he would never let her do such a foolish thing again.

And when he found the person responsible for putting her in danger, the person who had controlled him for so long, he would… His hands tightened on the reins and a growl escaped his throat. Whoever it was would wish they had never heard of Lucas Sinclair by the time he finished with them.

He fed his anger as they wound up the incline to the palace, held onto it like a shield against other, more dangerous, emotions. Guilt and shame over the things he had done while cursed, fear for Madeline and his family—they stalked his thoughts, waiting to slip through his armour and pierce his flesh. But he would not let them.

No. The sharp edge of rage was his best option now, the most useful.

The palace gates were closed when they arrived outside. At their approach, the double guard detail formed up, hands on hilts, faces set in stone.

The captain reined in and murmured, "Let me do the talking."

He dismounted and approached the lead guard on foot, looking back at Luc with a gesture for him to stay put. Luc shrugged and studied the men behind the one in charge. They glanced at each other and shuffled about in a manner that made the hair on the back of Luc's neck stand on end.

"Give me a weapon," he whispered to Jocelyn.

"I don't think so." She walked her mount a few steps forward and dismounted as well.

Luc did not hear what the captain said to the guard, but a moment later, the stout man drew his sword. A chorus of rasps filled the air as the rest of the detail followed his lead and surrounded the captain and Jocelyn.

Luc's hand reached to his hip, only to clasp at empty air. Once more, he cursed the captain for taking his sword. He spurred his horse forward, but the captain called out, "Your Majesty. Don't."

Torn between riding over the guards to get inside and discovering what under the Creator's sun had made them draw weapons on their own leader, Luc pulled up and clenched his jaw. Rushing in without all the facts and a sound strategy got people killed, so he tossed his leg over the back of his horse and swung down to the ground.

"What's the matter, Captain?" he asked, hiding a wince of pain. "Lost control of your troops?"

Any reply the captain might have made was drowned out by the clatter of hooves—the rest of the group from Oslengil arriving. Parker rode at the front, a horse bearing one of the slain men tied to her mount, and when she came level with Luc, she reined in and glared at the guards surrounding the captain and Jocelyn. "How dare you draw swords on the princess!"

"Stand down, Parker," the captain said.

"But Sir!" She slid from her horse, quickly followed by the rest, but halted when he raised his hand at them.

The lead guard stepped forwards. "The captain, um, well…" He grimaced and straightened at the same time. "We have orders to bring the captain and Princess Jocelyn in for, um, for treason."

"What?" Luc, Jocelyn, and several others said at the same time.

The princess snorted. "That's ridiculous. How have we committed treason?"

Eyes on the ground, the guard mumbled, "Conspiring to steal the throne from your sister. Your Highness."

"But she gave me rule over Tyrrath, to save it from the curse she's under. I didn't even want it."

"It's true," the captain said. He gestured to the group beside Luc, who rumbled their agreement. "We were all there. But we're wasting time. Princess Madeline is in grave danger. Let us through so we can sort this out."

A pained look crossed the poor man's face. "I wish you hadn't said that, sir." He turned to his men. "Take them into custody."

They closed in, and the group from Oslengil started to advance but stopped at a command from the captain. Jocelyn, however, struck out at the first guard to approach her, dropping him to the ground and taking his weapon. The rest paused and eyed their leader, who shuffled in place, the point of his sword wavering.

Luc made a disgusted sound in his throat. His men would never fail to apprehend their target. Then again, his men would never go against him. What in the blazes had happened inside the palace?

"Please don't make us fight you," the lead guard begged, though to whom was unclear.

The captain swept his gaze around the group and blew out a breath. He stepped closer to Jocelyn and covered her hand with his, forcing her to lower the stolen weapon.

"Stop now, Joss. This isn't their fault."

"But—"

"We won't resist," he told the guards. "But give me a moment first."

The leader nodded, and the captain strode towards Luc, scattering the others like sheep before a dragon. He closed the distance between them until they stood toe to toe, then angled his body to shield his movements from the guards' view and slid the dagger from his waist.

Straightening, Luc accepted the weapon as the captain whispered, "Save Maddie."

His eyes bore into Luc's, the resolute gaze promising retribution should Luc fail him. Luc nodded, and the captain spun on his heel and marched over to the Oslengil party.

He whispered something to Parker, who gritted her teeth but gave a single nod. She remounted, and at a flick of her hand, the rest of the group did the same, then followed her around the side of the palace walls in the direction of the barracks.

The captain, meanwhile, returned to the waiting guards. Without a word of protest, he handed over his sword and allowed his wrists to be bound.

Jocelyn's protests withered in the face of his steadfast calm, and the guards visibly relaxed as they formed up to escort their prisoners through the gate.

Luc gripped the hilt of the hidden dagger, contemplating how to gain entry without the captain or princess speaking for him. He was about to steal a better weapon when the gates opened and a group of Craeickish soldiers walked out.

They veered in his direction, and for the second time in an hour, the back of Luc's neck prickled. How were they able to move about so freely when the Tyrrathians had locked down Redcairn Palace? Did they have something to do with the captain's capture?

"Your Majesty." The leader gave a perfunctory bow. "We've been asked to escort you inside."

None of the Tyrrathian guards complained, so Luc followed the soldiers through the gate. One step closer to his wife and the dragon-cursed fiend controlling her. As they crossed the courtyard, four of the six men dropped back to surround him, and he absently noted their relative positions and weaponry.

They did not belong to his elite force, but all had seen active service before joining the royal household and appeared at ease in the protective formation. If it came to it, they would be able to help him free Madeline and get her to safety while he roused Aiden and his most trusted troops to battle his nemesis.

Muscles loose and the pain from his injuries barely registering, Luc climbed the steps to the main entrance, confident in his abilities and the dagger hidden within reach.

Chapter 36

Maddie

Tears slid down Olivia's cheeks, and the tremors shaking her limbs tore through Maddie's soul. "It's all right, Mouse," she said, relieved to be able to speak. "Do as he says."

"Please." Olivia sobbed. "Don't hurt Maddie."

Gabriel's head reared back. "Of course I won't. Quite the opposite, in fact. As long as you keep our connection a secret, I intend you all to live for a long time." His eyes narrowed. "But should you need a demonstration of my resolve… Madeline, dear, unsheathe your—"

The doors at the end of the great hall swung open, and Gabriel's men marched in with Lucas between them.

Maddie's heart twisted at the sight. Bad enough that he had been controlled so cruelly from such a young age, he would soon discover that his own stepfather was the one behind it. Worse still, in her attempt to break that hold on him, it seemed she had only tightened the shackles on them both.

If she could have told him to turn around and flee, she would have.

But she could not.

The words stuck in her throat, trapped there by Gabriel's earlier command. All she could do was watch her husband walk towards her, surrounded by men he probably thought were loyal to him.

Thunder clouded his expression, and as they covered the length of the room, his every movement was that of a predator ready to strike. Despite the situation, she swallowed a frisson of fear. Would he unleash his fury on her as well as the one who had cursed him?

It mattered not, and neither did Gabriel's schemes. Lucas was the Wolf of Craeick, and he was no longer bound to another's will. If anyone could save her kingdom, it would be him, even if he could not save her as well.

The group stopped a few strides from the base of the dais where she sat, and Lucas's eyes finally met hers. The molten silver burned with an emotion she could not quite place. Anger? Betrayal? Pain? He blinked, and it was gone, leaving her oddly unsettled.

The rest of his face appeared pale, and blood stained the bandage visible through the hole in his sleeve. Had his wound opened again on the ride back to the capital? Or had he fought to get inside the palace?

Whatever the cause, he needed to be well to stave off Gabriel's attacks. Instinct urged her to go to him, but the curse held her immobile. She would have to find another way.

She tested the bounds of Gabriel's control and found it loose enough for her to voice her concern.

“He needs a healer.” She faced her master. “Please allow Bronwen to tend his wounds.”

He looked at one of the soldiers and flicked a hand in the direction of the side entrance. The man peeled off from the group and hurried through the curtained archway, his footsteps thudding loudly in the otherwise quiet hall.

Lucas’s gaze bounced from her to Gabriel and back, a deep vee etched between his brows. Her stomach writhed as she watched him piece together the truth.

“Gabriel. What are you doing here? I—” His expression flattened, and he continued in a voice edged with ice. “You cursed me.”

Gabriel shook his head. “No. Not cursed—”

Lucas lunged forwards with a curse of his own, but the soldiers on either side of him closed in, capturing him in their strong grip before he had taken more than a single step. He strained against them, snarling and swearing, but quieted when steel rang and one of the men behind him held a sword to his neck while another patted him down and removed a dagger from his waist.

“Then what?” Lucas levelled a fiery glare at his stepfather. “You took my will. Forced me to obey you like a mindless slave.”

Gabriel winced as though struck. “Lucas, no. It wasn’t like that. I made sure you didn’t feel a thing.”

The truth of his words hit Maddie hard. No wonder Lucas showed no emotion to anyone beyond his immediate family. The cold calculation. The ruthlessness. He had not been able to feel anything. For years.

Gabriel stepped down from the dais. “The first instruction I ever gave you was to forget—”

“So you could control me without anyone finding out.” Lucas bucked against his captors, but their grip remained firm.

“I told you, it wasn’t like that,” Gabriel snapped.

“What was it like then? How much of my life was real? How much of my character…”

“Don’t be ridiculous. I would never change who you are.” He exhaled and scrubbed a hand down his face. “I was already advising you. This was just a way of protecting our people’s interests and ensuring you made the right decisions for our future.”

“The right decisions?” Lucas gaped at him, then jerked his chin at Maddie. “You made me invade another kingdom.”

Gabriel clenched his fists. “Yes, and I’d do it again. My family died because they”—he pointed at Maddie—“did nothing. They could’ve sent help—Brunland has more than enough dragons to fly aid in over the mountains, and Tyrrath is rich enough to cover any expenses—but they sat in their fat lowland palaces and let us perish instead. My boy wasn’t even a year old.

“Think what we’ve accomplished together. We’re on the brink of taking it all. Nothing can stop us. I just need you to trust me and wear your ring a little longer.”

Lucas snarled. “Never.”

“Then you leave me no choice.” Gabriel flicked a hand at the men holding Lucas, and they stretched his arms out to the sides, one prising his left hand open. "You will wear the ring, whether I have to force it on you or…" He swivelled his head towards Maddie, his eyes glinting. "Maybe use your wife as leverage."

"Don't you dare touch her."

Lucas jerked against the soldiers' hold, managing to throw one off and swing his fist at the other. The man stumbled backwards, his face bloodied, as Gabriel retreated to the safety of the high table and the others closed in. Blows fell left and right, and though it was four against one, Lucas fought so fiercely that it seemed he might break free—until the man behind him drew a dagger.

He rammed the hilt into Lucas's temple before Maddie could warn him of the danger, and she sucked in air as Lucas fell to one knee.

"That's enough," Gabriel said. "Help him up."

Lucas pushed off the floor unaided and stood to his full height, eyes fixed on his stepfather in a glare sharp enough to pierce a dragon. Fresh blood dribbled down his face and dripped from his stubbled jaw to disappear into the black fabric of his shirt.

Was that why he preferred that colour?

A shudder rippled through her at the stray thought even as she searched for signs of further injuries. She released the breath she had been holding. Aside from a few minor cuts and bruises, he appeared unharmed.

"You sent for me, Your Highness?"

She turned towards the voice and found Bronwen fidgeting with her skirts just inside the entrance leading to the royal apartments. The healer's gaze flitted around the room, alighting on the soldiers surrounding Lucas, Olivia cowering against the wall, Gabriel standing beside Maddie at the high table.

Her head ducked low, shoulders hunched inwards, and pity washed over Maddie. If she had any other choice, she would not have involved another innocent soul, but she did not.

"Yes, thank you, Bronwen."

Again, Bronwen cast an anxious glance between them all. Then she smoothed her skirt, lifted her chin, and asked, "What do you need, Your Highness?"

"Lucas requires your attention," Gabriel said. "Heal him."

"O-of course."

Darting a confused look at Maddie, she scurried over to Lucas and inspected his wounds. Mumbled phrases slipped from her lips as she held her hands over the gash on his arm and then his face, ribs, and leg, healing each injury in turn.

He sagged at one point, and the soldiers on either side of him tightened their hold, but by the time Maddie had finished mentally reciting the Creator's blessing for the second time, Bronwen was finished. She stood back and perused her handiwork, gave a satisfied nod, and turned towards the high table.

"Is that it?" Gabriel demanded.

"I— Yes, milord. I think so."

He huffed. "Is he healed or not? Speak, woman."

"Y-yes. He is." She studied her hands, twisting them this way and that. "My power's been growing stronger every day since I came to the palace, and I can do much more now than I ever could before. King Lucas will need to rest, but his wounds are fully healed."

Gabriel waved a hand through the air as if batting away a fly. "Then you're dismissed."

Bronwen frowned. Then, in an act bolder than any Maddie had seen, she lifted her chin, looked directly at Maddie, and said, "Will that be all, Your Highness?"

Under normal circumstances, Maddie would have cheered the woman's brave act of loyalty, but right then, her life was more important. "Yes, thank you, Bronwen."

The healer hesitated for a moment, her mouth twisting as if suppressing the urge to speak, but she bobbed a curtsey and headed for the archway through which she had entered.

She was three or four paces from it when the curtain opened and Flynn ducked through, causing Maddie's heart to trip in her chest. He beamed up at her and said, "Hello, Maddie. Have—"

"What are you doing here?" Gabriel asked at the same time as Lucas said, "Get out of here, Flynn."

Flynn started, his eyes jumping to his father. He lowered his head and rubbed one foot against the back of the other. "I heard people arriving and wanted to see who it was."

"How did you get past the guards?" Gabriel clutched the back of the chair beside him.

"I used the secret passageway Joss showed me. I'm sorry, Papa." Flynn peeked around him, pausing on Bronwen and then his brother, and his little face creased.

Straightening, he turned to Lucas and said, "Did you get hurt? Is that why those men are holding you up?"

Maddie winced. Before anyone could reply, the curtain rustled again, and Catriona swept inside. "My apologies, Madeline, dear. I told him not to—"

Silence gripped the entire room as she glanced around, until Gabriel made a strangled sound.

"You can't be here," he said, shaking his head, his features blanched. "Go back upstairs, both of you."

"Gabriel?" Catriona's eyes swivelled from her husband to the armed soldiers surrounding Lucas and back again. "What's happening here?"

"He's trying to steal our kingdoms," Lucas said.

"Shut up," Gabriel spat. "Dearest one, I—"

Her brow furrowed. "Is that true?"

"Yes. He cursed my signet ring." Lucas grunted, one of the soldiers having planted a fist in his stomach, but continued. "He's been using it to control me for years..."

"It's not like that," Gabriel said over him. He rounded the table, bumping into the corner and toppling one of the goblets in his haste. Ignoring the wine sloshing across the wooden surface, he advanced on his wife, hands raised in a placating gesture. "I'm doing it for us, for Craeick."

"...got two of them, one for me, and one for Madeline."

Gabriel reached for Catriona, but she grabbed Flynn and backed away from him, a mixture of horror and disgust pinching her face. They sharpened her tone as she said, "How could you?"

He stilled, his arm falling to his side, his expression bereft. Then he spun around, stomped back across the room, and scraped a hand through his grey hair. With a bone-deep moan, he faced her once more, something dangerous flashing in his eyes.

"You're not supposed to be here," he said, though whether plea or accusation, Maddie could not tell. "Everything would've been fine if you'd just stayed upstairs."

She caught her lower lip between her teeth. This was the flaw in his plan—it relied on absolute secrecy. Controlling her and silencing her sisters was one thing, but despite everything he had done, he loved his family. He would never harm them. And now they knew the truth. What would he do?

He shared a look with the lead soldier, and when the subordinate nodded and reached for his sword, every muscle in Maddie's body tightened. Would they kill Lucas to secure their escape? No. They could not. They—

Gabriel backed towards the servants' entrance, opposite where his family stood.

"There's no use running," Lucas growled. "I'll find you no matter where you hide."

"Not if you're busy elsewhere." As he retreated, Gabriel pulled the dragon stone from his pouch and held it up, drawing all eyes to it. Ice coated Maddie's insides as the entire room held its breath.

He whispered something, and her ring began to glow, the swirls rippling out around her until everything else disappeared behind the irresistible veil of red light. Then the voice, sickeningly powerful, slithered inside her mind, freezing her body in place and bending her will to its own.

"Madeline, my dear. As soon as I stop speaking, you will draw your dagger and use it to stab yourself in the heart."

"As soon as you stop speaking, I will draw my dagger and stab myself in the heart."

Yes. She must kill herself. That would solve everything. Lucas would be free, and the kingdom would no longer suffer under her incompetence.

The all-encompassing glow faded, and distant sounds buffeted her senses like butterfly wings against a thick glass window. Screams to stop, swords clashing, cries of distress—they were nothing compared to the strong certainty of the voice in her head.

She drew her dagger from its sheath, the hilt warm in her grip and the sharp blade promising release. Lucas's gift would serve her well today. She held it aloft for a single heartbeat, then swung it down towards her body.

Her arm stopped midair.

She strained to pull the dagger in, the compulsion urging her on, even as horror grew in the far recesses of her mind, but her limbs refused to move. Something held her immobile.

The buzz of a thousand insects crawled beneath her skin, and she shot wild eyes around her for the source of the invisible force. She must break free. She must stab herself. The voice had commanded it.

She frowned. Something about that reasoning did not ring true, but she must obey the voice. Nothing else mattered.

She searched again, part of her troubled by what she saw. Lucas fighting three of the soldiers. Someone knocking Flynn aside. His body crashing into the wall. Catriona, frozen, one hand covering her mouth, one holding Olivia. Her sister, crying, cowering.

There. Her eyes stopped on Bronwen. At the side of the hall, away from the chaos of battling men, the healer stood with both arms stretched out in front of her, hands splayed in a stopping motion. Icy heat rippled the air between them, and beyond it, she stared back at Maddie. Though horror filled her widened eyes, her mouth was set in a determined line.

Caught between relief and dread, Maddie felt like the curse would rip her to shreds.

"Let me go." The words tore, raw and desperate, from her throat. Tears burned her eyes and trailed hot streaks down her face as her body fought with all its might to comply and what was left of her will fought to regain control.

A tremor rocked Bronwen, and the force holding Maddie lessened slightly. Her arm moved a fraction. She strained harder, and it moved again.

"Stop her," Olivia cried, the anguish in her voice tugging at something deep inside Maddie's chest.

Sweat beaded Bronwen's brow. "I can't," she said. "I didn't even know I could do this."

"Please. You have to." Olivia staggered forwards and clutched Bronwen's arm, and the force slammed into

Maddie anew, stealing her breath and leaving her unable even to blink.

She was still struggling against the fresh onslaught when a body thudded into her back, strong arms wrapped around her, and the pungent scent of sweat mixed with blood invaded her nostrils. Lucas.

"Fight it, Maddie." He pried the dagger from her grip, one finger at a time, and flung it across the table before spinning her around and into his embrace.

"You scared me," he rasped into her hair.

As he held her, the force let go, leaving her free to search for another weapon. The compulsion could not be ignored—she needed to find a way to end her life.

His dagger lay discarded on the table beside them, so she eased her hands around his waist and reached for it, managing to snag the hilt before he noticed. Shoving away from him, she turned and raised the blade, ready to stab herself for the second time.

Agony tore through her as, once again, something stopped her.

Whether Bronwen's force or Lucas's arms mattered not. She struggled against it to no avail. The compulsion pulsed like a heartbeat in her ears, louder and louder, drowning out the voices raised in an indistinct, far-off argument.

Her husband held her close again, and the heat of his body against her back provided momentary comfort from the compulsion trying to overwhelm her senses. He swore. Then he nuzzled her neck, his cheek stubble-roughened and oddly damp, and his lips found her ear.

"I'm so sorry, Maddie," he whispered.

His hold on her hands shifted, and she managed to free one. Acting quickly, before she lost her chance, she raised the dagger high, plunged it inwards, and froze as cold, sharp metal sliced into her skin.

Pain bit deep, ricocheting through her body, and a scream ripped from her throat. Her vision blurred, the room tilting as she slumped against her husband and the world turned blessedly black.

Chapter 37

Maddie

Oblivion, thick and heavy, pressed down on Maddie, holding her deep within its suffocating grasp. She pushed against it, fighting to… to what? She paused in her struggles and sank back into the void's embrace. Why was she so desperate to escape? What was waiting for her beyond its reach?

Her sisters. Her kingdom. Lucas.

She redoubled her efforts. Slowly, agonisingly, she climbed out of the blackness and heaved her eyelids open. Her bedchamber came into focus, bright light shining through the open window and banishing the last of the nightmare. She turned her face to the warmth and started to stretch, but a solid weight trapped her arm in place.

When she tried to dislodge it, Lucas jerked upright, chair legs barking across the floor with his movement. His hair fell about his face in a tousled mess, and a crease from the bedding had turned the scar on his left cheek into a lopsided cross.

An urge to chuckle at his rumpled state flitted through her mind, chased by utter shock that he sat beside her, concern filling his eyes. She froze, staring up at him.

"Are you well?" he asked.

His question brought her back to herself. She swallowed against a raw throat and managed to croak, "Water."

He gave her elbow a gentle squeeze, then got up and crossed to the fireside table, where a jug and several goblets sat on a tray.

"What happened?" She tried to push herself upright while he poured her a drink, but her limbs quivered like a newborn foal, so she gave up.

Lucas set the jug down and turned to face her but made no move towards the bed. He twisted the goblet between his fingers, looking anywhere but at her, and her chest tightened.

"What's the last thing you remember?" he eventually asked.

Furrowing her brow, she pushed through the dense fog still shrouding her thoughts and grasped the closest wisps of memories. The great hall. Gabriel. A dagger in her hand.

She sat up with a gasp, clutching her stomach. "I tried to stab myself."

He was at her side within a heartbeat, taking her hand and ducking his head to meet her gaze. "You don't still want to, do you?"

The caution in his tone made her pause, think more carefully. "No." But she should. The curse should make her. She glanced down at his hand engulfing hers, then up at him. “Why is that?”

He closed his eyes, and his hold tightened at the same time as the muscle in his jaw ticced.

Unease stirred in Maddie’s gut. If his reaction was any indication, maybe she did not want to hear the answer. She searched for another topic and blurted, “Where’s Gabriel? Has he been caught?”

“Not yet,” he gritted, drawing his hand away. “But I’ve sent my best men after him, so he will be soon.”

Good. After what he had done, the idea of him wandering her land, free, made her stomach roil. But… “I would’ve thought you’d have gone with them.”

“Being here is more important.”

She stared blankly at him, but he did not look up, only rubbed a scar on the back of his knuckles with his other thumb and said, “You matter to me.”

His statement knocked all coherent thought from her head. “I do?”

Finally, his eyes snapped to hers and held. “Of course. You’re my wife.”

Ah. The marriage contract. It was only reasonable that he would be concerned about their kingdoms’ alliance after all that had happened. But he must also crave his freedom now he was no longer controlled by his stepfather. She would have to find a way to give it to him.

Someone knocked on the door.

They turned as one in time to see it open and Tabitha walk in. She was barely past the threshold when Joss squeezed around her, trailed by Olivia.

“You’re awake. I told you she would be.” Joss flew across the room and launched herself at Maddie, knocking her prone and eliciting a disapproving tsk from Tabitha.

Peering around her sister’s shoulder, Maddie found Olivia, who had stopped at the end of the bed, and gave her a reassuring smile. “I am. How long was I asleep?”

“An entire day,” Olivia said in a near whisper.

So long? Maddie looked out of the window, the position of the sun confirming it was indeed late afternoon.

“Are you feeling better now?” Olivia asked, her voice stronger.

Joss let go and sat back, giving Maddie enough space to consider the question. The dryness in her throat reasserted itself, and she put a hand up to her neck. “Yes, but I’m thirsty.”

“Of course you are. Let’s get you more comfortable.” Tabitha shooed Joss out of her way and helped Maddie to sit up, piling more pillows behind her and easing her back against them. She tugged the blankets higher and, when Maddie was settled to her satisfaction, turned to Lucas. “You didn’t fetch her a drink yet?”

Lucas narrowed his eyes at the elderly maid but picked up the goblet from the bedside table without commenting. He handed it to Maddie and stepped away, out of the circle of their conversation.

Maddie sipped the water, savouring the soothing cool that flooded her mouth and washed the burrs from her throat. She downed the rest and placed the empty goblet in Tabitha’s waiting hand.

"You must be hungry too."

As if conjured by Tabitha's words, an empty growl rumbled through Maddie's stomach. Tabitha patted her forearm and said, "I'll go and get you something from the kitchen."

She hurried away, and Joss returned to her seat on the bed. "How are you feeling now? How's your hand?"

"My hand?"

Maddie looked down at her hands, her gaze snagging on the left ring finger. Or rather, what was left of it. It ended where the second knuckle should have been, the skin meeting at the top in a thin pink line. How had she not noticed that before?

Voices floated around her, unheeded, as her focus narrowed to that one point. She lifted her hand, turning it this way and that, then tentatively touched the shortened digit, feeling the smooth skin, the almost imperceptible ridge of the scar, the knobbly end of the bone.

Her injury did not cause any pain—which was probably why she had not noticed it earlier—but strangely, when she closed her eyes, she could still sense the ghost of the missing section.

The bed dipped, and Olivia curled up beside her, linking their arms together. Unshed tears shone in her eyes as she asked, "Does it hurt?"

"No. Not at all."

The truth earned Maddie a watery smile. "That's good. Bronwen did the best she could—"

"Mouse helped too," Joss said, sitting on the edge of the bed with her back squarely to Lucas. "She's got the gift of magic. Increased Bronwen's ability somehow when they touched."

"But we couldn't save the tip. Sorry, Maddie."

"You helped?" Maddie stared, wide-eyed, at Olivia, who ducked her head. The youngest Dalbot sibling had run from the mere mention of blood since she was little. How had she managed to tend such a serious injury?

"I kept my eyes closed the entire time," Olivia mumbled, the tips of her ears turning pink.

"Mouse could be a powerful mage," Joss said.

Maddie pulled Olivia in for a hug. "Thank you. I'm so proud of you."

"Do you think it was passed down from that ancestor, what's her name?" Joss's gaze bounced back and forth between them, her eyes alight with a mystery to be solved.

"You mean Galisia." Olivia shrugged. "Maybe."

"How many generations are there between us? D'you know what she could do? We should ask Nessa about it when we get the chance."

Olivia's entire body tensed beside Maddie, her eyes widening. "Please don't make a fuss. I can research it in the library, or maybe the books you found at Oslengil—once I've translated them."

Maddie kissed the top of her head and chafed her arm. "Don't worry, we won't rush you, will we, Joss?" She searched through her hazy memories. "But I still don't understand how you stopped me."

Olivia nudged Joss, prompting her to explain what had happened after Gabriel issued his final command. How Bronwen had instinctively reached out towards

Maddie, completely taken aback when she froze without them touching. How the mage had quickly tired but found her power surging when Olivia clutched her arm, begging her to save her sister. How Lucas had fought free of his captors and rushed to Maddie's side, only to realise there was no way of stopping her until Gabriel rescinded the command. No way other than to sever her finger.

"…though I'm sure we could've found an alternative if he'd waited long enough for us to think it through," Joss said. Her mouth twisted in disgust, and she turned enough to side-eye Lucas.

He had remained quiet throughout their account, leaning against the fireplace with his arms folded and one heel propped up on the hearth, but he tensed at her comment. "You weren't there. Cutting the ring off was quick and definitive."

"You wouldn't say that if we'd cut it off you at Oslengil," Joss muttered.

"The situation wasn't as urgent then," Maddie said at the same time as Luc said, "You're not that ruthless."

She glanced over at him in time to see him wince and look away.

"I thank you for it," she said. "Truly. Things could've gone so differently…"

She loosed a steadying breath. What might have happened had Gabriel had his way did not bear thinking about. Avoiding that outcome was worth the loss of her fingertip, though it would take some getting used to, despite Bronwen's care.

The thought spawned another, and she looked to her sisters. "If Bronwen's powers have grown, can she heal Papa?"

They both slumped.

"No." Joss shook her head. "She tried, but she can still only treat physical wounds."

Oh.

Olivia snuggled closer into Maddie's side. "I'm just glad you're well. And that we're all together again."

A knock on the door heralded Tabitha's return. She walked in carrying a tray loaded with a steaming bowl of soup, three or four thick slices of bread, and a plate of griddle cakes. Maddie's mouth watered at the warm, buttery scent wafting towards her as Tabitha approached the bed, and her stomach rumbled again.

"Here you are. I had Cook prepare these as a little treat. No doubt you deserve it after all you've been through." Tabitha slapped Joss's hand away from the plate. "They're not for you. You can get your own from the kitchen. And Parker's looking for you."

Joss winced. With an exaggerated sigh, she stood and tugged at Olivia's hand. "Come with me, Mouse. She won't shout at me if you're there."

A chuckle escaped Maddie even as she shook her head at her sister's skewed priorities. "Will you ever grow up?"

"Never." Joss scrunched her entire face and shuddered. "But I can handle the necessities for a day or two, so take your time and rest."

She pulled Olivia to her feet, and they left arm in arm, Tabitha bustling behind them. Maddie glanced over at Lucas, but he remained still as a statue, only his eyes following the others' exit.

"Do you need to leave too?" she asked.

"No. I'm staying here."

Oh. They lapsed into an awkward silence, and she turned her attention to her food. When there was nothing left but a few crumbs, she searched for something to say.

"How are your mother and Flynn?"

His head whipped up at her question, and a vee formed between his eyebrows as if his thoughts had been elsewhere and he had to force them back to the present. "Mother's devastated. She's locked herself in her room and doesn't want to see anyone. Flynn's just confused. He doesn't fully understand what's happened, and I haven't had a chance to explain yet."

An image appeared in Maddie's mind of Flynn flying backwards across the great hall, landing in a crumpled heap beneath one of the windows. "Was he hurt?"

"Only a few bumps and bruises. Nothing a growing lad can't handle." His lips quirked, though his eyes remained sober. "He fought well for his age."

Maddie nodded, her gaze dipping to the empty platter and a snagged thread in the blanket. She picked at it as she said, "That's good. Would you like me to go with you when you talk to him?"

He gave no immediate answer, but though she did not look up, she could feel his eyes on her. The moment stretched until he cleared his throat and said, "Yes. I would. If it's not too much for you."

He crossed to the bed and sat in the same chair as earlier, leaning forwards with his elbows propped on his knees. An uncertainty she had not seen in him before diluted his usual intensity as he drew in a breath but clamped his jaw shut and dropped his gaze to the floor.

The silence between them became suffocating, choked with all the things she wanted to, needed to, but dare not say. If she did not speak soon, they would surely burst out of her on their own.

Mustering her courage, she said, “Lucas, I—”

“About everything that’s happened… I’m sorry, Madeline. More than you can imagine.”

Pain pierced her chest. “It wasn’t your fault.”

His shoulders hunched even lower. “But you must hate me.”

“No.” She reached out but stopped and pulled back, uncertain whether he would accept her touch. “Gabriel made you do those things.” Her hands curled into a ball on her lap as she added quietly, “And so many more.”

“I don’t know what’s real and what’s the curse. I’ve been thinking about it all night, and I just don’t know. Do you think it’s true that he didn’t change who I am?”

She considered the question. “I think so. He did seem to love you, in his own twisted way. But maybe there’s a way to be sure.

“Now the ring’s gone, some of my memories from the past few days are becoming clearer while others are foggy or disappearing altogether. I think those are the ones linked to the curse. If it’s the same for you, what you remember is the real you, and whatever’s hazy or blank is what came from him.”

He nodded slowly, then leaned back in the chair and tipped his head up to stare at the ceiling. His thumb rubbed the base of his pinkie finger as though unconsciously turning the ring he no longer wore.

Maddie caught her lips between her teeth, itching to ask what was going through his mind but determined to give him time to think.

Eventually, he dragged a hand over his face and lowered his head, returning his gaze to hers. "I want to change the contract for our marriage. If you'll agree. I want to start again."

"I understand." He wanted to put her, Tyrrath, and everything that had happened to him in the past. She could not fault him for that. But her heart ached at the prospect of his departure. If only she had not fallen in love with him.

She hid her pain behind a serene mask and said, "You must want to get your mother and Flynn back to Craeick as soon as possible. Besides, you were ordered to marry me against your will, so—"

"No, I wasn't."

Maddie stared at him, open-mouthed.

"The decision to come here is hazy, as is preparing for war with Brunland"—he winced—"and trying to kill you. But I remember every detail of persuading you to marry me. And getting to know you and your sisters. Our time together is the clearest memory I have of the past year."

She blinked. Frowned. "So… marrying me wasn't part of the curse?"

"What? No. Haven't you been listening?" He raked a hand through his unruly hair, then shifted across to the bed and gripped her shoulders, turning her to face him squarely. "That was me. And if you truly don't hate me, I'd like to have a real marriage with you."

It took a moment for his words to sink in, but when they did, her cheeks heated. She lowered her gaze and said, "That's what I want too. As long as you're certain."

He closed the distance between them, setting the air itself on fire. She clutched the blankets and swallowed. "Lucas?"

"Call me Luc."

She tested the name, rolling it around her mind before whispering it aloud. "Luc." It felt natural. Good. Intimate. So much so that she forgot what she had meant to say. "And you call me Maddie."

With his mouth close enough that she could feel his breath on her skin, he did. And then he kissed her. His lips were soft and warm. They caressed hers with the lightest of touches at first and then pressed deeper, stealing the air from her lungs and sending her thoughts spiralling.

When they broke apart, it took a moment to regain her senses. She smoothed the blankets in an effort to calm her racing heart and caught sight of her finger in her periphery. Her lips quirked as a memory popped into her head. "One more thing…"

"Mmm?" he murmured, stroking a lock of her unbound hair between his finger and thumb.

"I'd really like it if you stopped cutting me."

His gaze snapped to hers. Then a growl rumbled through his chest, and resolve hardened his expression.

"This was the last time, I swear it. No one will ever hurt you again."

"You can't promise that."

He studied her, silver eyes glinting. "No. But I can promise to kill anyone who does."

Chapter 38
Maddie

When Maddie woke the next morning, thin dawn light pierced the curtains and Lucas was nowhere to be seen. Tabitha sat by the fireplace, a pile of sewing on her lap, humming a folk song about reunited lovers. She looked up when Maddie stirred.

"Did you sleep well?"

"Where's Lucas?"

Tabitha pursed her lips, then said, "He's in the great hall. They caught Gabriel, and he—"

Maddie threw the covers aside and scrambled from the bed. "Why didn't you tell me? I need to be there." She snatched the dress hanging over the warming rail and shoved her arms into the sleeves, looking around for her shoes. "Help me tie my laces."

"Are you sure about this, Madeline. After what he did…"

She spun to the older woman, read the worry etched into her round face, and paused, her urgency ebbing. "After what he did, I need to see him punished with my own eyes." She straightened. "I owe that to my people, if nothing else."

Tabitha studied her for another endless moment, then nodded and set to work on Maddie's laces.

They managed to fix her clothing and hair in record time, and Maddie was soon racing along the corridor in the direction of the great hall. She did not allow herself to dwell on her last experiences in that room, nor did she allow herself to look at her left hand, even in her periphery.

When she arrived outside the curtained entrance the royal family used, she straightened her skirts, patted the knot of hair at the back of her head, and walked inside with her head held high.

Lucas stood on the dais in front of the thrones of Tyrrath, wearing the formal, silver-embellished regalia of the King of Craeick. The high table was gone, leaving his choice of outfit, and the wolf-headed sword he wore at his side, on full display.

Maddie wished she had taken more care over her appearance, though a glance around the room revealed that they were alone. She crossed the dais to join her husband, who watched her approach with a stony expression.

"You're here."

"Why didn't you tell me about it?"

He returned his attention to the main doors at the far end of the hall. "I didn't think you'd want to see him."

She faced the same direction, taking a moment to weigh his assumption. "I don't, in all honesty. But I need to, to be able to put this behind me."

The hard planes of his face softened, and he brushed a stray wisp of her hair away from her face. "I'll be right here the whole time."

"Will anyone else be joining us?" she asked, more to break the heavy tension than anything else.

"I'm not giving him the satisfaction of an audience."

She had not considered that—or anything beyond capturing the vile man—but on reflection, she agreed with Lucas's decision. "Do you know what you'll do with him?"

His hands balled at his sides. "I'll have him executed as quickly as our laws allow."

As expected. But… She caught her lower lip between her teeth as she worked out how to word what she needed to say.

"I don't think you should."

He spun to face her, brows lofted high. "Why in the blazes not?"

"You'd kill the father of your only brother? Your mother's husband?"

"Execute, not kill. It's not the same thing."

She rested her fingers on his arm, felt the strain in his muscles beneath the black velvet. "Even so. What will that accomplish? He should be punished, and I'd very much like to know he'll never set foot in Tyrrath again, but death? Don't act in hatred, Luc. My father always said that how we treat our enemies says more about us than them, and I think he's right."

He only grunted, but she could not press him further because the doors at the far end of the hall swung wide and a contingent of Craeickish soldiers marched in. She recognised Aiden, and Rheann's red hair behind him. Then Gabriel came into view, and she clutched the folds of her skirts as the others blurred into a single, armed mass.

Lucas stepped closer to her and ordered them forward.

As they made their way down the centre of the hall, in a scene remarkably similar—if reversed—to that two days' prior, she saw how different Gabriel appeared. Streaks of mud shaded his scruffy beard, his clothing was rumpled and torn in one or two places, and dried blood splattered his cloak.

He must have put up a fight, or those working with him had done so on his behalf. Despite his bedraggled state, when they came to a stop several paces from the dais, he stood erect with his chin held high.

"Do you have anything to say for yourself?" Lucas asked.

"Only this. Whatever you think of me and whatever you're planning to do, know that I've only ever acted in the best interests of Craeick, and I would never harm my king."

A low growl rumbled through Lucas's chest. "I beg to differ on that point. You've done more harm to me than any sword or dragon I've ever faced, including the one that left this." He pointed to the scar on his cheek.

Gabriel stared up at them silently for a long moment, then slumped and bowed his head at last.

"Do you admit your guilt? Or will you force Mother to sit through your trial?"

His head jerked up. “Please leave her out of this. She’s done nothing wrong.”

“Of course not,” Lucas gritted out. “You lied to her.”

“Loving her wasn’t a lie. Nor loving you. I only did what I needed to for our kingdo—”

“Do you admit your guilt or not?”

“I admit it. Just, please, spare your mother and Flynn.”

Lucas clenched his jaw. “Then for your crimes, of which there are too many to recount, I sentence you to banishment at Drakes Ridge Fortress.”

Gabriel looked up, visibly stunned, but Lucas gestured to Aiden, who walked forwards and took the small bundle Lucas held out to him. He opened the cloth to reveal the signet ring Lucas and then Maddie had worn. The black stone lay dormant, though she could have sworn she heard faint echoes of its whispers.

Her palms began to sweat as Lucas whispered something in Aiden’s ear, and she forced herself to focus on them instead of the evil object. Aiden met Lucas’s eyes and nodded before returning to Gabriel’s side.

Straightening, Lucas continued his instructions aloud. “You will set out for Drakes Ridge immediately, where you will live under the watch of Friar Utham and never set foot outside the fortress’s walls again. To ensure you obey this command, you will wear the signet ring you forced on us and be bound by its power.”

The soldiers on either side of Gabriel gripped his arms, and at first, he did nothing to prevent them. Then he gave a jerk that rippled through his entire bulky frame and struggled in earnest, but it was too late. The ring was soon forced onto one of his fingers, and the fight went out of him like a candle in a rainstorm.

Aiden produced the control stone from a pocket and offered it to Lucas, but he shook his head and gestured for them to leave. Rheann plucked the stone from her superior's hand, and the malicious grin she cast at Gabriel said she would give him no quarter. Though Lucas had vouched for her loyalty, only now, seeing how she loathed one who had betrayed him, did Maddie appreciate its depth.

The soldiers escorted their prisoner back outside, closing the doors behind them, and it was over.

Maddie dropped onto the throne behind her. Gabriel's punishment was at once more lenient and far harsher than she could have envisioned. She peered up at Lucas, who raised one brow.

"Does that meet your approval? I didn't kill him."

She swallowed bile. "Will you use the ring to control him?"

"Of course not. As soon as Aiden issues his orders, I'll lock the stone and the second ring in the bottom of my strongbox, where they'll stay till I can get them to my castle vault." His brow furrowed. "I would've tossed them in the ocean, but I'd rather know exactly where they are, just in case."

A slow smile spread across her lips, and his scowl deepened. "What are you grinning for?"

"I knew you'd do the right thing."

He huffed. "I'm not a good man, Madeline."

"No, you're the Wolf of Craeick."

"Exactly." He strode to the steps down from the dais but paused and looked back over his shoulder. "Are you coming?"

"Give me a few minutes."

She leaned back into the soft padding of the throne as he left through the side entrance and allowed the events of the previous few days to drain away. Her husband was, indeed, a wolf. "But," she added quietly, "wolves don't kill unless they have to."

Chapter 39

Maddie

Maddie waited outside the great hall for the signal to make her entrance and did not feel a single urge to pat her hair or smooth the skirts of her dress. A sizeable crowd gathered on the other side of the curtained archway, but only she and Luc stood in the small antechamber.

With a stretch of his neck to the left and right, he moved into position beside her, his arm brushing against hers. Though his presence banished any qualms about what was expected of her, awareness of his body so close to hers brought heat to her cheeks and set her hands fidgeting for a different reason.

He leaned closer and whispered, "Only worry about the people who matter, remember?"

She recalled the last time he had said those words and smiled ruefully at the reminder that their marriage was born of convenience and a curse-driven invasion. But no longer. Over the month since Gabriel's exile, they had grown much closer, learning each other's habits and working together to solve any lingering issues related to the curse.

Fortunately, Gabriel's plot to have Luc invade Brunland had been foiled before it became public knowledge. The men captured for the Craeickish army had been released, most under the impression they had been conscripted only to build the fortress, and Luc had personally visited the families of the guards he had killed at Oslengil to make restitution. It was an ongoing process, but one he was determined to see through.

It took time to work through ruling the two kingdoms together as a married couple, and eventually, Maddie and Luc decided to split their time between the capitals while encouraging free movement across the border. Many Craeickish families had already begun the journey south, but a surprising number of young Tyrrathian men had conversely chosen to travel north. Their stated intention was to join the Craeick army, which Luc vowed would be much more discerning in future about the roles they undertook.

Maddie had discovered during the month that they complemented each other well. Luc was decisive and a keen strategist. She was measured and diplomatic. She smoothed his sharp edges, and he challenged her to be bolder. If only she were as certain of his feelings as she was of hers.

"I love you," he said, the low rumble of his voice and the brush of his lips against her temple pulling her from her musings.

"What?"

She spun her head to stare at him, and the wicked grin tilting the corners of his mouth told her he had purposefully caught her off guard. Before she could formulate any further response, he swept the curtain aside and ushered her through.

"But—"

How could he admit something so important and not give her time to digest it, or reciprocate?

Over the drone of the lord chamberlain's introduction, he whispered, "Later, sweetheart. Time to greet our guests now."

Pasting a bright smile on her face, she pierced him with a sideways look. "I'll pay you back for this."

He stepped up onto the dais, a chuckle drifting over his shoulder, and she had little choice but to follow. She mounted the stairs, walked in front of the table, and stopped in the centre, allowing her gaze to wander the room.

Her sisters stood at one side with Tristan as their shadow. The necks and cuffs of their gowns, sage green for Olivia and a sunny yellow for Joss, twinkled in the torchlight where they had been embroidered with fine gold thread. Maddie's eyes caught and held on Olivia's hair, pinned up for the first time, before taking in Tristan, who had eschewed his uniform in favour of a deep blue doublet over black trousers. She flashed them a brief smile and moved on.

Beyond them, farther along the wall, stood Catriona, recently returned from Craeick for the occasion and appearing as serene as ever in a pale lavender gown with silver embroidery. Flynn leaned against her, stifling a yawn with one hand, and a handful of Luc's men flanked them, including Rheann in a deep blue dress. Maddie suppressed a laugh at the redhead's scowl, and another at the weapon strapped to her waist.

The centre of the room held the requisite dignitaries from the other kingdoms of Egrea along with Nessa and another mage, both of whom wore their guild medallions prominently displayed. And at the other side, Bronwen stood between Olivia's favourite tutor and the librarian, and a distant cousin on Maddie's mother's side that they could not leave out of the celebration.

It was a smaller guest list than usual, but Olivia did not like large crowds, and they were there for her that evening. She would have preferred a private gathering in their solar, had argued for that, but a formal reception was required for a princess's seventeenth birthday.

If only their parents had been present as well, it would have been perfect. Tears stung the backs of Maddie's eyes at the thought, but she blinked them back and stepped forwards to address the group at large.

"Thank you, all, for joining us tonight to celebrate the seventeenth birthday of Tyrrath's youngest princess, Olivia Grace Dalbot. Olivia?"

She gestured for her sister to join her, and with a little push from Joss, Olivia inched up the steps and out onto the dais. She fixed her eyes on the floor and clutched her hands together at her waist, but there was no hiding the blush that swept up her neck and turned even her ears pink.

Maddie took her sister's hands in hers, gave them a little squeeze, and spoke directly to her, though loudly enough for everyone present to hear.

"If our mother were here, she would be so proud to see you reach your majority, to see the beautiful, compassionate woman you've become, and I know she would wish you every happiness in the year to come. On behalf of our father, King Johnathan, I would like to present you with our grandmother's pearl brooch and the whole family's sincerest love and affection on this special day."

Luc handed her the embroidered pouch containing the precious heirloom, and she placed it in Olivia's trembling fingers. She longed to wrap her sister in a tight hug and tell her the worst of the formalities was over and she had done well, but there were too many eyes on them. Instead, she faced the gathered witnesses and said, "Let the feast begin."

By the time they had taken their places, a line of servants waited to serve the food, and the high table was soon piled high. Steamed fish, broad beans and buttered carrots, creamy leeks, roasted pork with spiced apple sauce, and herbed potatoes—all Olivia's favourites, all delicious. The scents made Maddie's mouth water, and she stabbed her eating dagger into a generous slice of pork, thus allowing the others to also dig in.

An hour and a half later, she leaned back in her chair, her stomach completely full, while the servants cleared the tables and the rest of the guests milled around the edges of the hall. She was about to get up and join the throng when the main doors opened at the far end.

"Lord Elland and... guests," the lord chamberlain announced.

Luc straightened, and Maddie slid her hand around his beneath the table. As part of his vow to make full restitution to those affected by his actions while cursed, he had offered to find generous positions for anyone taken by his army who had nowhere to go, and Lord Elland had been tasked with bringing them with him to the capital.

He strode down the central aisle between the rows of tables with a contingent of men trailing behind him. Dressed in tunics and trousers of varying quality, they shuffled forwards, heads alternately lowered and swivelling left to right with awed expressions.

When they came within three paces of the high table, Lord Elland stopped and bowed, the bow rippling through the men behind him like a wave.

"Your Majesty. Your Highness," he said on rising. "It's good to be home."

"We've missed you," Maddie said, standing and skirting the table.

The general hubbub restarted when she joined him and moved a couple of steps to the side of the room.

"How was the journey, Lord Elland?" Olivia asked, appearing at Maddie's other side. "Shall I ask for some more food to be brought?"

"No thank you, little one," he said, then pressed his lips together. "Not little any longer. Look how you've grown while I was away. And so like your mother now, a truly beautiful young woman."

Maddie found Olivia's hand and gave it a surreptitious squeeze, knowing without even looking that her sister's face would be aflame.

"Are these the men you mentioned?" she asked, casting a welcoming smile over the group clustered behind him.

"Yes." He gestured to a knot of men, who separated to reveal a familiar face.

Bronwen's husband, Finley, stepped forwards and dipped into a low bow. "Your Highness. I—"

"Finley!"

The cry from the other side of the hall cut him off, and a moment later, Bronwen flew into his arms. He picked her up and swung her around, lowering her to her feet after a full turn. Tears streamed down her face, and he brushed them away with the pads of his thumbs, whispering assurances that he was there, he was well, and he would never leave her again.

"Thank you, Lord Elland. Thank you for bringing him back to me," she said, clasping her hands to her chest. Then she looked behind Maddie. "And thank you, Sire."

Maddie half turned to find Luc approaching on silent feet. He locked eyes with Lord Elland and gave him a single, slow nod that was reciprocated in kind, then focused on the reunited couple.

"I owed you far more," he said.

"A new cottage an' a dozen sows is more'n we could dream o'. Thank you, Sire." Finley bowed again, tugging Bronwen into a curtsey beside him, but when he rose, he fidgeted with his sleeve. "Um, if you don't mind, Ma'am, Sire, I'd like to find me daughter."

"Go," Maddie said. "She'll be happy to see you. And take some caeldon berry tarts with you, too."

"Yes, Ma'am. Thank you."

With one last bow, the farmer-turned-messenger-turned-army-conscript tucked his arm around his wife and left the hall through the side entrance leading to the kitchens.

Olivia sighed. "I'm so happy everyone's home and together again. This is the best birthday present I could have."

"But not the only one." Luc grinned as he pulled an old, leather-bound book from behind his back and handed it to Olivia.

From her gasp of delight, it appeared to be a precious volume, so Maddie bent for a closer look. The gold embossed on the front had flaked away in places, but she could make out the form of a dragon beneath the title, its wings extended in flight. The text was written in the old tongue, which she had never taken the time to learn, so she looked to Olivia to translate.

"Terheart's treatise on the five forms of original magic. Where did you find this?"

Luc shrugged one shoulder. "It's been in the library in Lochanack for as long as our records go back. I thought it might help with your research into the books from Oslengil."

Sheer joy swept all traces of shyness from Olivia's features, and she hugged the book to her chest. "It will. This is perfect. Thank you, Luc."

"A fine present, indeed," Lord Elland agreed.

She eyed the curtained entrance leading to their private rooms, her feet taking half a step in that direction, and Maddie reached out to gently tug her back.

"Later, Mouse. This is your celebration banquet. You need to stay for a few rounds of dancing at least."

"Did someone mention dancing?"

Joss appeared at Olivia's other side, and Maddie could have sworn she gave Luc a conspiratorial wink before looking around the rest of the group. Much to her dismay, they often schemed together since she had recovered, Luc covering for her sister whenever she snuck out of the palace on one of her adventures.

Maddie almost wished they were still squabbling. At least then Joss would have fewer opportunities to escape.

Low strains of music interrupted her thoughts, and she spun to Luc as soon as she recognised the tune. It was the one they had danced to during their formal wedding reception when they had first returned to Faerstolmere.

"Shall we start the dance?" he asked.

Taking her hand in his, he kissed the knuckles and led her out into the centre of the hall. The guests cleared aside as several more couples joined them, and Luc linked her arm through his to begin the first promenade.

They walked forwards, swept out in opposite directions, came back together, and wove between the other dancers as one before breaking apart again. When she returned to his side for the lift, she tilted her head to his ear and said, "So, you love me."

His lips twitched as he lowered her to the floor. "Did you need me to repeat it?"

"I wouldn't mind hearing it again."

"I love you, Princess. I've known it since you took the ring in my place."

Her cheeks heated, and she ducked her head to hide the smile spreading across them. "Hmm."

They separated once more, and she forced her features back under control. She had promised revenge for the abruptness of his heart-fluttering confession, and the upcoming section of the dance would be the perfect opportunity.

He walked towards her, and as they circled each other in hold, she slid her hand across his shoulder and behind his neck to twirl her fingers in the thick waves of hair at his nape. He lifted her, and on the descent, she trailed her fingers down his chest to rest over his heart.

Stepping closer, close enough for their breath to mingle, she waited for the moment they would part and whispered, "I love you too."

She moved back, ready to switch partners, but he did not let her go.

Instead, he stood like a rock in the river of the dance, gripping her hand while the other couples flowed around them, his eyes burning into hers. Then he strode out of the dancing area, tugging her behind him.

He headed directly to where Olivia sat in one of the window alcoves with her old tutor and Nessa and said, "Happy birthday, Olivia. We're leaving early."

Then he made his way around to the royal entrance without stopping for anyone, and the moment the curtain swung closed behind them, he spun her against the nearest wall.

Darkness had stolen over the world outside, and only a single torch burned on the opposite wall. But the lack of light only heightened Maddie's other senses as he pressed the entire length of his body against hers—his solid warmth through the layers of clothing between them, the slap of his hand landing on the wall beside her head, the ragged puffs of his breath, the musky scent of his skin.

She did not wait for his next move. Throwing her arms around his neck, she tilted her head up to his and kissed him. His arm slid around her waist, and his lips moulded to hers, capturing her breath and setting fire to her insides, but he broke away far too soon.

"Say it again," he said, his chest heaving.

"I love you, Lucas Sinclair."

"You mean it?"

She cupped his face between her hands, her finger touching his scar, physical proof of the battles he had faced and overcome. "Yes. I do. I want to rule with you, have children with you, grow old with you. I want to heal your wounds and share your burdens. I love your—"

He pulled her into a tight embrace, muffling the rest of her confession in the crook of his neck. "You've no idea how much you mean to me." Letting go, he leaned his forehead against hers. "I'll protect you with my life, Maddie, and give you everything you ever dreamed of."

He eased back, far enough for her to see the promise shining in his eyes. Then her Wolf King kissed her tenderly, took her hand in his, and led her up the stairs to their room.

Acknowledgements

This is hard to write. Which is why I left it till the last possible minute, in case I missed anyone.

There are so many people without whom this book would never have seen the light of day. First, my nieces, Alice and Katelyn, who insisted I tell them stories while we walked around Quarr Abbey, a monastic pig farm near their home, and then insisted the pigs *and* wolf got a happy ending. Thanks to that, I now have another entire series of ideas swirling around my mind.

Then, in no particular order, Mary and C.J., for the courses that have taught me so much, the retreat where I rediscovered my love for this story, and the advice and inspiration you never fail to provide.

My writing friends, Cathy and Sophia, who cheered for these characters, helped me work through the sticking points, and were present through the darkest moments of the last year. You're as dear to me as my biological sister.

My family, Mum, Dad, Kate, El, and Ame, for listening to my excited—and often nonsensical—ramblings and reading countless versions, and Gabe for keeping my secret and sharing your name with one of the characters. Welcome to the wild side.

Vanessa, who is an absolute gem both inside and out. Despite your own overwhelming deadlines, you took the time to make me believe in myself and my ability to write again. I doubt I would've picked up my pen to finish this if it weren't for you, never mind publishing it so soon. Also, thank you for introducing me to a whole new world of fellow creatives.

Jourdan, whose insights into this genre were exactly what I needed, and who gave me a reason to push through at exactly the right time.

Jasmine, for boosting my confidence with your kind words during the edits. You're my kind of people, and I know we're going to become fast friends.

Bianca and Andrés, who made this book so pretty, I can't stop looking at it. You are artistic geniuses.

And David at the Royal Armouries Museum. Thanks for answering my questions about medieval weaponry. Any errors in their usage here are entirely on me.

My critique group—I'll see your twin swords and raise you one buckler—street team, and online writing community, who kept me aimed towards publication.

Finally, I can't leave without acknowledging my husband, Dave, without whom I wouldn't be writing at all. There simply are no words, and you know how much you mean to me. Thank you, for everything.

They say every author ultimately writes alone. I disagree. This book is testament to the many people in my life who refused to let me give up, and it's theirs as much as it is mine, though I'll keep the royalty cheques, all the same. ;)

Thank you, all, for your support, encouragement, patience, and love. And thank you to my Father in heaven for your continued grace while I rediscover the gift of your inner peace. Like Maddie and so many others in the real world, in your eyes, I am enough.

Coming Next

THE DRAGON STONE

Tales of Tyrrath 2

She's looking for a cure… but will finding it heal her heart or break it?

Jocelyn Dalbot has spent the last two years supporting her sister's rule while longing to escape the suffocating confines of palace life. Desperate for a way to break the sleeping curse on their father, she sets out to find a magical dragon stone with the power to restore him to health.

Unfortunately, the stone has been lost to the ages, and only a few scribbled notes in the margins of an ancient text provide a clue to its whereabouts. She ventures south, where she meets Theo, an enigmatic stranger who appears whenever she is most in need and also seems to be searching for the stone.

With war brewing and hidden parties working against them, Jocelyn must decide where her heart lies before the dragon stone, and her chance at happiness, is lost forever.

www.ingramcontent.com/pod-product-compliance
Lightning Source LLC
LaVergne TN
LVHW041101080826
845145LV00007B/1641

* 9 7 8 1 9 1 5 4 3 8 0 4 1 *